Silver Spells

Silver Spells

Kate Moseman

Silver Spells

First Edition

ISBN 978-1-7345144-4-5 (ebook)
ISBN 978-1-7345144-5-2 (paperback)

Published by:
Fortunella Press

Find out who you are and do it on purpose.

—Dolly Parton

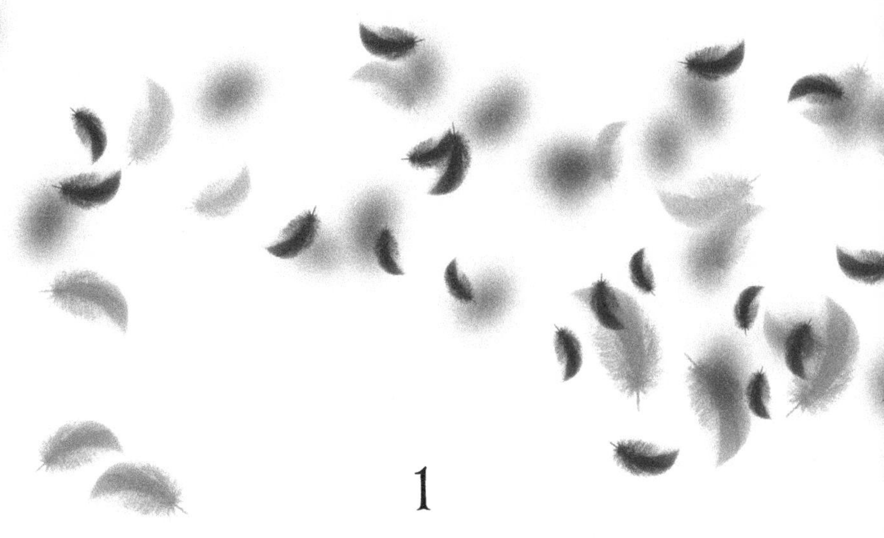

1

My boss couldn't escape this time. I'd been trying to catch her all week to ask if I could ride on the Suntan Queen parade float, and now I'd spotted her across the employee parking lot getting out of her vintage teal convertible. Oversized sunglasses and a driving scarf obscured part of her face, but I would know Queenie Russell anywhere—I'd worked for her for over twenty years.

"Queenie!" Everyone at the Suntan Queen sunscreen factory, high and low, was on a first-name basis with our fearless leader.

She looked around. When she spotted me, she staggered back against the side of her car, then righted herself and rushed toward the red-brick factory building.

I hurried after her. "Wait!"

She disappeared through the revolving door, which spun wildly, sending drafts of cool, sunscreen-scented air outside.

I increased my speed to a jog as I passed through the door and into the reception area. Coffee sloshed in my cruiser cup, making me glad it had a tight lid.

From the reception area, I could swerve to the factory side or the office side of the building. I veered toward the factory side, knowing Queenie liked to walk through the factory first thing in the morning.

Machinery whirred and clicked, dispensing filled bottles of sunscreen. Workers in white coats and hair nets loaded the bottles into boxes to be shipped from Sparkle Beach to vendors all over the world.

I skidded to a stop and looked in all directions, hoping to spot Queenie somewhere among the large steel vats.

A black-haired woman with dark red lipstick and a piercing gaze hailed me. "Luella! What are you doing on the factory side?"

"Did you see which way Queenie went?" Normally, I would have paused to shoot the breeze with Rose—one of my oldest and dearest friends—but I needed to catch Queenie first.

Rose lifted her safety goggles, displaying nails painted with tiny white skulls on glossy black polish. "I don't think she came in here."

"Nice nails."

"You like?" She waggled them proudly.

"They go with your outfit. Well, the outfit under your lab coat, anyway." Rose's dark clothing walked a fine line between office-appropriate and graveyard-appropriate. The occasional dog hairs stuck to her clothes revealed her softer side—a weakness for taking in rescue dogs. "I can't stay. Gotta catch Queenie before she locks herself away again."

Rose nodded. "Good luck."

I backtracked through the reception area and entered the office side. My other bestie, Pepper, occupied a cubicle on the main aisle, around the corner from mine. She would have spotted anyone who had walked by.

Pepper's brow wrinkled as she stared down at the latest spreadsheet on her desk, her brown curls still wet from her usual morning surf. Those curls always dried down to enviable beachy waves within a few hours, but until then, they'd surely leave a few water spots on the papers scattered in front of her.

"Pepper, did you see Queenie go by?"

Pepper looked up and swept her damp hair away from her face. Crow's-feet highlighted her eyes as she smiled. "A minute ago. Why?"

"I tried to talk with her, but she ran off."

Pepper leaped out of her seat, game for excitement as always. "You want me to help you look for her?"

"No, no. I'll find her. I don't want to drag you away from your work."

"Catch you later, then." She dropped into her seat with loose-limbed grace.

I jogged down the main aisle and up the stairs, heading for the executive offices on the upper floor. When I reached Queenie's outer office, the secretary jumped up and barred me from going any further.

"Could I speak to Queenie briefly? It's about the parade."

"She's not to be disturbed."

"She just got here."

"I'm sorry. She left strict instructions that she was not to be disturbed."

I glanced at Queenie's closed office door. "Could you call her real quick? I'm sure she wouldn't mind." Of all the times for her decades-long open door policy to change, it had to be on the morning I needed to talk to her.

"I'm sorry." The secretary didn't budge.

"Could you give her a message?"

The secretary raised her eyebrows without speaking.

"Tell her Luella wanted to see her about the parade. I usually get to ride on the float, but I didn't get the invite this year."

"I will pass along the message."

"Thanks." With no other recourse, I trudged downstairs and ran through a mental list of things to do that sunny Friday.

One: Get through my workday at Suntan Queen.

Two: Enjoy a date night with Dan, my boyfriend of the last month.

Another sip of coffee brought home the fact that my daughter, Lily, had gone off to college in New York—making it unnecessary to keep stocking almond milk creamer in the fridge—and yet I kept on buying the stuff like it was me, not her, who got an upset stomach from dairy. I added one more item to my to-do list: *Don't cry over Lily's unoccupied room.*

I set the insulated tumbler on my desk and noticed a red light flashing on my office phone. I mashed the button to listen to the message.

It was Rod, one of the managers on the office side of the operation. "Luella, I need to see you in my office when you arrive." Rod supervised the marketing team, which included me as the person in charge of social media.

On my way to Ron's office, I stopped by London Russell's desk.

Queenie Russell's family was full of aspirational names alluding to royalty and capital cities—such as Kingsley and Rome, for example—but Queenie's niece, London, was the only member of the clan who'd shown genuine interest in the business rather than plain old greed. Queenie was allowing her to shadow staff members in every department in hopes that she would learn the company from the inside out.

She'd spent the past few months with me.

"Morning, London."

London glanced up from her selfie camera. "One sec." She puckered her lips just so. The phone clicked in rapid succession, capturing a series of photos. She slipped the phone into her designer bag. "What's up?"

"Rod wants to see me about something, but when I get back, I thought we'd go over the copy for the upcoming posts."

London saluted with a manicured hand. "Yes, ma'am."

I hid a smile. She didn't mean any harm by calling me "ma'am," and I didn't particularly mind it. I chose to view it as a sign of respect from one generation to another—and despite her self-obsessed rich girl appearance, London was a sharp cookie with a natural talent for navigating the subterfuge and in-fighting of the Russell family.

I presumed Rod wanted to talk to me about the new marketing push we'd be doing to position Suntan Queen as the hip, new brand of the twenty-first century. A name like "Suntan Queen" made it an uphill battle, harkening as it did back to the old days when a tan was considered perfectly healthy. Queenie did not want the company—or herself, God forbid—to be thought of as an aging grand dame.

I couldn't blame her.

When I pushed open the door to Rod's office, I caught the distinct tang of fear in the air, cutting through the ever-present scent of sunscreen and the bland cologne Rod favored. You don't get to be a single parent for umpteen years without developing a sixth sense for smelling trouble.

"Morning, Rod." I settled on the chair facing his desk. I'd been with Suntan Queen since I was in high school and didn't need permission to take a seat.

"Luella." Rod fidgeted with an ugly digital clock on his desk.

I waited.

He put the clock down but didn't make eye contact. "Luella, I have some bad news."

My stomach dropped like I was on that five-story flume ride my daughter made me go on once at Walt Disney World.

He shifted his weight. "Apparently, some of the higher-ups think it's time for a change."

"What do you mean?" My fingers curled over the arms of the chair. I was liable to snap one off if I wasn't careful.

Rod met my gaze with an earnest expression. "You know how it is these days, with the kids and their phones—"

"Everyone has a phone, Rod."

He tried to smile, but only succeeded in looking flustered. "Exactly."

An idiotic statement like that didn't deserve a response.

He looked away again. "Anyhow, they want to take your position in a new direction."

"What direction?" Whatever direction this was going in, it didn't sound like a good one.

Rod sighed. "A direction that doesn't include you."

My toes tingled. Anger fizzed right up my legs, churned through my belly, and seized my chest. It's a wonder I didn't burst into flame on the spot. "Rod, I have worked for this company since—"

"Since the earth cooled. I know." He raised his hands in a placating gesture, possibly to stop me from punching him in the nose.

"I want to talk to Queenie. Right now."

"Well, Queenie doesn't want to talk to you."

"Why's that?"

"It's been decided."

I laughed. I couldn't help it, even though the situation was far from humorous. "You think Queenie would fire me after all these years without so much as a word of explanation? You're joking." I leaned forward. "Queenie herself moved me into this position when websites were first getting big and social media wasn't even around yet. I know this company backwards and forwards. Every raise, every accolade I've ever had came from her. And now you're telling me she's throwing me out without an explanation?"

"Look, Luella—you know I don't have anything against you. I just do what I'm told."

"That's a copout. Show me my bad performance reviews. Oh, wait—there aren't any." I sat back and folded my arms. Sometimes, silence was the best way to get someone talking.

He opened and closed his mouth like a landed fish.

"What now? You going to put me in handcuffs and escort me out?"

"Don't be dramatic—"

I lowered my voice to a soft purr. "I'm not being dramatic. I'm slightly perturbed that I put so many years into this company and now I'm out without so much as an explanation."

He winced. "It's not technically required to give a reason to fire someone."

"And if I wanted to be dramatic, I could walk right out of here and make a big fuss on my way out. But I won't. I'll just say I'm highly disappointed by this treatment."

Relief spread over his face. "You'll need to clean out your desk. Then I'll escort you out."

"Great. Bring the handcuffs." I stood. "I better get my accrued leave in my last check, Rod. You hear me?"

He nodded without meeting my gaze.

"I'll let you know when you can 'escort' me out." I pulled the door open with considerable force and let it bang into the wall before striding out.

I headed straight for Pepper.

Pepper took one look at my face and sprang from her desk, her curls bobbing. "Luella? What happened? What did he say?"

I shook my head. "I'll explain after we get Rose."

Pepper darted around her desk and followed me.

Rose's kohl-lined eyes widened as we approached her on the factory floor. "Are you okay?"

"Can you come to my office?"

Rose handed her clipboard to a nearby employee and followed.

In my cubicle, Pepper dropped into an extra chair and rubbed at a stray smudge of sunscreen on her arm. Rose remained standing.

I sat on the edge of my desk and lowered my voice. "Rod fired me."

Pepper bolted up. "What the—"

Rose gasped and covered her mouth with both hands. The tiny skulls on her nails grinned at me.

"He didn't even give me a reason."

"That's not right," said Pepper, shaking her head with vehement disapproval. The black pearl on her leather necklace glinted green under the fluorescent lighting. "In fact, I'm going to go tell Rod—"

I snagged her shirt as she attempted to charge out of the cubicle, causing her to boomerang. "No, you're not. He's just the messenger. Sit down."

She huffed and sat.

Rose frowned. "Why would Queenie do that to you? You always get good performance reviews."

"I don't know. Maybe she thinks I'm too old for running the social media?"

"Damn ageism," muttered Pepper, who was clearly still peeved about being stopped from assaulting Rod.

Fine lines appeared on Rose's forehead as she raised her eyebrows. "I didn't think that was Queenie's style. After all, she's much older than you—and she's still running her own company." Rose tucked her hair behind her ears, revealing delicate silver earrings shaped like miniature daggers.

"I didn't think that was her style either, but now I don't know anything." The adrenalin backwash left me hugging myself as my stomach turned slow flips.

Rose embraced me. "I'm so sorry."

Pepper threw her arms around both of us. She smelled of salt, sunscreen, and the neoprene wetsuit she wore while surfing. "We'll help you. I bet there are a hundred companies dying to hire a clever lady with ninja social media skills." She released us and her face lit up with determination.

Rose let go and nodded decisively. One of her dagger earrings flashed in the morning light.

An abrupt laugh escaped my lips, the sound dangerously close to a sob. "Yes, a middle-aged empty nest single mom is certainly a hot commodity these days." I pressed my fingertips to the outer corners of my eyes. "It'll be okay, right?"

Our conversation was interrupted when London knocked on the cubicle wall. When she entered, her facial expression indicated she'd caught the vibe in the room. "Am I interrupting something?"

"My firing," I said.

London gasped. "Oh, my God!" She paused, then continued breathlessly. "Why would Aunt Queenie fire you? I thought everything was going super. Who's going to do your job?"

"Not me, apparently."

She gripped my arm with surprising strength. "You know what? I'm going to talk to my aunt."

"You don't have to do that—"

London flipped her hair over her shoulder. "I'm part of the family. I might as well use the influence I have." She mimed texting in midair. "I'll be in touch."

Rose, Pepper, and I exchanged glances after London swept out.

I shrugged. "I guess there could be worse things than an advocate on the inside."

Rose made a dubious face. "London?"

"Lay off, goth queen. She's not as shallow as she looks."

"Hmph," said Rose, clearly unconvinced.

I picked up a framed photo of Lily, my mother, and me at the beach.

Pepper reached for it. "Let me see." She held the frame and examined the photo within. "Isn't Lily precious? They grow up so fast. I remember holding her in the hospital the day after she was born."

She passed the photo to Rose, who trailed a fingertip around the edge. "Seems like yesterday. You look more like your Mama every year. So does Lily."

I took it and carefully put it in a box. "I'll have to tell Mama about losing my job."

They both chuckled. They'd known Mama so long they called her "Mama," too.

Sometimes, Mama was too wrapped up in her own hijinks to mind what I got up to—but you never knew when she'd be in between motorcycle rallies and out of cigarettes and in enough of a mood to latch on to something. Mama was a lot of things—many of them positive—but she was the last person anyone with sense would turn to for advice on a technology career.

The photo of Pepper, Rose, and me at a long-ago Suntan Queen company picnic went in the box next. On that day, the three of us ate cold watermelon till our fingers got sticky, then took over the karaoke machine and sang songs by The Cure—Rose's choice—until we got dragged off, giggling unrepentantly.

Mama had kept an eye on Lily, who could stuff herself with watermelon but couldn't touch most of the other treats for fear of her celiac disease flaring up. I promised to bake her a whole raft of gluten-free treats later to make up for it. I made good on that promise with chocolate chip cookies, strawberry shortcake, and a whole pan of brownies—everything she'd missed out on.

It's funny, the things you remember. And the things you take for granted until they're gone.

With Lily, I figured as long as we avoided gluten, we'd be golden. Then it turned out she was pretty sensitive to dairy, too, and I had to go back to the drawing board on all the recipes I'd assumed were keepers.

With my career, I'd always thought I'd retire from Suntan Queen, covered in glory—or at least a few free bottles of sunscreen—then ride off into the Sparkle Beach sunset to enjoy my retirement.

It made me want to give Queenie a piece of my mind.

I dropped stray office supplies into an empty desk drawer. No point in being accused of stealing company property on top of the other indignities foisted upon me. There was nothing else left to pack.

I reached out to Pepper and Rose. They took my hands, then joined theirs, completing a circle. "Whatever happens, we have each other." I squeezed their hands and a strange jolt shot through me. "The static is crazy in here!"

We released each other and laughed.

Rose tapped the metal desk to discharge electrical buildup.

Pepper attempted to zap herself by touching her index fingers together.

I tried to shake off the electrical sensation, but stopped in mid-gesture when I heard a sound like a slingshot being spun at high speed.

It was coming from the reception area.

All three of us turned in the direction of the noise.

Beyond the reception desk, the revolving door rotated wildly. A blast of air shot into the building and sent everything in its path airborne. Papers and folders took wing and flew across the reception area.

"What in the—" I couldn't finish the thought. A flock of Suntan Queen flyers pelted past my head as the wind howled into the offices.

Rose ducked a flying folder and stayed low.

Pepper joined her in a crouch behind the cubicle wall. "Get down, Luella!"

I remained standing, but I braced one hand against the desk and used the other to keep my hair from being whipped into my face. A glance out the far windows revealed no sign of a storm.

Shrieks echoed from the cubicles around me as my former coworkers dodged the projectiles that shot through the air. Coffee mugs tumbled to the floor as the wind increased.

Then, I saw it.

A white dog—no, not just white, a white and *silver* dog—ran through the spinning door and loped past the reception desk. The wake of its passage knocked over chairs as it barreled through the gauntlet of cubicles.

I could tell its location by the debris blasted upward as it passed. Closer and closer it came, yet I couldn't move. I didn't want to move.

Silver eddies spiraled upward from its path like argent smoke.

I'd never seen anything so breathtaking.

The dog skidded to a halt before me, the wind still howling outside the gentle calm that enveloped me like a soft blanket.

I let go of my hair. It lifted and tossed in a gentle breeze, a quiet contrast to the chaotic tempest in the office surrounding me.

She—for I immediately conceived of her as female—sat on her haunches and looked up at me with self-satisfaction, as if to say *See what I did?*

I held out my hand to the strange canine before me.

She trotted closer. Her hair glimmered with a thousand streaks of silver under the fluorescent lights. She nudged her head under my hand.

I nearly withdrew in shock. Instead of feeling plain animal hair under my fingers, it felt like I had placed my hand over a hairdryer made of fur. It blasted my palm with a tepid but steady current of air. I smoothed my hand over her elegant head. "Hello, girl. Who are you? Where did you come from?"

She turned in a playful circle, her fluffy tail waving jauntily—then she bolted.

My heart contracted. "Wait!" I ran after her as she bounded through the cubicle maze much faster than I could follow.

She plunged through the lobby like a white and silver cannonball.

I could only watch as she blew through the revolving door and disappeared.

The wind died and everything fluttered to the floor, leaving the entire office in utter disarray.

I picked my way past the reception desk, pushed through the revolving door, and stumbled outside into the ferocious heat and humidity of a summer morning in Florida.

No dog in any direction. The only sign of life was a blue-black crow perched on a nearby planter.

Tears of frustration pricked my eyes. "Come back," I whispered.

Pepper and Rose pushed through the revolving door and joined me on the sidewalk. The three of us moved into the scant shade of a palm tree.

"Who let a dog into the building?" Pepper said.

"You saw it?"

Pepper scrunched up her nose. "Of course I did. Big fluffy thing. How could you miss it?"

Rose peered down the street. "That was no normal dog."

"Rose—you saw it, too?"

She gave me an are-you-kidding look.

"Great. At least it's not just me who's cracked from the stress."

Rose treated me to one of her trademark stares. "What do you mean?"

"You didn't notice?" I looked from Rose to Pepper and back again. I lowered my voice. "No one else was looking at the dog. It was like they couldn't see it."

Pepper made a noise of disbelief. "That's impossible."

"See if anyone mentions it when you go in."

Pepper put on a police officer voice. "Excuse me, ma'am, have you seen a dog that looks like a white German shepherd with silver hair plugs?" She dropped the voice. "You're the dog expert, Rose. What kind of dog is that?"

Rose arched a dark eyebrow. "A mythical one?"

I squeezed my eyes shut and opened them again. "I know what I saw. And I'm pretty sure we're the only ones who saw it. Her."

Rose quoted her favorite play. "'There are more things in heaven and earth, Horatio, than are dreamt of in your philosophy.'"

Pepper scratched her head. "Who's talking about philosophy?"

"Science," Rose clarified. "The line refers to things science can't explain."

"Oh," said Pepper.

"Rose, does that mean you think we're not crazy?"

"We're not crazy."

"I'm glad you don't think I'm turning into Hamlet. But don't say anything about this to anyone, okay? I'm not sure other people would react so calmly. I don't want someone to get the wrong idea and decide we need to be committed."

They both shook their heads vehemently.

"Maybe we could talk about it some more, though—later? Figure out what it was?"

They agreed. Pepper rubbed her hands together.

We returned to the office to find the damage even worse than it first appeared. The wind had sent not only papers flying, but also scores of the morning's full cups of coffee from every desk in sight. Brown stains decorated the cubicle walls, the carpet, and—by the looks of it—Rod's white shirt.

I collected my box and approached him. "Looks like you have your hands full. How about I see myself out?"

Rod shot me the haunted look of a man about to have to do a whole lot of explaining to the higher-ups. He groaned, then gestured with flailing hands. "Look at this mess."

I'd left any sympathy for Rod back in his office. "Sorry, Rod. Looks like none of this is my problem anymore."

All I had to do now was find a new job, figure out why I was seeing dogs that weren't there, explain everything to Mama and Lily—and come up with a polite way to ask Lily's dad to pitch in extra for Lily until I got my income flowing again.

Piece of cake.

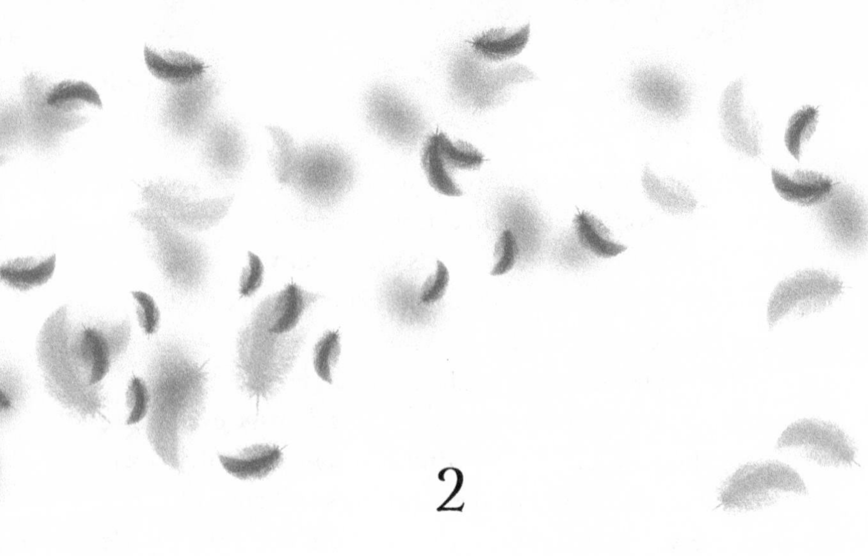

2

I promised the girls I'd meet up with them later at Shelly's Place—Sparkle Beach's one-of-a-kind mermaid-themed bar—but first I had to head home and do some serious communicating. Home was a bland but serviceable two-bedroom, second story apartment in a decent complex located much closer to the interstate than to the beach. Real estate prices being what they were, I'd never been able to afford to rent a fancier apartment, let alone actually purchase a home.

I sank into the sofa and put my feet up. First, a text for my ex-husband—Lily's dad. *Hey, Bradley. Got some bad news today. Call when you get a chance.*

He was pretty good about getting back to me, especially when something was urgent.

I'd have to call Mama later. Of course, she refused to own a cell phone. She insisted the government would listen to her calls. I tried to tell her the government didn't want to overhear any of her throwdowns about the relative merits of Harley-Davidson versus Indian Motorcycles, but she just shook her head and muttered something ominous about the truth being out there. She also disliked banks—presumably for similar reasons. She probably had pirate treasure hidden somewhere in the walls of her trailer.

I sent a text to Lily. *How are you, kiddo?*

I wasn't about to tell her about my bad day until I had gotten the situation firmly under control. She had enough on her plate, starting college in a faraway city, and I didn't want to burden her.

The phone buzzed in my hand as a text came in from Pepper. *You okay?*

Her concern warmed my heart. *I'm fine*, I wrote. *Don't worry. I'll see you later at Shelly's.*

The phone rang and displayed Bradley's name. "Hey, thanks for calling." We'd been divorced for almost a decade, and despite some early bumps with child-raising decisions and his remarriage, on the whole we'd been able to communicate like civil adults.

"You all right? Lily okay?" he said.

I pictured him way out in Montana, far from the Florida shores where we'd lived while we were together. "Lily's fine. But I got fired from Suntan Queen this morning."

"That's terrible. Why'd they do that? You've been there since—"

"Since the earth cooled, I know. People keep telling me that. But for some reason, Queenie decided to let me go."

"That doesn't make any sense."

"I know." I paused. The next part wasn't easy to say. "Listen, this puts me in kind of a situation." Understatement of the century. "Lily's expenses are pretty high right now. I know we were sharing the costs her partial scholarship didn't cover, but I'm going to come up short soon if I can't find something else right away."

He sighed. "That's bad news. I needed to talk to you, too."

My heart skipped a beat.

"I tore my ACL."

I pressed my free hand to my chest. "Oh, my God! How did it happen?"

"Jumped down from my truck bed like a fool. I'm all right—but I'm staring down the barrel of a full reconstruction on that knee. Surgery, physical therapy, the works. And my insurance stinks. I'm gonna be paying out of pocket for a lot of it."

"So you're going to be short, too."

"I'm gonna be short, too."

We both fell silent.

I closed my eyes. "What are we going to do for Lily?"

"I don't know. I was hoping you could take up a little slack while I deal with these medical bills." A dark chuckle rippled over the line. "Guess that's not gonna happen."

I took a deep breath and blew it out. "I guess I better come up with a new job."

"Luella, I'm not trying to leave you in the lurch, here. You know Lily's education is more important to me than anything."

"I know. I'll figure it out. You take care of yourself."

"Thank you. You too."

"Bye." I hung up, then set the phone down and pressed my fingertips to my temples in an attempt to massage away an oncoming headache.

Maybe going to Shelly's Place wasn't such a great way to blow off steam. Drinks and snacks cost money, and if I didn't come up with a plan, I would soon be as broke as the Ten Commandments.

My phone buzzed. Lily was texting me back. *I'm fine, Mom. You?*

Super duper, baby. You eating safe up there?

You know I am, she wrote.

I know. I just worry.

No gluten, no problem. She added a smiley grin emoji. *Gotta get going. Love you.*

I love you, too. I tapped out the letters and added a string of heart emojis before sending the message.

I lay on the couch and my gaze drifted to the window where a large oak tree filled the view. The leaves flapped wildly, then settled. I watched as one cardinal, then two, landed in the branches. Then a blue jay. Then a mockingbird. Then a woodpecker. There was even a brown thrasher, a type of bird that usually hid in the underbrush.

I sat up abruptly. This wasn't normal.

I rubbed my eyes as I stood. I walked to the window, moving slowly to avoid startling the birds.

More birds landed. I spotted a robin, which was unusual for the time of year, and a beady-eyed crow.

The crow cocked its head and eyed me directly, then let out a raucous caw. The other birds burst into a cacophony of songs as if I'd walked into my own personal version of

Walt Disney World's Enchanted Tiki Room—only with backyard birds instead of toucans and parrots.

I pressed my hands against the window glass.

The crow left his perch and flew to the windowsill. He tapped insistently on the glass while the chorus of birdsong continued.

Visions of broken windows, irate landlords, and expensive repair bills flashed through my mind. "Shoo! Go on, shoo!" I flapped my hands.

The crow looked insulted.

"Look, bird, if you break my window, there's going to be hell to pay. Literally. So unless you have some money tucked under your wing, knock it off."

The crow let out another caw, then turned away and flew back to the tree. The entire host of birds flew off like miniature synchronized stunt planes—leaving behind silver contrails that glittered in the sun before fading away like they'd never existed.

Indoor whirlwinds. Mystery dogs. Birds trailing silver. This was getting weirder by the minute.

I turned away from the window and considered calling Mama to break the job loss news, but decided I wasn't up for it. Better to recuperate at Shelly's Place, and on my date with Dan, before I attempted anything so fraught.

I padded down the hallway to change clothes before going out. I tried not to look in Lily's room, but I couldn't stop myself.

She'd left more than a dozen teddy bears on the bed. I resisted the urge to give one a hug.

Instead, I resolutely turned away and went into my room. A quick rummage in the closet produced an acceptable pair of shorts and a pretty top. Shorts would show off my calves, especially when paired with a pair of sandals. High heels were not my friends.

Casual Florida living had its advantages.

I touched up my makeup and brushed my hair. I'd need a trim soon—the ends looked ragged. Maybe I could do it myself and save a few bucks.

I hadn't bothered to dye it yet. I used to be afraid of going prematurely gray like Mama, but when it actually started happening, I liked it. I'd found myself stopping in front of a mirror more than once to watch the silver strands catch the light in contrast with the brown.

I put it up in a French braid to show off the colors, then I texted the girls. *Heading over. See you in fifteen.* Thanks to their part-time work schedules, we could meet up for a late lunch without conflicting with my dinner date.

I drove the usual route between my apartment and the beachside peninsula. The mainland strip malls gave way to a hodgepodge of buildings spanning every decade from the late nineteenth century all the way up to modern day. I loved the Craftsman cottages, the shotgun houses, and the two-story Victorians.

A broad bridge carried me across the wide Intracoastal Waterway. Even safe and secure in a car, my nerves jangled at the sensation of height. The feeling passed as the car leveled out on solid ground, and one block later, I pulled up to Shelly's Place and parked under the weathered wood sign featuring a plump, purple-tailed mermaid with a sea-green shell bra and thick waves of blue hair.

The heavy door creaked as I pushed it open. I bypassed the hostess stand and headed straight for our usual high-top table in the bar.

Rose and Pepper sat under strings of white Christmas lights that trailed from the ceiling in a glowing crisscross pattern. The sound of Sparkle Beach's classic rock radio station crackled through the overhead speakers.

"I made it. I can't stay long, though. I'm supposed to meet Dan for dinner later."

Rose raised her usual—red wine and Diet Coke over ice—the dark drink accented by flashes of light like smoldering embers.

Pepper hoisted an oversized concoction with both hands. "Check out today's drink special." The drink reflected the precise shade of the Caribbean Sea if the Caribbean Sea were made of neon.

I gave it a sideways look. "If I drank that, I'd probably die."

"Oh, come on, a little laundry detergent won't kill you." Pepper took a sip.

When the server approached, I slid the remaining menu across the table. "Can I get a glass of water with lemon?"

Rose raised an eyebrow. "You don't want a soda? Or an iced tea?"

"How about some food?" said Pepper.

"Just water for me."

Pepper stopped the server. "Can I get a triple play platter for the table, please?" She waved away my thanks. "I got this."

Rose smirked. "We should all have married dentists."

"For a relationship you can sink your teeth into, marry a dentist." Pepper wiggled her eyebrows like Groucho Marx.

"Speaking of marriage—I talked to my ex-husband. I called to tell him he might need to pick up the slack for Lily's living expenses for a while."

Pepper leaned in. "And?"

I sighed. "And it turns out—he's wrecked his knee. ACL tear. Going to be out of work, in surgery, or doing physical therapy for the foreseeable future."

Pepper set down her glass with a thud. "Oh, my God!"

"That's what I said."

"Is he okay?" asked Rose.

"He's okay. But it's going to cost a mint."

"Doesn't he have insurance?"

"You know how it is. Some of those plans barely cover a doctor visit, let alone anything extensive."

They both nodded.

Suntan Queen's health plan had been good. That reminded me of something else to lose sleep over—my own health insurance, considering I was way too young for Medicare. I pushed the thought away.

"Mozzarella sticks are the perfect food," said Pepper, submerging one in a small ramekin of tomato sauce.

"Chocolate is the perfect food," countered Rose. She took a mozzarella stick.

Pepper nibbled her mozzarella stick thoughtfully. "Maybe we should dip mozzarella sticks in chocolate."

Rose pushed the platter toward me.

I snagged a fried chicken finger and dunked it in honey mustard sauce. "Bradley's short on cash. I'm short on cash. Lily needs money for groceries and rent. She's going to be working all hours on her courses and I can't ask her to get a job on top of that. Her education comes first."

Rose brandished a half-eaten mozzarella stick. "Absolutely."

"I need a new job, stat." I leaned back and nibbled the chicken finger.

"I still want to know what the hell happened this morning," said Pepper.

"That's not the only weird thing. Wait till I tell you what happened at home."

"Yes, please." Pepper propped her chin on her hands.

I let my gaze drift over the kitschy fishing nets lining the walls, gathering my thoughts before I spoke. "I was at home, getting in touch with Bradley and checking on Lily. I was sitting there on the couch, minding my own business, when I looked out the window and saw all these different birds sitting in the big oak tree."

Rose made a skeptical face. "Isn't that what birds do? Sit in trees?"

Pepper hushed her. "I wanna hear the story!"

"I got up. I went to the window. And all these birds started singing at full volume—"

"Like the Tiki Room show at Disney World," said Pepper.

"Exactly. This big black crow flies over to the window, looks at me—I mean really looks at me—and starts banging its beak against the glass." I made a bird beak with my hand, like a shadow puppet, and gestured to indicate the force of the blows.

Rose shivered with delight. "Creepy."

"I tried to shoo it away before it broke the glass. The whole time, the other birds are whistling and singing and making a racket. Finally it flew off the windowsill, and all the birds took off together." I leaned back. "And here's the kicker. When they flew off, they left behind these bright silver trails in the air—which promptly disappeared before I could think to try to take a picture."

Pepper put down a potato skin she'd picked up. "Was there a bunch of wind this time, too?"

"As a matter of fact, yeah. I remember seeing the leaves moving in the tree outside the window, like there was a high wind."

Rose drained the last of her drink. She drummed her skull fingernails in thought. "Did you tell your mom yet? About any of it?"

"No." I covered my face with my hands.

Pepper snorted into her neon drink. "She's going to love this."

I groaned. "Don't remind me."

"Are you going to tell Dan the Man?" asked Pepper.

"I'm not even telling Mama—why would I tell him? Besides, Dan . . . " I paused to gather the right words. "Dan is very . . . "

"Boring?" said Rose.

"Dull?" added Pepper.

Their opinions on Dan were well-known to me. I soldiered on. "Because Dan is not prone to flights of fancy."

Rose and Pepper rolled their eyes in near-perfect synchrony.

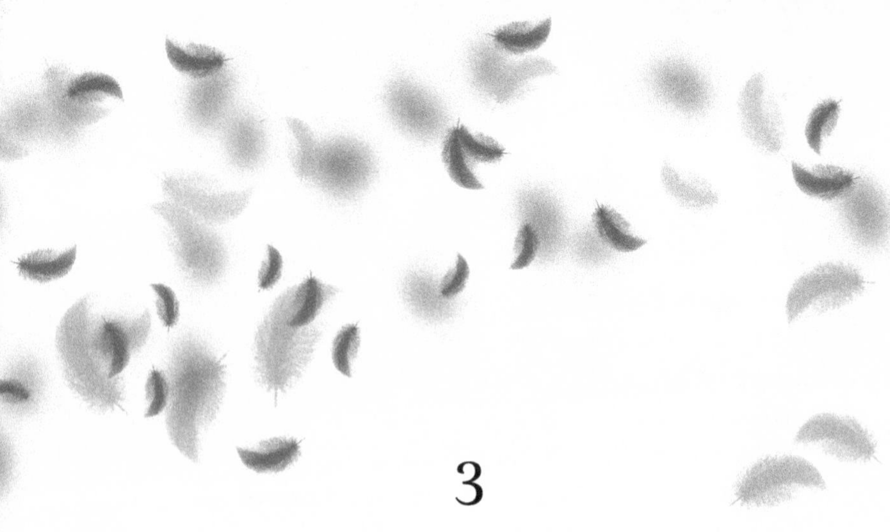

3

Dan was also never late. Given the option, he'd arrive early, corral a table, and wait for everyone else to show up. It was one of the things I liked about him, especially in comparison with the large number of flaky middle-aged men still running around loose trying to find a combination wife/mother. He wasn't the soul of excitement—in fact, he tended to call it quits when he reached some sort of recommended daily allowance of fun—but I enjoyed his company. He was reliable, and good-looking in a square-jawed, clean cut kind of way.

We'd made the local Tex-Mex restaurant our spot. La Tierra y el Mar boasted a mariachi band with a harpist, just the right thing to set the mood. I entered the restaurant and passed the colorful Mexican pottery adorning the wall. Sure enough, Dan was already seated at a table with a basket of tortilla chips and a crock of salsa. I wove through the tables and took a seat across from him. "I see you got a head start on the chips."

He swallowed a bite. "Freshly fried. Have some."

"Don't mind if I do." I scooped up some salsa and bit into the chip with an audible crunch. "Although I did have a snack already with the girls."

Dan slid the chips away from me.

I arrested the motion by touching the rim of the basket. I pulled the basket closer and grabbed a handful of chips, depositing them in a heap on a side plate. "Anyway, my day has not been so good."

His forehead wrinkled as he raised his eyebrows. "How so?"

"I got fired."

"What? No!"

I told him the story, leaving out the part about the indoor tornado and the white-and-silver dog. "I can't see why Queenie would fire me. It doesn't make any sense."

Dan had opened his mouth to respond when the server interrupted. He turned his attention to the menu. "I'll have the steak fajitas—add shrimp."

"I'll have the smothered enchilada, please." I closed the menu with a snap and handed it to the server.

Dan gave me a look of concern. "Are you sure?"

The server looked back and forth between us.

"Of course I'm sure. Why?"

"I thought... maybe it was too much food."

I laughed. "I know my limitations, and a smothered enchilada ain't one of them." I sounded like my mother.

"Thank you," I said to the server. When she left, I went from being amused that Dan thought I couldn't finish a smothered enchilada, to wondering if he'd actually been implying that I *shouldn't* finish a smothered enchilada.

"You were saying," he prompted.

I eyed him speculatively, but put aside the question of the enchilada and returned to the subject at hand. "I was saying it didn't make sense why she would fire me."

He nodded, then rubbed his chin. It was clear he had something to say, but was hesitating to say it. "Your performance reviews were good?"

"They were fine. Every year I've worked there they've been fine."

"Have you considered they might have thought your performance was lacking in some way, even if they didn't ding you on your review?" He sipped from his glass of water with lemon.

I blinked. Had I heard what I thought I heard? "Are you saying I wasn't doing a good job?"

We were interrupted by the cheerful tones of the mariachi band, led by a fellow with an enormous harp on a tiny rolling stand. The music seemed much louder than I remembered it. I forced a smile and nodded along with the song, which, admittedly, was lovely—I just wasn't currently in the mood for it.

Unfortunately, after they finished the first song, they launched into another.

I dug in my purse, past assorted crumpled receipts, loose change, keys, a single peppermint, and an emergency chocolate bar that was only half-melted, and pulled out a five-dollar bill. I laid the money on the edge of the table.

The harpist acknowledged it with a nod without skipping a beat. When they wrapped up the second song, he pocketed the tip, tipped the harp back, and wheeled it away, allowing our conversation to continue.

The look I gave Dan was hotter than the salsa, and not in a good way. "You were saying?"

"I mean, nobody's perfect." He bit into a chip.

I'd never noticed the sound of his chewing before. It grated on my ears. "Are you saying it's my fault I got fired?"

His mouth said, "No"—but the expression on his face said, "Yes."

"Don't sugar coat it, Dan. If you think I did something wrong, say so." The smell of the chips, so appetizing upon my arrival, turned my stomach.

He rolled his eyes. "Stop picking at this and let's enjoy our date, okay?"

I threw my napkin down on the table. "You started this, and now you're blaming me for picking at it?"

He held his hands up. "Calm down, Luella."

"Don't you dare tell me to calm down. Not when you're the one who pissed me off in the first place."

His gaze darted around the room. "People will hear you . . ."

"Good. Maybe they should! Then they'll know what kind of a man—no, *worm*—you are, blaming someone for getting fired when they didn't do anything wrong."

The sound of sizzling meat drifted from over my shoulder. The server approached with Dan's surf and turf fajitas, then set the hot pan down with a flourish. An accompanying runner parked my plate on the table in front of me. "Can I get you anything else?" said the server.

Snap decisions weren't my bag, but I was about to make an exception. "You know what? Bring me a box, and bring me another smothered enchilada to go. I'm going to take everything home and smother my enchilada with *another* smothered enchilada. Alone!" I glared at Dan.

"Oh, come on … " His tone turned wheedling.

He knew he was in the wrong. I could at least enjoy that as the sauce on my takeout dinner. "I'm leaving as soon as I have my enchiladas."

He had lifted a single shrimp to his mouth, seemingly at a loss to do anything else, when I saw movement out of the corner of my eye.

The white dog had returned! She trotted across the dining room, past the mariachi band, and sat on the floor next to my chair. No one else had noticed a thing.

I tried not to look.

She placed her paws on my thigh, then boosted herself into my lap, nearly crowding me out of my chair. She felt heavy as a real dog but light as air at the same time, as if she were only the idea of weight rather than the reality.

What are you doing, dog?

I don't know if I expected a response, but what I got certainly wasn't the response I would have predicted.

The dog sneezed, sending a blast of silver sparkles across the table that shot Dan's entire dinner onto his shirt: shrimp, steak, peppers, onions, rice, beans, sour cream, salsa, and tortillas, plus the entire basket of chips.

My mouth fell open.

Dan gasped. “What the—”

Mischief complete, the dog hopped down and ran away, quickly disappearing from sight before I could even think to run after her.

The server returned with a full box and an empty box, took one look at Dan—then dropped the boxes on the table and scurried off, clearly eager to be anywhere else.

I scraped the enchilada from my plate into the empty box and closed it up. I tossed some more cash on the table and stood. “It’ll be a cold day in hell before I share a table with you again.”

I carried my two dinners out with my head held high.

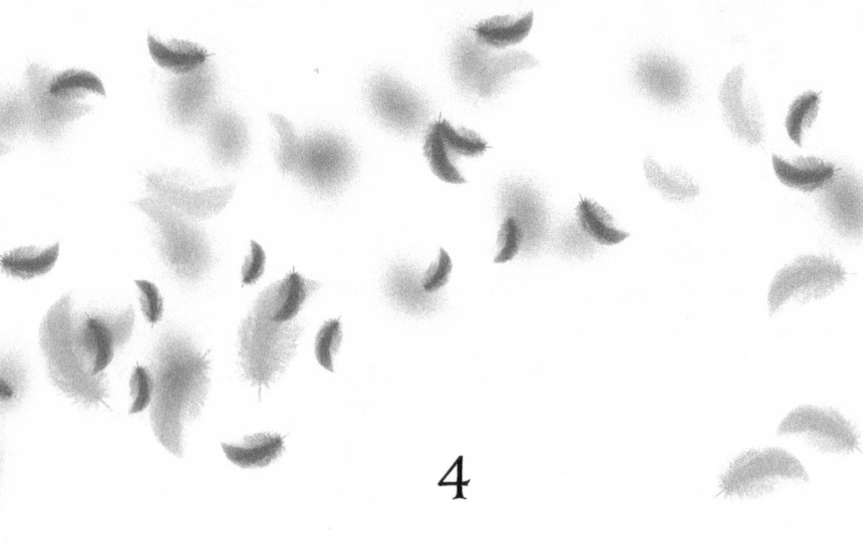

4

I detoured to Mama's on my way home. I needed to talk to her—and after the disastrous date with Dan, I craved moral support.

The gravel crunched under the wheels as I pulled into the driveway. I walked past Mama's beloved motorcycle and tried the door of the trailer.

Unlocked.

For a woman so paranoid, she was remarkably lax about locking the front door. I stepped inside and shut the door behind me, conscientiously turning the lock. "Mama?"

Her voice floated from deeper within the trailer. "Luella? That you?"

"You left the door unlocked, Mama."

Mama emerged from the hallway in cutoff shorts and an ancient Bike Week tank top, her white hair pulled tight in a bun. "Me and my Smith & Wesson ain't scared of nobody." She cackled.

"Well, that's dandy, but I worry."

"That's your father in you, baby. He always was a worrier, bless him." Mama touched an old family portrait on the faux wood wall with affection. "Come on and sit down. Can I get you something? Did you eat yet?"

"I just came from a dinner date with Dan."

"You want some iced tea? Water?"

"I'm good." I sat on the old but clean couch, which creaked as I sank into the cushions.

Mama took the recliner and retrieved a pack of cigarettes and a lighter from the side table.

"Mama, please?" I gave the cigarettes a pointed look.

"Oh, sorry! Force of habit." She set them down. "I'll have one after you go."

"I wish you wouldn't have one at all."

"When you're my age, girl, you'll understand—something's going to kill you soon, so you might as well enjoy yourself." She settled back in the recliner and threw the lever to pop out the footrest.

This was an old argument I was too wise to continue. "All right, Mama. You do your thing. I don't have to like it."

Mama nodded contentedly. "How was your date?"

I looked down at my hands. "I broke up with him."

She sat up so hard she nearly shut the footrest. "You broke up? Why?"

"It's a long story."

"I ain't got nothing but time."

"It has to do with what I really came here to talk about: I got fired from Suntan Queen."

She seemed less surprised than I thought she would be, but her wrinkles deepened as she frowned. "You got fired? What's that got to do with Dan?"

"Dan implied getting fired was my own fault. So I dumped him."

Mama's eyes narrowed. "I'm sorry that happened to you."

"Which part?"

"Suntan Queen, mostly. If your boyfriend said that to you, well—he deserves to get dumped. Why do you think you got fired?"

"I don't know. I got good reviews, Mama. Queenie always seemed to approve of the job I was doing. It doesn't make sense." Something tickled my memory. "Weren't you friends with Queenie, back in the day?"

"Me?" Her eyes widened. "Not so's you'd notice. We went to the same school, that's all."

"I see." The tickle of memory became an itch, but I ignored it. "Anyway, it puts me in a pretty bad spot, financially speaking. I called Bradley to see if he could pitch in more for Lily, but he can't—he got injured real bad, and he's paying for it out of pocket."

Mama shook her head back and forth. "When it rains, it pours."

"Tell me about it." I let my head drop back onto the couch cushion.

We sat in silence, the only sound the roar of the overworked air conditioner.

"I tell you what, baby. Maybe I can help out."

"You don't have that kind of money, Mama."

"I know I don't, girl. Be quiet and listen." She shut the footrest and sat forward in the recliner. "A woman of my acquaintance, Mrs. Millefleur—"

"Millefleur? Isn't that the family with their name on all the buildings? How do you know them?" The social difference between Mama and the well-connected Millefleurs wasn't just a gap—it was a canyon.

"I've been in this town since before you were born. I've known lots of people. Now hush and listen for a minute. Mrs. Millefleur is taking an extended vacation. She wanted somebody to personally look after one of her more special rental properties while she's gone. I was thinking about doing it, but if you want, you could pack up and move over there rent-free while she's gallivanting around the world."

"Leave my apartment?"

"What's keeping you there?"

I opened my mouth, then shut it. The landlord was about to raise my rent—again—and being able to cross rent off my monthly budget would be a godsend, even if it was temporary. "Where is this place?"

Mama's eyes twinkled. "On the peninsula."

She had me there. She knew I'd always dreamed of living on the peninsula rather than the mainland. "Is it a nice place?"

"I don't know if it's *fancy*." Mama said the word with disdain. "But Mrs. Millefleur is particular in her ways. I expect it's kept up real nice. Got two bedrooms and everything." She stood and walked to the kitchen, where she opened a drawer and took out a stack of papers. "In fact, I think I have an old picture here somewhere." She withdrew a photograph and brought it to me.

"When was this taken?"

"Roundabout 1960-something, I'd reckon." She sat next to me.

The faded photograph depicted a tidy shotgun house with heart-shaped cutouts in the white picket fence surrounding it. It looked too good to be true. "This is adorable. Have you seen it in person?"

"Not recently. But I trust Mrs. Millefleur if she says it's ready to move in."

I held the photograph in my hands and glanced out the living room window. As I looked, hundreds of dandelion seeds drifted into view, trailing tiny, twinkling silver motes like a field of pinpoint stars. I bit my lip to keep from making a startled noise, half-expecting a crow to bang on the window or a silver-white dog to come pelting through the door. "Do you see that?"

"See what?" Mama turned to follow my gaze.

I blinked.

They were gone. At least, the silver motes were gone.

"Oh, how pretty. Dandelion seeds!" Mama moved to the window and adjusted the curtain. "So what do you think?"

"I think… I'll think about it." I stood and went to the kitchen. I tidied the pile of papers and placed the photograph on top. Another photo popped out of the pile sideways, so I pulled it out entirely to make a neat stack—but I froze as I was about to place it on top of the house photo.

The old photo depicted three women—one of whom was definitely Mama—standing side-by-side with big grins and their arms around each other's shoulders. I turned the photo over. The handwriting on the back was hard to read, but I could make out the words: *When shall we three meet again?* I looked at the front again. "Mama, what's this?"

Mama turned from the window and joined me in the kitchen. "What's what?" When she caught sight of what I was holding, she snatched it and returned it to the drawer, piling the other papers on top. "That's nothing. Just an old picture." She herded me back to the living room.

"Who were those ladies?"

"I don't recall. Guess I got a little old-timer's disease, right?" She laughed and reached for her cigarettes again.

"Mama—"

"Oops, sorry." She withdrew her hand from the cigarettes. "You probably better get a move on. Let me know what you wanna do about the house."

Mama knew I never made snap decisions.

Or did I?

Visions of white picket fences danced through my mind accompanied by the imaginary caress of a fresh ocean breeze. I could almost taste the salt on my lips. "I'll take it."

Mama did a double take. "You will? You sure you don't want to go home and think about it?"

"Nope." My doubts would have to take a long walk off a short pier.

"Well, I'll be darned. Guess you can still surprise your mama after all. I'll get the keys for you and leave them under the rabbit by the wind chime."

Mama's outdoor hidey-holes transformed the trailer yard into something like a treasure hunt, if you knew where to look. "Under the rabbit by the wind chime. Thanks." I hugged her.

She patted my back like I was a baby. "You're gonna be all right, Luella. Don't you worry." She released me and walked me to the door.

I was halfway through when I turned back. "Don't forget to lock up."

"You worry too much." Mama shook her head and shut the door.

I waited, listening.

It took a full ten seconds until the lock clicked home. I smiled and walked to my car.

Thanks to the sun, the heat inside the car had reached the level of nuclear fission. I gingerly lowered myself to the driver's seat, tugging my shorts to cover my thighs so they wouldn't fry on contact. The air conditioner kicked in as I turned the key in the ignition.

I stopped at the nearest gas station to pick up the Sparkle Beach Journal. I knew job listings would be primarily found online—but I still liked the feel of a real paper in my hands. I'd start with the paper and move on to the internet job sites later.

Rather than drive home, I pulled into a riverside park where I could overlook the Intracoastal Waterway. Comfortably ensconced with the air conditioning on full blast, I opened the paper—which flapped like a bird in the cooled air—and turned to the help wanted section. I got a little distracted by the rainbow sail of a catamaran that drifted across my view, but I returned my attention to the paper after the catamaran passed.

There were only four jobs listed: liquor store clerk, bus mechanic, bartender, and some sort of questionable party-hosting job that seemed to be more of a pyramid scheme than an actual job.

Where were all the jobs? I closed the paper and tossed it on the passenger's seat, then pulled out my phone and typed "jobs" into the search bar.

Dozens of websites popped up. I stared at the screen as I scrolled. How was I supposed to know which ones were legit and which ones were a scam? There were so many! Thanks to my formerly lifelong employment at Suntan Queen, my job-hunting skills had hit their sell-by date sometime during the Clinton administration.

I cast the phone aside to join the newspaper and let my forehead fall to rest on top of the steering wheel. Lacking a wall to bang my head against, I let it strike the steering wheel. The closed space of the car interior amplified the sound—*bang, bang, bang.*

I heard an answering noise.

Tap, tap, tap.

I looked up.

A crow perched on my windshield wiper and batted the glass with its beak.

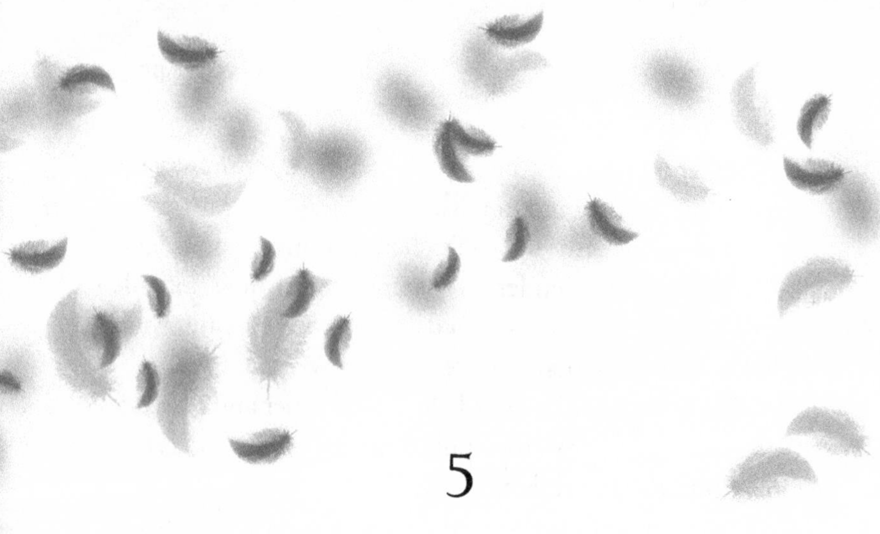

5

Later that night, I used my computer to visit every job search website I could find, making notes on a yellow notepad as I slogged through the listings. There were few unique job listings—most of them were the same spammy handful of listings mirrored across dozens of websites. I painstakingly created account after account to submit my short résumé to any job that looked both genuine and plausible.

I exhaled and tossed my ballpoint pen on the notepad, then leaned back to close my eyes.

I needed a break.

I got up from the desk and went to Lily's room. I sat on the edge of her bed, scooped an armful of stuffed animals out of the way, and fell backwards into the pillows. It felt good to rest. I was tempted to close my eyes and sink into sleep.

Instead, I opened them and looked around.

Once, Lily was a tiny little thing who cradled comfortably in the length of my hand and forearm. Then she outgrew her crib and we had to take the side off to turn it into a toddler bed. After that, we set the crib on the curb and replaced it with a twin bed.

After that, it was a sweet blur of days that swept by quickly no matter how you tried to slow them down.

Now she had gone away to a good school, and I was happy for her. She'd make it through college—I knew she would—and she would have a more secure future. I hoped.

But I still missed her. Newborn, toddler, child, preteen, teenager—I loved every evolution of Lily and would have gladly hopped in a time machine to hug each and every one of them. When she left for college, I felt the same pang I had when I dropped her off at kindergarten on the first day. There's a moment where you want to say, "Wait—come back!" but you let them go anyway, because it's their time to fly.

And now it was mine, and I didn't even know if my wings worked anymore.

I gave a teddy bear a hug and sat up, strangely energized. I walked to the kitchen as if in a dream. I pulled out all my gluten-free baking supplies and laid them on the counter. I started with an easy recipe for brownies, quickly mixing them in one bowl and popping the square pan into the oven. While they cooked, I turned out two dozen cowboy cookies and placed them in the fridge while I waited for the brownies to finish.

Once the oatmeal cookies went in, I started on shortbread cookies. The pattern pricked into the tops of the cookies pleased me to no end, such that I hardly noticed I'd barreled right past the midnight hour.

I ran to the computer and looked up a recipe for bird treats, improvising substitutions from what I had on hand.

By the time I finished, it was closer to dawn than to midnight. A giddy feeling spread through me, partly from staying up half the night, and partly from being surrounded by brownies, shortbread, oatmeal cookies, multiple loaves of bread, bird treats, and a half-gallon of lemonade I'd somehow managed to make in between all of it.

I cut a brownie and ate it straight from the pan, staining my fingers with the reddish-brown chocolate.

I'd missed baking for Lily, but it turned out baking for myself was pretty fun, too. I smiled as I imagined the looks on my friends' faces when I brought them a share of the goodies.

Since I'd polished off the brownie and didn't feel like sleeping yet, I picked up the tray of bird treats and quietly slipped out the door. I tiptoed quietly down the stairs, not wanting to wake anyone in the predawn hour, and crossed the grass to the oak tree outside my window. I set the treats among the exposed roots, hoping the bird chorus would find them on a return visit. It seemed right to pat the tree before I made my way back upstairs to my apartment, so I did.

In the silent darkness of the living room, I heard a quiet bird call. The gentle cooing soothed my fluttered heart. I let the fatigue I'd been holding off wash over me as I stretched out on the couch and slipped into the darkness of sleep.

When the continuous buzzing of the phone finally woke me, I nearly fell off the couch. I blinked at the clear light streaming through the windows.

What time was it? Had I really stayed up most of the night baking?

I stumbled around looking for the phone, until I found where it had slipped between the couch and the side table. I mashed the button to pick up before the call went to voicemail. "Hello? Hello?"

"Luella? Where've you been? You didn't answer any texts." Pepper's voice carried a tinge of worry.

I rubbed my eyes with my free hand. "I'm sorry. I must have slept through it."

"You sound rough."

"I was up half the night baking."

"Baking?"

"Yeah, I... got on a roll. I must have used everything in the house." I confirmed this by spotting the empty egg carton and butter wrappers on the counter.

"Well, put your pants on, 'cause we're going out."

"We are? Now? I've hardly slept—"

"Yes, now. After everything that happened yesterday, Rose and I decided you need a mojo boost. Bring some dessert—it'll help. Can't hurt, anyway."

"Where are we going?"

"Downtown. Make yourself decent and we'll pick you up in half an hour. It's not like you've got anything better to do." Pepper hung up.

"Except maybe try to look for a job," I said. Fuzzy memories of applying to dozens of positions floated into my mind—I'd applied to just about anything. If I didn't go out with the girls, the alternative was to mope around at home and stuff myself. If I was going to stuff myself, it would be more fun to do it with friends.

I gulped a cup of coffee and a handful of vitamins and supplements, figuring I'd need all the help I could get to power through the day. Then I showered, changed my clothes, and packed up the baked goods in record time, no doubt helped by the caffeine as it kicked in.

When I got Pepper's arrival text, I locked up and headed down the stairs with two totes filled with cookies and brownies. I set the totes on the floor of Pepper's SUV and slid into the back seat, shutting the door. "Where are we going?"

"We're going to the downtown art murals." Pepper threw the vehicle into reverse and backed out.

"We thought it would be fun to take pictures." Rose turned and fished around in a tote. She retrieved a brownie and waved it triumphantly before taking a big bite. "You need to bake for us all the time, Luella," she said around a mouthful of brownie. "I'd pay good money for these."

"Would you?"

Rose closed her eyes. "Mmm."

"What made you think about the downtown murals, Pepper?" I retrieved a cookie—breakfast of champions—and glanced at the oak tree by my apartment as we drove off.

"Big article in the paper. Apparently, they bring lots of customers downtown. Did you finally talk to your mom?" Pepper glanced at me in the rearview mirror.

"I stopped by after the disaster date."

"Did you tell her about the dog?"

I laughed. "No, are you kidding? But she did offer to hook me up with an unoccupied house for a while, to save money. I'm going to take her up on it."

Rose finished her brownie. "That's big. You've been at that apartment since—"

"Since the rent on my previous apartment got jacked sky high, yes. Can't keep one for more than a few years, it seems."

Before the bridge to the beachside, Pepper turned off on a stretch of road that ran along the edge of the river. Restored two-story buildings lined the mainland side of the street, and wrought iron streetlamps punctuated the sidewalk at regular intervals. Palm trees swayed over the riverside walkway.

Pepper eyed an open space. "I hate parallel parking."

Rose and I stiffened as Pepper pulled in and nearly hit the vehicle in front, then reversed and nearly hit another vehicle behind us.

"Damn it." Pepper turned the wheel and tried again.

When the car finally reached an acceptable angle—only slightly hanging into traffic—we disembarked to the cobblestone sidewalk.

Rose tugged her metal-studded denim skirt into place and smoothed her black blouse. "I have a map."

"Lead on," I said.

We strolled past gift shops and downtown's Thai restaurant—Thai Fi—to find the first mural: a large red rose painted in the style of a tattoo.

"You have to go first for this one. Give me your phone," Pepper said to Rose, slipping her own phone into a large pocket on the side of her loose-fitting cargo shorts.

Rose handed it over and stood in front of the mural. She rolled up her sleeve and exposed a similar tattoo on her bicep, then posed making a muscle. "Like this?"

Pepper raised the phone higher and snapped the photo. "Perfect!"

Before Rose could roll down her sleeve, I came close to admire the artwork on her skin. "That's so pretty. It really suits you."

"You should get a tattoo!" said Pepper.

I laughed ruefully. "Sometimes I feel like I'm the only person left in Sparkle Beach who hasn't gotten a tattoo."

After the rose mural, we visited the lighthouse mural, the rainbow mural, and the cupcake mural. We took turns taking pictures, striking various poses until we found our favorite angles.

I forgot all my troubles until my phone rang. "I have to take this. It might be for a job interview."

Rose raised an eyebrow. "On a Saturday?"

I ducked into an alley for quiet and picked up. "Hello?"

"This is the Social Security Administration. We are calling to inform you that your Social Security card has been suspended for suspicion of illegal activity—"

"Oh, for heaven's sake!" I hung up. "Stupid scammers."

A breeze whipped through the alley. An empty red cup rolled past, making a hollow rattling sound.

A white dog stood in the shadows at the other end of the alley.

I didn't dare look away. "Rose, Pepper," I stage-whispered without turning my head. "The dog is back." I took careful steps down the alley.

The dog sat on her haunches.

"Good girl," I murmured. "Stay where you are."

She barked, the sound like a penny tossed in a coffee can.

I drew near and sank to the damp ground of the alley. "Good girl," I repeated, beckoning her closer.

She approached and nudged my hand with her head, then turned away and walked a few steps out of the far end of the alley.

"So pretty," whispered Pepper, who had come up behind me with Rose.

The dog raised one paw and hesitated, apparently waiting for me, then darted away out of sight, down the undecorated rear of the row of buildings.

I slung my purse back and ran, cursing my sandals as a terrible choice of footwear, following the dog down the row of buildings and around a corner into a different alley—a dead end with black walls on all three sides.

The dog sat and looked up at me with the same *See what I did?* expression she had at Suntan Queen.

I bent and placed my hands on my knees, huffing at the exertion. I wasn't in bad shape, exactly—but I wasn't about to qualify for the Olympic running team, either.

My friends' footsteps echoed in the alley as they caught up.

"Be careful," said Rose.

"Of what? The worst she's done is blow a few things around." After she'd jumped in my lap at the Mexican restaurant, I wanted nothing more than to find her and convince her to stay with me.

The dog turned a circle, then—unbelievably—leaped and ran vertically out of the alley on nothing but air before pivoting over the roof and disappearing.

The three of us gasped in unison.

I stifled a shriek. "Did you see that? The dog ran up. Straight up. Into the air."

Pepper clapped her hands. "This is awesome!"

Rose stared into the sky, in the direction the dog had gone—then, seeing nothing, she shifted her gaze to the dead end of the alley. "What's that down there?"

We walked closer.

Faint black tracings marked the wall.

Rose ran her fingers over them. "There's a shape to this." She traced the lines as we watched. "Wings?"

Sure enough, they were wings—wide and tall, and even darker than the black walls of the alley. "With some kind of filigree design on the inside. I can't make it out, though."

Pepper took out her camera and snapped a picture. The shutter sound effect echoed. She lowered her phone and stared at the screen. "It's actually easier to see on the phone than it is when you're looking straight at it."

I leaned close to the wall and felt the snap of a static charge in my hair. I recoiled. "What in the—"

"A secret mural?" Rose stepped back and surveyed the wall from a distance.

Pepper's eyes lit up. "Do you think we get a prize for finding it?"

Rose examined her map, front and back. "It doesn't say anything about a secret mural."

"Luella, stand there so I can take a picture." Pepper gestured for me to stand in front of the wings. "So we can prove we were here. And maybe win something," she added hopefully.

I centered myself in front of the midnight-colored wings. Pepper raised her phone. "This is going to be so cool." Then I leaned against the wall—and everything changed.

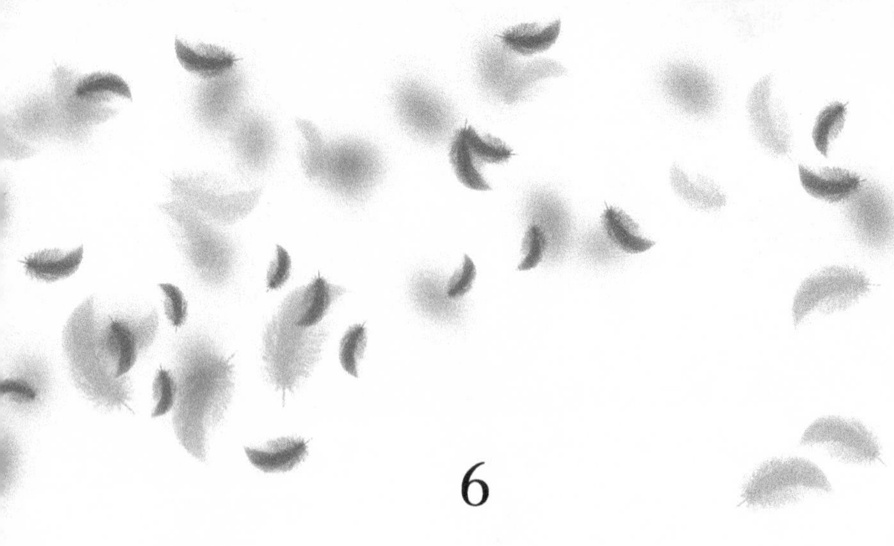

6

Electricity shot through my shoulder blades the instant my back touched the wall. My vision went white and a roar filled my ears. I couldn't gather enough air into my lungs to speak, let alone cry out, and without sight, I couldn't tell if Rose and Pepper were still nearby or not.

Was I being electrocuted? I wasn't going to die in a heap in a downtown alley, that was for sure. Not without a fight. I pressed my hands against the wall and pushed as hard as I could, ignoring the zapping sensation that shot through my fingers. If only I could get free of whatever it was, the shock would stop.

I gritted my teeth and twisted my torso back and forth, wriggling like a fish on a hook. Whatever mysterious force held me in its grip broke, and I collapsed to the ground.

My vision returned.

Pepper and Rose leaned over me.

"What happened?" My voice came out as a croak. My back felt cold.

I'd landed in a puddle.

"Are you okay?" Rose offered her hand to help me sit up.

I waved her hand away. "Don't touch me. I might still have a charge."

They looked at each other, then back at me.

"A charge?" said Pepper.

"Didn't you see? I must have leaned against a frayed wire." I turned my head awkwardly, feeling the loose gravel under my head, to look toward the wall.

Instead, I caught a glimpse of glowing silver in my peripheral vision. I sat up in a panic. "Get back! There's still electricity!"

Rose—calm, cool, level-headed Rose—raised a shaking hand and pointed at something over my shoulder. "Luella . . . "

Pepper's eyes widened as she looked at me. "Luella, you have wings!"

"What?" I turned my head from side to side in a frenzied attempt to comprehend the glow expanding from my shoulder blades. "I have *wings*?" I scrambled unsteadily to my feet, then turned like a dog chasing its tail, trying to see them in full.

"Whoa, girl." Pepper grabbed my arm to steady me.

Whorls and swirls of silver cascaded behind me, forming a pair of wings that seemed to be growing larger by the second. "Are they getting bigger, or am I seeing things?"

Rose swept her gaze over my wings. "They're getting bigger." She approached the wall and leaned in without touching it. "The whole mural is gone."

Pepper let go of my arm and dug into her pocket for her phone. She pulled up the photo she'd taken minutes before.

We peered at her photo of the wall and the black-on-black designs that resembled filigree made of fractals. Then I pivoted to show them my back.

Identical.

The wings were growing brighter, increasing in definition and luminescence. Even at half-mast, they were at least as wide as I was tall.

Pepper scrunched her nose as she studied me. "Can you do anything with them?" She flapped her hands. "The wings?"

"Like fly? I highly doubt it." I plucked at my shirt, the back of which remained soaked with puddle water, then let it fall back into place. The wet fabric stuck to my back. "If I have wings, I should at least be able to use them to fan this shirt dry." I shifted my awareness to my wings the same way I would concentrate on an aching knee to find the source of discomfort. The more effort I put into it, the more the wings seemed to shimmer and vibrate.

"I feel something!" Pepper hopped in place. "Like a tiny breeze. Do it again!"

I put my mind to it. The wings extended even more, so far the tips nearly touched the walls of the alley on either side. "Look how big they are—they must be at least ten feet across!" I laughed in delight and my wings quivered, making Pepper's curly brown hair and Rose's straight black hair visibly flutter in the wind.

"You did it!" Pepper punched the air.

Relief and dizziness washed over me. I staggered. "I feel—a little—"

They rushed to my side and helped me stay upright.

I glanced over my shoulder. The wings were gone, as if they were never there. Disappointment tightened my throat. "They're gone." I nearly choked on the words. Stars swirled through my vision. "My wings . . . "

Rose pulled my arm over her shoulder. "You probably tired yourself out."

I looked at Rose and Pepper with hope in my heart. "You think they'll come back?"

Pepper bore me up on the other side. "Your dog friend came back, didn't she? So don't worry. Let's go, wild woman." She took a maternal tone. "You've had enough excitement for one day."

We made our way to the car like we were doing a wobbly impression of The Monkees. They maneuvered me into the front passenger's seat, then Pepper took the wheel and Rose slid into the back seat.

I let my head loll against the headrest. The cool air tamped down the flip-flopping sensation in my stomach.

Rose handed me a cookie, then helped herself to one.

"Good idea, Rose," said Pepper. To me she added, "Put that in your face, quick. Maybe your blood sugar's low." Pepper craned her neck in an attempt to not cause an accident as she pulled out of the parking place.

I responded with my mouth full. "My blood sugar's fine."

"You didn't sleep last night, either," Rose pointed out.

"What are you, my mother?" I held my hand open over my shoulder. "More, please." As I took the cookies Rose placed in my palm, I snuck another look at my shoulders, hoping the wings would reappear.

They didn't.

I ate the cookies too fast and coughed on the last mouthful. "Where are we going?"

Pepper looked at me out of the corner of her eye. "You need a doctor?"

"You two are a couple of mother hens. I'm fine. Just got a little woozy, that's all. I'm forty-five, not a hundred and two. And I feel a lot better after the cookies."

"Are you sure you don't want to see a doctor?" Rose asked.

I turned and gave her a look. "I'm sure. Y'all are probably right—I didn't sleep enough, and I needed some food. All better now."

Rose made a skeptical noise.

"I'd feel better if someone was with you for a while." Pepper glanced in the rearview mirror. "You got anything to do, Rose?"

"The dogs will need feeding, eventually, but I have plenty of time before that."

"Let's go to my place. I got cold cuts in the fridge—we can eat something more substantial than this sugar rush." I gestured to the bags in the back seat.

Pepper treated us to a loud, off-key, a cappella version of "Sugar, Sugar" by The Archies, all the way back to my apartment.

When I got out of the car in the apartment parking lot, I felt steady enough to detour to the side of the building without assistance. I checked the ground under the oak tree outside my window.

Pepper hit the button to lock the car. "What are you doing?"

"I left some bird treats out here this morning. Looks like the birds got 'em."

Rose bent over the gnarled roots. "They didn't leave a single seed behind."

We trooped up the stairs.

Pepper stopped halfway up. "Look!"

I followed her gaze.

A crow perched on my welcome mat with something shiny in its beak. It dropped the item, made a series of clicking noises, then flew over our heads and out into the open air.

I sprinted up the last few steps and looked down at the welcome mat.

The mat held several dozen small items, arranged without any pattern but neatly spaced apart. I knelt and gathered the items into my hand as Rose and Pepper watched. There were single earrings, bits of smooth glass, small weathered stones, shiny metal bolts, assorted buttons, and a solitary Lego piece.

Rose examined the pile in my hand. "Presents."

Pepper looked confused. "Presents?"

Rose nodded. "Birds do that, you know. They leave things as presents for people they like."

"Add it to the list of mysteries." I stood and stuffed the items in my pockets so my hands would be free to unlock the door. Inside, I dropped my purse on the table, then emptied my pockets on the coffee table.

Pepper sank to the floor next to the table and eagerly poked through the items. "Where did all this come from?" She held a dangly earring up to her ear. "Arrr, I'm a pirate."

Rose walked to the window. "Look at this." She pointed at the windowsill.

A second set of odds and ends awaited me. I opened the window and retrieved the items, then added them to the stash on the coffee table. "This is officially weird." I closed the window and sat on the couch.

"This was officially weird yesterday morning." Pepper sorted the pile into smaller piles.

Rose went to the kitchen and rummaged in the fridge.

"I'll get that, Rose—"

"Sit." She pulled her black hair into a sleek ponytail, then piled sandwich fixings on the counter. "I got this."

I sat on the couch. "This is crazy."

Pepper looked up at me. "Crazy *fun*, you mean."

Rose paused her sandwich-making. "I'll go with crazy *and* fun. But we still don't have any explanation for what's going on."

Pepper pulled her legs into a pretzel shape and drummed her fingers on her knees. "There's gotta be an explanation."

"Everything started yesterday morning. I got fired. Then there was that big wind. Then the dog showed up."

"And then he ran away," Pepper put in.

"She."

"Right, she."

"Then she came back and blew Dan's dinner in his face. And the birds showed up and did their Tiki Room impression. Oh! I forgot to tell you—I saw glowing dandelion seeds outside the window at Mama's place."

A clanking sound came from the kitchen as Rose dropped a knife on a plate. "Glowing dandelion seeds?"

"Like silver embers, but dandelion seeds. Oh, and a crow showed up and banged on the windshield."

Pepper un-pretzeled her legs and lay on her back, stretching her legs into the air. "And today you saw the dog again, and got zapped, and got wings."

Rose carried a sandwich in and placed it on the coffee table in front of me. "And a bird—or birds—brought you presents."

I picked up the sandwich. "Thank you, Rose. You didn't have to do that."

Pepper rolled upward and bounded to her feet. "I'm gonna get me a sandwich. Keep talking."

I looked over my shoulder, wishing I could see that glow behind me one more time. It didn't seem fair for the wings to disappear right after I first saw them. It felt like someone had stolen my Christmas. "Makes me wonder how that design got on the wall. I mean, who put it there? And why?"

Rose paced with measured steps. "And why did the dog lead you to it?"

"To find it, obviously," Pepper called from the kitchen.

"Well, yeah. But why Luella?" Rose paused her attempt to wear a groove in the carpet.

I shrugged. "Because the world needs a forty-five-year-old ex-sunscreen marketer with glowing silver wings?"

"Why not?" said Pepper.

We helped ourselves to more sandwiches and baked goods until we were all too full to move. Pepper stretched out on the floor while Rose and I took the couch.

Rose took out her phone and tapped it rapidly.

"What are you doing?"

"I'm looking up the murals: the lighthouse, the rose, the rainbow, and the cupcake." Rose stared at the screen.

"Looks like they were all painted on commission for the Downtown Merchant Guild. It says so in this article in the Sparkle Beach Journal." She passed me the phone.

I scanned the text. "But who painted them?"

Rose shrugged. "It doesn't say."

I handed the phone back. "I want to find out."

Pepper inspected one of the polished stones on the coffee table. "Why don't you call the Downtown Merchant Guild?"

"I will, on Monday. Right now I gotta swing by Mama's and get the keys to the rental. Tomorrow's my day to work on sending in more résumés. What are your plans for the week?"

"The usual shifts at Suntan Queen," said Rose. "Plus, I have a decent number of dog-training sessions booked this week."

"How about you, Pepper?"

"The kids are busy at summer camp, so I'll either be at Suntan Queen or helping out at Peter's office."

My gaze met Rose's. She grimaced.

Pepper had previously sworn up and down that working for your spouse was a terrible, no good, very bad idea—and then, somehow, he'd convinced her to work part-time at his dental office while also working part-time for Suntan Queen and being the primary caregiver for their kids. It seemed like a lot to put on one person.

I chose my words with care. "How are you handling all that?"

Pepper blew out air. "It's fine." She caught me observing her, and her worried expression immediately altered. "Did I tell you I saw a dolphin this morning?"

Mama raised me with manners, so I didn't stop Pepper from not-so-subtly changing the subject. "No kidding?"

"Came right up alongside me while I was paddling out. At first I thought it was a shark! Then it bobbed out of the water and I saw its nose and blowhole. Coolest thing ever."

"Dogs, dolphins—what's next?" Rose threw her hands up in mock exasperation.

"I'll take my wings coming back, for a start." I cast a forlorn look over my shoulder. "We all deserve a little magic."

The words hung in the air like a spell.

"Truer words were never spoken," said Rose.

"Hugs!" Pepper scrambled off the floor and threw her arms around both of us. "I can't bear to see my friends with long faces."

It felt good to be loved.

When we released one another, Rose gestured at the crow's gifts. "Whatever's happening to you—it means something. Even if your first priority is finding a job, don't let this go."

"That's right." Pepper pointed a finger at me. "We want more magic stuff. Keep us posted."

I handed them the remaining packages of baked goods. "Cross my heart. Now take these with you, before I have to eat them all."

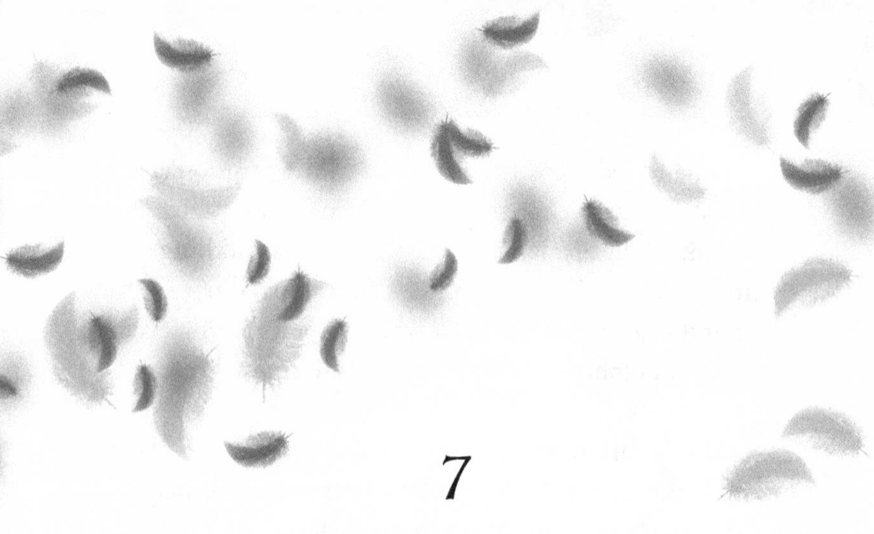

7

After they left, I swung by Mama's to pick up the keys to Mrs. Millefleur's shotgun house. Mama wasn't home, but since she'd already told me where I could find them, all I had to do was check the appropriate hidey-hole like a squirrel retrieving a nut.

I passed the bird feeder and the oversized gazing ball on my way to the rickety garden bench. When I turned over the statue of the rabbit, I found a set of keys labeled "Seabreeze Lane."

With the set of keys safely stashed in my purse, I hopped back into the car and punched the address into my phone.

"Turn right in one thousand feet," it said.

"That's not right." I drove past the recommended turn.

It made a chastising noise like a quarter dropped in a large glass jug. "Recalculating."

"You do that."

"Take the next right," the voice commanded.

"No thank you, Miss Bossypants." I hit the main drag, knowing it would get me to the neighborhood faster. After ignoring several more commands—and several more of those chastising noises—I started following the directions as I got closer to the destination.

The final turn took me onto a side street with barely enough room for two cars to pass each other. Long, skinny houses in various states of decay lined the street, their short ends facing the lane like shoeboxes in a row. Some boasted fresh paint and colorful garden decorations. Others sported sagging porches and broken-down cars in the yard.

If I could have taken my hands off the wheel, I would have crossed my fingers. Instead, I counted the street numbers until I found the property at the far end of Seabreeze Lane.

The picket fence remained—or had been replaced at some point—heart-shaped cutouts and all. The exterior of the house glowed with a fresh coat of eye-wateringly purple paint. Red begonias filled the planters around the petite front porch. Since it was a shotgun house, the long side stretched beyond a taller white fence that cut off any view beyond the front porch.

Anxious to see more, I threw the car into park and pulled the key ring out of my purse. When I opened the car door, loud music boomed through the air.

Perhaps my neighbors were music fans.

My steps echoed on the hollow wooden steps as I passed under the gingerbread trim bordering the ceiling of the front porch. I inhaled the salt air and tried to calm my nerves as I slid the key into the lock on the front door.

Strangely, the music only got louder as the door swung open.

I crossed the tidy living room, admiring the wood floors. A bar created a partial separation between the living room and the small but sparkling kitchen, which appeared to have been recently updated. The hallway led to a clever space-saving layout of a bathroom and two bedrooms in the back.

The window in the back door rattled in time with the booming music.

I twitched the curtain aside and peeked out. A small aboveground pool—more like an oversized outdoor bathtub—took up a good deal of the space in the backyard.

I had trouble focusing on details of the outdoor space, however, due to the fact that the pool was currently crammed with half a dozen teenagers.

I was pretty sure Mama hadn't said anything about the house coming with its own set of noisemakers.

I eyed the backyard one more time from behind the door. An extension cord thrown over a fence powered the boombox. They'd even brought two-liters of soda and red cups. And was that a bottle of vodka?

I put on my best parental face and flung open the back door. "What do you all think you're doing here?"

Thanks to the loud music, they didn't even notice me.

I crossed the yard with quick strides and disconnected the boombox power cord, bringing the music to a halt. "I said, what do y'all think you're doing here?"

That got their attention, but they didn't seem to know whether to sink into the water in shame or make a run for it.

I upended the vodka bottle and let the contents pour onto the fine green grass in a clear stream.

"Hey!" said a red-haired girl with a healthy spray of freckles across her nose. "What're you doing?"

Bold as brass. "What does it look like I'm doing? I'm pouring out your vodka. Your *illegal* vodka, I might add. There's no way you all are old enough to be drinking this stuff. Get your things and scoot, right now, before I find your parents and tell them what you were up to."

The teenagers clambered over the sides of the pool, dripping water everywhere as they rushed to gather their towels.

Except for the redhead. "My mama don't care what I do." She climbed out of the water in a leisurely fashion, like a queen with all the time in the world. While her friends slipped away, she patted her hair with a towel and looked me up and down. "You ain't Mrs. Millefleur. You ain't old enough. Or fancy enough."

Trust a teenager to give you a frank and not exactly flattering appraisal. "How do you know Mrs. Millefleur?"

She tilted her chin up. "I know she pretty much owns this whole street."

"Well, I may not be Mrs. Millefleur, but I will be living here for the foreseeable future—and as far as I know, this house didn't come with teenagers included."

"Didn't mean no harm." She covered her fair skin with a brightly colored beach towel. "Why have a pool if nobody's gonna use it?"

I raised an eyebrow and tried my best to look judgmental.

She grinned. "Just saying."

"What's your name?"

"My friends call me Red."

"For your hair?"

"Of course for my hair. What'd you think, it was for my bathing suit?" She looked down at her red two-piece with white polka dots, then shot me a look of disdain. "How about you?"

"What about me?" I felt like I was getting behind in the conversation.

Red rolled her eyes. "What's your name?"

"Luella."

"Luella." She stretched my name out like taffy with an even more exaggerated Southern accent. "That's pretty."

"Thank you." I regarded her as she leaned comfortably against the pool. "Shouldn't you be getting home?"

"I ain't in no hurry."

I cleared my throat. "Well, I best be getting back to things—"

"Can I see inside?" She wrapped her towel firmly around herself. "I promise I won't drip on the floor."

"I think you ought to be getting home before somebody worries about you."

Red bustled past me to the back door, where she laid her hand on the doorknob and peeked in the window. "Why do they call these shotgun houses, anyway? Because they're long and skinny like a shotgun?" She opened the door.

"Because you could fire a shotgun through the front door and the bullet would go out the back door. They're built to stay cool." I reached over and carefully shut the door. "Unless you let all the air conditioning out."

Her shoulders slumped. "Maybe next time I could see inside?"

"You live on this street, don't you? Isn't your house just like this one?"

"On the outside it is. I like seeing inside other people's houses. It's fun." She looked up at me, emphasizing her big hazel eyes.

What can I say? I'm a sucker. "Next time, Red."

"Okay!" She rewarded me with a smile. "Next time, Luella." She sashayed out of the backyard and let the fence gate slam closed behind her.

I went inside and examined the layout of the house again. Sure enough, there was a clear path from the back door to the front. I propped the back door open and walked the length of the house to the front door. As soon as I opened it, a breeze whooshed through like I'd turned on a fan. "Not bad." Right then it was pretty swampy, but I could imagine how fresh and sweet the air would be in the fall, when the weather cooled down.

I was about to close the door when I noticed a flash of white down the sidewalk.

The dog!

I thought to run outside, but the dog closed the distance and bounded up the front steps before I could even set foot on the porch.

She trotted into the bare living room, carrying the breeze with her, and sat on the wooden floor.

I slowly closed the front door. "Stay." I kept my eye on her and crept down the hallway, then carefully closed the back door and returned to the living room. "Good girl."

She barked, the hollow sound echoing in the empty house.

I sat on the floor. “Come here, baby.”

The dog came close. She flopped down and lay her head on my leg.

I could barely breathe for fear of startling her. Her warm, bright fur emitted its own subtle airflow, which tickled my hand as I rubbed her head and down her back. “You need a name. If I give you a name, will you promise to come when I call you?”

She made a sound like a cross between a snort and a snuffle.

I grinned. “I’ll take that as a yes. Now what am I going to call you?” I ruffled her silver and white fur.

She blinked at me. Her eyes were blue like the midday sky over the river.

“I’ll call you—Zephyr, after the west wind. You like that, Zephyr?”

Zephyr rolled over playfully and licked my hand.

I felt a jolt, then a tingling that spread over my whole body. Something sparkled in my peripheral vision. I turned my head slowly, then stifled a cry as my wings—my wings!—unfurled anew from my shoulders, billowing out like a queen’s train made of light.

I burst into tears. I couldn’t help it. She’d given them back to me.

Zephyr stood and walked into my outstretched arms. She rested her head on my shoulder.

As I held her, my tears disappeared into her fur and quickly dried. “Thank you,” I whispered.

She wiggled away and stood before me.

I felt a rising breeze swirl around us.

Zephyr took off from a standing start and ran to the back door, following the path of the wind that had blown through the house.

I scrambled to my feet and ran down the hallway after her.

She plunged through the door like it wasn't there.

I had to throw it open to follow her.

Zephyr spiraled into the air as if she was running up the invisible ramp of a thermal updraft, until she was lost to sight in a passing cloud.

Not caring who heard me, I shouted into the sky, "I'm not going to say goodbye, Zephyr! I'll see you again soon!"

And I meant it.

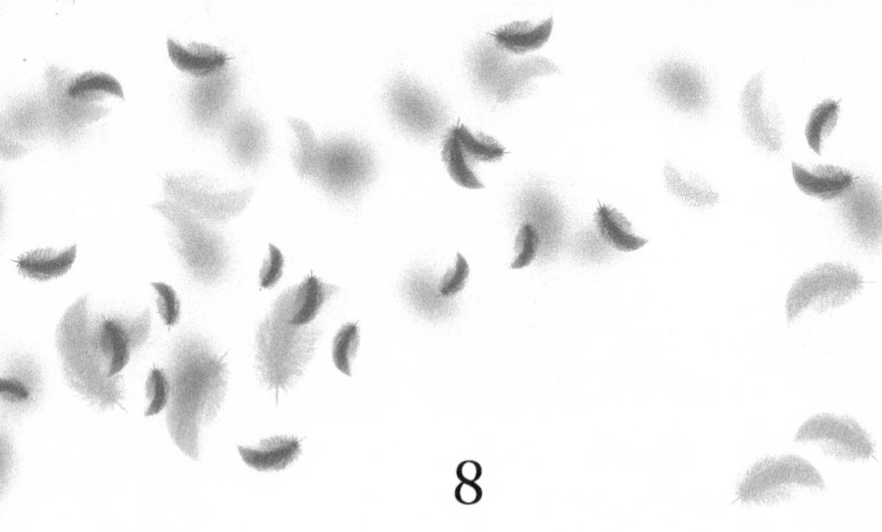

8

On Monday morning, I woke from dreams of a crackling bonfire on a windswept beach to the sound of the phone ringing. The rainbow numbers of the alarm clock flashed across my vision: nine-thirty in the morning. I'd slept later than I ever slept on a weekday. Grabbing the phone from the nightstand, I swung my legs down from the bed and sat up, clearing my throat in an attempt to sound fully awake.

"Hello?" My voice sounded sleep-roughened, but perhaps the caller wouldn't notice.

"Good morning! May I speak to Luella Campbell?" The man sounded so enthusiastic I half expected him to burst into song.

"This is Luella."

"This is Alex from Ultimate Crate, the fitness subscription box company. You sent in a résumé over the weekend, for the social media manager position?"

I racked my brain. "Ultimate Crate, yes! Absolutely."

"Luella, how do you feel about fitness?"

My mind blanked. The only thing about fitness I could think of involved a funny meme. *Yeah, I'm into fitness. Fitness whole pizza in my mouth.* The silence lengthened, so I blurted the first thing that came to mind that matched his enthusiasm: "I love fitness!"

Very smooth.

"Great! Can you come in for an interview later today? We've had a cancellation this afternoon and we would love to talk to you."

"Absolutely." I kicked myself for repeating the word I'd just used. It sounded stupid—but then, it also sounded wildly excited, which Alex might appreciate. "I'd love to."

"We will see you at three-thirty, Luella!"

"Thank you so much. Bye." I hoped I sounded friendly, competent, and self-assured, but since my brain didn't fire up until after my first cup of coffee, I feared I came across as a groggy idiot. I shuffled into the kitchen and turned on the coffeemaker, then rummaged in the cabinet for the usual handful of vitamins and supplements.

Caffeine and pills acquired, I settled on the couch in my pajamas. Ultimate Crate was the first nibble I'd had. I needed to make a good impression. My financial future—and Lily's—was on the line.

My thoughts drifted back to the shotgun house on Seabreeze Lane. I glanced around the apartment living room, already mentally arranging my possessions into boxes. Silver light floated into my peripheral vision. My glorious wings had curled up like loosely rolled lace, as insubstantial as light and air. I breathed a sigh of satisfaction and returned my attention to the logistics of moving.

I'd never felt so excited at the prospect of moving to a new place.

With my thoughts in gear, I turned to the mystery of the downtown mural. I pulled up the Downtown Merchant Guild website on my phone and made a mental note that the association met every Wednesday. Then I dialed the phone number listed at the bottom of the page.

"Sparkle Beach Downtown Merchant Guild. How may I help you?" The sweet, reedy voice over the phone made me think of my long-ago first grade teacher, with her tightly permed gray hair and eyeglasses on a chain.

"Good morning. I'm calling with a question about the downtown murals. Can you direct me to the right person to talk to?"

"Why, I can try to answer your question. What did you need to know?"

"I'm trying to find out who painted them."

"Oh, that's easy. He's a local artist—Raphael." She let out a girlish giggle. "Like the Renaissance artist."

Or the Teenage Mutant Ninja Turtles. "Do you know his last name?"

"Let me check."

I sat quietly and listened to the sound of rustling papers and tapping keys.

"Andalucia." She pronounced it with care.

The floor dropped out from under me like the Twilight Zone Tower of Terror ride. I hadn't heard that name in years. "Raphael Andalucia? Are you sure?"

"I'm sure."

"Thank you for your help." I hung up.

That name—it wasn't possible for it to be someone else. The sound of it revived a heat in my blood I hadn't felt in ages.

I rubbed my arms self-consciously. He was probably married with four children by now. He probably wasn't anything like the boy I knew in high school. I bet he wasn't even recognizable. I was not going to search for him on the internet.

I lasted ten seconds before typing his name into a search engine. I scrolled frantically, looking for more information—and photos.

There he was. Dark hair, dark eyes, arched brows and thick lashes, with cheekbones that could cut glass, and a closely trimmed beard.

I fanned myself. Then I sent a message to Pepper. *Did you know Raphael Andalucia was back in town? I thought he was still out of state!*

Pepper replied within seconds. *No! Is he married?* She added a few laughter emojis for good measure. *If not, you're in trouble, girl.*

Shut up, I texted. *He's the mural artist.*

No way, she replied.

Way. He's in a show in some downtown gallery this week.

A minute passed before she responded. *Looks like you'll be able to get a hold of him soon. LOL.*

Don't tempt me. I set down the phone and closed my eyes. With everything I had on my plate, the last thing I needed was a distraction.

Although maybe I could enjoy thinking about him for one more minute.

Or five.

I shook myself. I was being silly. I stood, stretched, and turned my thoughts to getting ready for the interview—not the high school crush who got away.

Behind the vintage exterior of its downtown office, Ultimate Crate sported a sleek modern look and what appeared to be pieces of high-end Scandinavian furniture. On closer inspection, I recognized several pieces from the budget furniture line at IKEA. Whoever decorated the office clearly believed in the "fake it till you make it" philosophy, but the fifteen-dollar office chairs weren't fooling me.

I gave my name to the receptionist and settled into one of the chairs, which wobbled precariously. I'd already done my homework on the company, but while I waited, I scrolled through their social media accounts one more time.

Their messaging was on point, although some of their images appeared to be used without attribution—a big no-no for any serious company—and some of the conversations in the comments had suspicious gaps, as if someone had been deleting negative remarks. I cringed. A company with that much of a need to control the conversation might have deeper problems than unattributed photos.

"Luella?"

A surge of panic seized me. What if the interviewer saw my wings?

I dismissed the nonsensical thought. Of course he couldn't see them. No one could, except for Rose and

Pepper. Even still, I couldn't help a brief glance over my shoulder as I stood. My wings remained quietly furled against my back.

The man who stood before me didn't line up with my expectations. Instead of the usual business attire, he wore workout pants with racing stripes and a crew neck t-shirt that emphasized his bulging chest muscles.

"I'm Alex!" His voice sounded like an aerobics class was about to begin. "Come on back!" He jogged down the hallway.

I shifted into a fast walk and followed him into an office with one small window—and fewer pretensions of grandeur than the reception area. The coffee cup on the desk said *It's A Great Day to Be A Founder. Founder* seemed a little grand, but who was I to judge?

Instead of having a seat, Alex began stretching in the space behind the desk. He bent in half, and his head dropped below the level of the desktop, making his stridently cheerful voice sound like it was coming from the bottom of a barrel. "So, how did you hear about Ultimate Crate?"

I remained standing. "Online. You seem to have a lot of fans." I didn't add that a lot of them seemed upset.

"Oh, yeah! The 'Craters.' That's what we call them."

Possibly the worst customer nickname ever. "How cute," I said, with what I hoped sounded like sincere admiration.

He unfolded. "Come on and stretch with me, Luella."

"Stretch with you?"

Alex shot me a wide, toothy grin. "Yeah! Love the body you have and you'll get the body you want, I always say."

I was one hundred percent sure that phrase wasn't original, but anything for a job, right? I un-flexibly imitated his deep lunge.

"So you have experience as a social media manager?"

The position compressed my diaphragm, making my words sound short. "Yes, I worked for Suntan Queen—"

"The sunscreen maker? How awesome is that?"

I wasn't sure if the question was rhetorical. "Pretty awesome. Can you tell me a little more about Ultimate Crate?"

Alex dropped into a full knee-bending crouch that would have sent me to the hospital. "Craters sign up for a one-month, six-month, or twelve-month subscription. Every month, we send them a box of fitness-related merch. Clothing, gear, vitamins—oh, and snacks! Gotta nourish to flourish, am I right?"

I lowered myself into a semi-squat in a hopeless attempt to match his movement.

Thank the Lord I had worn slacks.

"Anyway," he continued, "we're looking for someone to handle our social media accounts on a remote basis. We need content regularly posted, and—most importantly—content moderation."

He finally returned to an upright position, and I thanked any and all deities who might have been listening to my prayers for mercy.

"How frequently do you think you'd be able to monitor the comments?" he asked.

I hesitated. I had to sleep sometime, but I also needed the money this job could bring. "I'd try to monitor it as frequently as possible." I sensed my success hinged on being available every waking hour. "How frequently did you want it checked?"

"Every hour or two." He stretched his muscle-bound arms while waiting for my response.

I suppressed the urge to laugh. It took a lot of negative comments to need that kind of supervision.

A flutter of shadowy motion at the window caught my attention.

The crow had returned. It hopped back and forth on the windowsill and fixed me with a stare from one tiny black eye. There was no doubt in my mind it was the same bird that had been following me around town.

I gathered my thoughts and projected them at the sassy corvid. *Go away. You're distracting me. I need this job. I need the money.*

The crow turned its head, gave me one last look with a single beady eye, then flew off.

I couldn't help thinking it had left in a huff. *Sorry*, I thought belatedly, hoping my apology carried to wherever the bird had flown. I grasped for the last shred of the conversation. "Every hour or two? Sure, I can handle that." It was patently absurd, but I wasn't in a position to be choosy.

"Awesome." He jogged in place. "Salary?"

"What was in the job posting works for me."

He kept jogging in place. "Are you sure you can keep up with the technology? I know it's a lot." *For someone your age*, he didn't say—but the concern, bordering on pity, that crossed his face was a dead giveaway.

I forced myself to smile. I couldn't afford to slap an interviewer across the face, but imagining doing so helped my smile get bigger and more sincere. "I'm sure I can handle any of the technology."

"Well, thank you for coming out, Luella. We'll be in touch." He stopped jogging. Instead of holding out a hand to shake, he held it up for a high five. "Nice work!"

"Uh, thanks." I gave him a high-five. "Nice meeting you." I showed myself out of the Ultimate Crate office and returned to my car, where I threw my purse on the passenger seat with more force than was strictly necessary.

A scratching noise made me look up from digging in my purse for my sunglasses.

The crow had returned—and was currently scratching grooves into the hood.

"Hey, knock that off!" I flapped my hands, to no effect.

The crow dropped something shiny from its beak and retreated down the hood to the hood ornament, which it pecked industriously.

"That does it." I put on my sunglasses and threw the car door open. Just as I was about to confront the disrespectful bird, a flash of yellow caught my eye.

A gold coin sat on the hood, winking in the overhead glare of the late afternoon sun.

"What in the—" I picked it up, then tossed it from hand to hand. It was already hot to the touch from sitting on the scorching hood of the car.

The crow cocked its head at me, then went back to attacking the hood ornament.

The front of the coin displayed a woman with a torch in one hand and a branch in the other, superimposed over the rays of the sun, with the word "LIBERTY" printed across the top. It was unmistakably real gold. Estimating its weight to be around half an ounce, I calculated it was probably worth a thousand dollars or so.

I tucked it securely into my pocket and addressed the persistent bird. "Hey, you. Crow."

It paused its attack and looked up.

"I think I owe you an apology."

It hopped from side to side.

"I'm sorry I told you to go away."

It preened itself.

"Thank you for the presents." I patted my pocket. "I'd like to give you something in return."

It ruffled its wings and regarded me with one eye.

"Would you like a name?"

It spread its wings and flew to my shoulder.

I steadied myself, adjusting to balance the weight of the bird. "You're heavier than you look."

It ignored the comment and leaned over my shoulder, tapping my wings with its beak. The wings unfurled to half-mast and glowed brighter than before.

"That's a neat trick. Are you friends with the dog? With Zephyr?"

The crow made a clicking sound and squeezed my shoulder lightly with its claws.

"How about I call you—Midnight? Would you like that?" It was absurd, asking a crow how it felt about a name, but it seemed the least I could do after it had brought me a thousand-dollar gold coin.

Midnight made another clicking noise and took off, angling over the Ultimate Crate building and out of sight.

I touched the coin in my pocket once more, then checked over both shoulders. My wings looked so brilliant I could hardly believe no one could see them but me. Impulsively, I pushed them to their full span and concentrated on moving them like I had in the downtown alley.

To my shock, the resulting wind knocked over three garbage bins lined up behind the building.

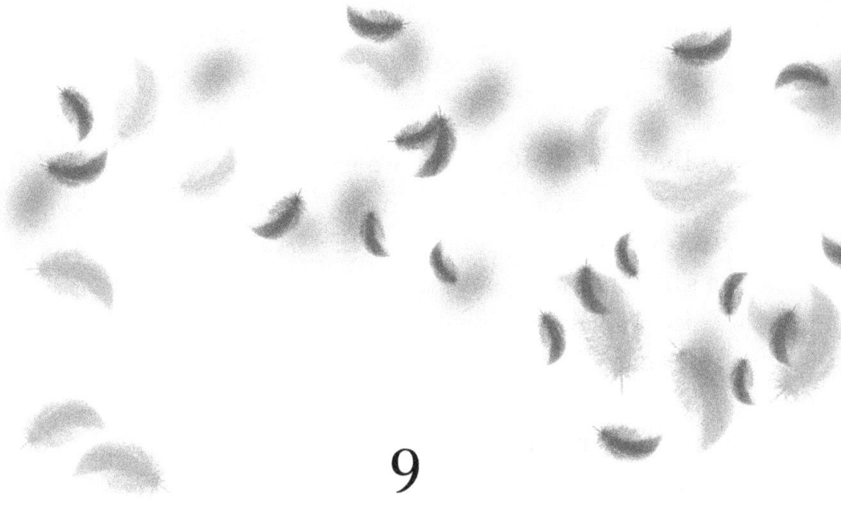

9

To use up the nervous energy I'd accumulated during the interview, I spent the rest of the day hauling boxes from the apartment over to Seabreeze Lane. After a handful of trips, I took a glass of iced tea and sat on the steps by the back door, watching the evening breeze riffle the surface of the little pool.

I closed my eyes and felt the warmth of the sun, now soft instead of oppressive. "Midnight and Zephyr," I whispered, trying out the names, half-hoping I'd summon them. I opened my eyes.

The wind increased, sending tiny wavelets across the surface.

I realized my wings were vibrating. "Oops." I concentrated on calm and the wind ceased. "Zephyr?" I kept my voice low. "Here, Zephyr."

Nothing.

I tried again, louder. "Zephyr!"

The fence gate banged open and I nearly fell off the steps.

It was Red, clad in a bathing suit and draped in a towel. "Who're you talking to back here? I could hear you from the sidewalk." She nonchalantly clambered into the pool, sending a small wave of water over the side.

"Make yourself at home."

She missed—or ignored—the sarcasm. "Thanks. You gonna show me the house this time?"

"I'm going home for the night. You can't stay, Red. I can't leave you unattended in a pool."

"I ain't gonna drown."

"I don't know that."

Red sighed like her infinite patience with the world had finally run out. "All right. If you say so." She climbed out as easily as she'd climbed in and stood next to the pool, water dripping from her hair. "Can I see inside now?"

I eyed her up and down. "What do you think?"

"Oh!" She hastily rubbed herself down with the towel, then wrapped it around herself like a sarong. "I'm ready."

I remembered when Lily was that age, between childhood and adulthood, with many of the troubles and charms of each. "Come on, then." I stood and led the way into the house.

Red padded behind me on bare feet. She poked her head into the empty bedrooms, then the tiny bathroom.

"Does it look like your house?"

"Kind of." She shuffled past and entered the kitchen and living room area. "Isn't this fancy!"

I smiled to myself. Her description was exactly what Mama had denied.

She patted the counters and the cabinets with one hand and used the other hand to keep her towel in place. "It's real nice," she concluded. "You cook?"

"I do." I went to the front door. "You can go out this way so you don't have to go around the back again."

Red lingered in the kitchen a moment longer, then crossed the wooden floor, leaving damp footprints. "Will you be back soon?"

"Soon as I can."

"Can I come swim sometime?"

"Not if I'm not here."

"Okay." She stopped halfway down the front porch steps. "Bye, Luella."

"Bye, Red." I watched her go, then turned away and went inside.

Talking to Red reminded me of how much I missed Lily's daily presence in my life. I didn't mind being alone, exactly—especially considering I had Mama, Rose, and Pepper to keep me company whenever I reached out—but a home can be so quiet with only one person in it.

I needed to tell Lily at least some of what was going on. I couldn't up and move without letting my own daughter know. I drew the phone from my back pocket with a certain measure of reluctance, then opened my messages and typed. *How are you, baby? I miss you.*

When an answer didn't appear right away, I tucked the phone in my pocket, locked up the house, and drove back to the apartment. The sun sank in the west, turning the sky the color of an orange creamsicle.

The phone vibrated once as I made the turn at the last stoplight. Inside the apartment, I settled on Lily's bed and read the text.

Miss you too!

I smiled. *Can you call me? Or would another time be better?*

The phone rang and I picked up instantly. "Hey, baby! How are you?"

Lily's warm voice carried over the phone. "I'm good. I was about to go out with some friends."

I could hear her smile in the way she spoke. "Oh, I don't mean to keep you—"

"No, no, it's okay. I have a minute. Mama, you would not believe the bakeries up here. I am going to spend all my money on eclairs, I think. And cheesecake. And cookies. And cupcakes. It's like a gluten-free heaven. There's this one place on Madison Avenue that is to die for. Of course, it costs a ton, but it's so good I can't help myself. There's this other place down the street that makes gluten-free rugelach—apricot or strawberry—that you can get by the bag. I bought *two* bags and ate all of it right away."

Her chatter washed over me like a warm ocean wave. She sounded so happy. "I wish I was there. But we would probably go broke from buying all the sweets."

She laughed, bright and clear. "I know, right?"

I retrieved the gold coin from my pocket and flipped it as I spoke. "Listen, pumpkin, I have some news. Your grandma found me a new place to live for a while, to save on rent. It's over on the peninsula and it's real nice."

"Wow! Beachside? That's amazing." Lily paused. "How many bedrooms?"

I heard the unspoken question—she wanted to know if I still had room for her. "Two, of course. What'd you think, I'd kick you out?" I chuckled softly.

Lily released a relieved laugh. "Just checking."

"And . . . I have a little bad news."

"Oh, no! What is it?"

"Suntan Queen let me go."

"They let you go? But why? You've been there for—"

"Ages. I know. Guess they wanted some fresh blood." It struck me as a gruesome phrase, but I'd said it anyway. "But don't worry—I'm already looking for a new job. I even interviewed with a fitness company that needs someone to handle their social media for them."

"Which one?"

"Ultimate Crate."

"Never heard of them," she said cheerfully.

"You doing okay for money? Eclairs aside?"

"I'm fine. I can slow down on the bakeries, if you want."

I rubbed the gold coin between my thumb and forefinger. "We never had any bakeries like that down here. You enjoy yourself up there, baby. I mean, don't buy a hundred a day, or anything—but you deserve treats that are safe for you to eat." I couldn't bring myself to limit her, not yet—not with the hope that something might yet come through. "You ready for class to start?"

"Mmm-hmm."

I could feel her attention drifting as the sound of laughter increased in the background. "Are your friends ready to go?"

"I think so."

"You go on, then. I love you."

"Love you. Hug Grandma for me."

"I will. Bye."

"Bye." She hung up.

I cradled the phone in my hand and pulled up my photo roll, scrolling through the pictures. The roll went back several years, through the latter half of Lily's time in high school. Funny how I reckoned time by her milestones. I allowed myself the indulgence of scrolling back in time, marveling over the still frames of happiness, until I reached the end of the roll—a breathless selfie of Lily and me at the trampoline center she'd insisted on visiting weekly. She loved it so much I didn't have the heart to tell her I lived in fear of injuring a joint during one of our bouncing sessions.

The memory of jumping—of hanging in the air for one weightless moment before returning to the trampoline—triggered a lightning strike of inspiration.

I retrieved the step stool from the kitchen and set it on the living room carpet. I climbed onto the step and found my balance. My wings rested in a furled position, as they seemed to do when I wasn't actively using them.

I set my mind to unfurling them, verifying their dazzling glow as they expanded fully. The wings gave off a light hum, like summer crickets, a sensation I felt rather than heard. I hoped that meant I had a full tank of gas, magically speaking.

I concentrated on the idea of fanning the air down, instead of out. I didn't want to knock over my own furniture—I wanted to lift myself up.

I wanted to fly.

I readied myself and jumped off the step.

Thump.

I hit the ground flat-footed. I stepped up and tried again.

Thump.

One more time.

Thump.

I hadn't managed to slow my fall in the slightest, and I'd probably annoyed the daylights out of my downstairs neighbor. At least my wings hadn't dimmed, and I didn't feel dizzy. I sighed and carried the step stool back to the kitchen, figuring I'd go ahead and pack up the detritus in the upper kitchen cabinets.

I placed a recycled box from the grocery store on the Formica countertop, then stepped on the stool. The high shelves held infrequently used mugs and various tchotchkes accumulated over the years. I grasped a cracked porcelain dog and stepped down to place it in the box.

On my next grope through the cabinet, my hand found an old Suntan Queen mug emblazoned with the company logo: a crowned woman surfing an enormous wave. I had looked forward to riding the wave, so to speak, of the campaign that would relaunch the brand. The marketing side of my brain swung into action and fresh ideas percolated with no conscious effort.

I shook my head to drive the thoughts away. There was no need for that sort of thing, not anymore. Even when I worked there, I just followed orders—campaign decisions were made above my head. I only carried them out.

I stepped down and let the mug clatter to the counter, intending to donate it at the first opportunity. When I climbed up again, the lower step wasn't high enough to reach all the way into the back of the cabinet, so I mounted the second step without realizing I'd placed my foot wrong.

The fall happened faster than I could cry out.

The step stool flew sideways. My hand flailed for purchase on the cabinet but caught only splinters. I fell, and fear surged through me as my body stiffened for impact—

BOOM.

Silver exploded in my vision. When it cleared, I found myself staring up at the ceiling. My heart pounded. I couldn't feel the floor underneath me. I couldn't feel any pain. Had I broken my back? Was I paralyzed? I reached out and felt the floor, its vinyl surface solid and cool, if a bit sticky, under my fingertips.

If the floor was there, why couldn't I feel it under me? And what was that buzzing sound?

Fearful of causing greater injury, I turned my head with infinite care.

My wings were vibrating so hard they blurred, emitting a hum like a hive of angry bees.

My back didn't touch the ground. My wings were holding me aloft inches above the floor.

They'd arrested my fall.

The second I realized what was happening, the humming stopped—and I dropped to the kitchen floor like a sack of potatoes.

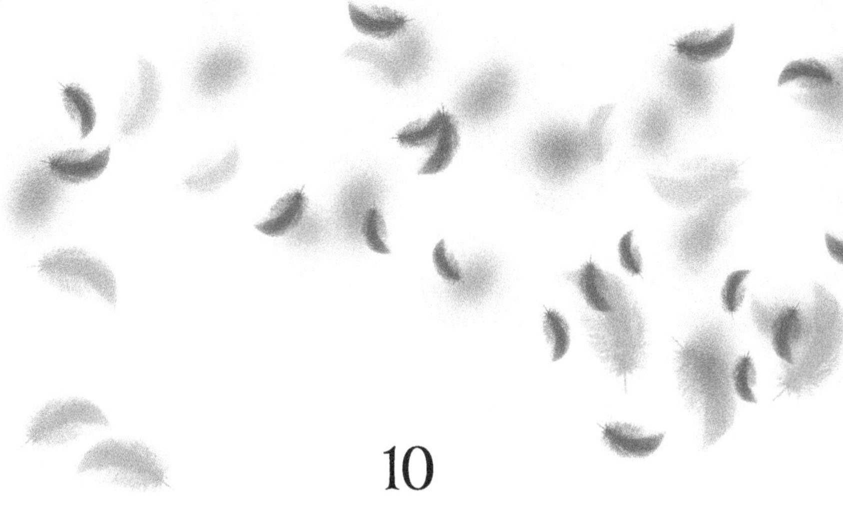

10

Morning revealed no lasting damage from the fall, only a lingering sense of shock that my mysterious wings had snapped into action without any conscious thought on my part.

Coffee in hand, I checked all the job search sites. There weren't a lot of new listings. Not too surprising—Sparkle Beach was a small town, with only a handful of major companies. I considered broadening the distance on my search, but decided to give it one more week.

In an impulse more hopeful than realistic, I checked Ultimate Crate's most recent social media posts to see if I could gain any insight for future use.

Complaints piled up in the comments: *Where is my crate? When will my crate ship? Why don't you respond to your emails?*

A muscle twitched in my eyelid. The idea of sweeping problems under the rug made me uncomfortable. I wanted a job—desperately—but between the shady approach to customer service and the interviewer's casual ageism, I was beginning to think I'd dodged a bullet by not getting hired on the spot.

I worked the rest of the morning, first sprucing up my résumé, then customizing cover letters to send to the new positions that had popped up.

After I got caught up on job searching, I got down to the other business of the day: Raphael's art show. Like most small-town art events, anyone who wanted to attend could show up. The average art show had too few guests, and almost never too many. I'd be a welcome visitor even if I didn't know one of the artists.

I rifled through the clothes hung up in my closet, finding plenty of acceptable outfits but nothing that wowed me. I needed to be wowed.

I tossed half a dozen work dresses on the bed. I paced back and forth, trying to decide which one was the least boring, before concluding that the whole task was impossible. Getting gussied up didn't play to my strengths.

"Who would have best dress advice?" Mama would veer toward biker chic. Lily would try to dress me in some cutting edge look. Pepper and Rose—well, maybe somewhere between goth gal and surfer chick they'd balance each other out and I'd turn out looking like a fabulously elegant beach babe. A Sparkle Beach femme fatale, if such a thing could exist.

I pulled up our group text on my phone. *Mayday. Outfit required. Likelihood of shopping: high.*

Pepper replied first. *Goody! I was looking for an excuse to skip out of the office.*

Rose replied a minute later. *Can I bring a friend?*

I grimaced. *Not sure I want my trials observed by a stranger. No offense.*

Rose texted a string of laughing emojis. *It's a dog.* She sent several dog emojis to drive the point home.

"Sure, bring the dog, you crazy woman." I typed the words as I spoke, then added, *P.S. I'm broke. Or I will be soon if I'm not careful. Any ideas for saving money on this?*

A message from Pepper appeared. *Don't you have store credit at the consignment shop?*

I'd forgotten all about it. *Pepper, you're a genius.*

We met at Fifi's Secondhand Salon, Sparkle Beach's answer to Rodeo Drive. The shop combined a hair salon with a consignment store, all housed in a repurposed two-story Victorian house downtown. The sign out front depicted a black poodle standing on two legs, wielding a comb and wearing a fifties-style fit-and-flare dress and a string of pearls.

The door swung open to reveal a frou-frou interior complete with pink walls, chunky crystal lamps, and tiny chairs with throw pillows edged in marabou feathers.

A black poodle bounded up and licked my hand. It had been a long time since I'd been to Fifi's, but the shop's namesake hadn't forgotten me.

"Hello, Fifi, old girl. How are you?" I bent and patted the poodle's thick hair. The store smelled, not unpleasantly, of dogs, permanents, and other people's closets.

Fifi's owner bustled up in a voluminous robe and a satiny turban with a costume jewelry brooch affixed. She blinked at me in a friendly, assessing way. "What'll it be today? Hair or flair?"

I straightened. "Flair, please. I'm looking to use up some credit on a dress."

"Let me know if I can help you find anything." She settled on the stool behind the counter and began rearranging an assortment of sequined masks next to a framed flyer promoting the Sun Festival.

The door chimed. Fifi swished her pom-pom tail.

Rose walked in carrying a tiny Chihuahua with caramel-colored fur.

"You made it! And who's this little guy?"

Rose shifted the dog in her arms. "This is Peanut. I'm helping him learn how to make new friends."

Peanut may have had a different agenda—he spotted Fifi and promptly went berserk. The little dog barked wildly, attempting to wiggle free from Rose's hold.

Rose kept her cool and spoke calmly. "Hush, Peanut." She set him down on the floor with enough leash to move but not enough to reach Fifi, then briskly walked him away. At the back of the shop, Rose turned on her heel and led Peanut to the front of the store again.

This time, Peanut shook himself, but did not bark.

Fifi sat like a Sphinx and regarded the intruder with regal hauteur.

Rose lavished Peanut with pats and murmurs of approval. "Such a good boy." She turned to me. "He's getting the hang of it."

Pepper pushed the door open and found the two of us with Peanut and Fifi. "Dog party!"

"The best kind of party," Rose said. "Watch this. Peanut, play dead."

Peanut flopped on his side and looked up at us with black, marble-round eyes, his tiny tail twitching.

Rose praised him and rubbed his belly.

Pepper watched with awe. "How do you *do* that?"

"It's a knack." She elbowed Pepper. "Like what you have with children."

"Dogs don't beg you for the latest video game machine," Pepper said with matter-of-fact cheer. She held up a blindingly pink sequined dress from the nearest rack. "What do you think? Is it me?"

"Get serious." I grabbed the dress and returned it to the rack. "This is a code red. I have only a few hours until I have to see this guy in the flesh."

Rose ran her fingers over a black dress. "Don't get your hopes up, Luella. He's probably married."

"You're missing the point." I rapidly flicked through another rack. "Do you know what it's like to be compared to the memory of your high school self? I don't care if he's married or if he's the pope. I want him to stagger back in admiration. That's not too much to ask."

A faint smile touched Rose's lips. "Vanity, thy name is woman."

"Damn right it is." I soldiered through another row of dresses while Pepper launched into an impromptu rendition of "You're So Vain" by Carly Simon.

Rose found yet another black dress and held it up for my approval. "Size sixteen, right?"

"More or less." I took it and held it against my body. "It's a maybe. I'll add it to the try-ons."

"How about this?" Pepper held up a cherry-red wrap dress.

Rose's eyes lit up. "I have a lipstick that would go with it."

I eyed the dress. "You don't think it's too young?"

"No!" they chorused.

Peanut barked for good measure.

"Fine, I'll try it." I retreated to the fitting room, with its tiny pouf chair and gilt-edged mirror, to wrestle my way into the dresses. I discarded several without even showing them to the girls—one had an unflattering neckline, and the other fit too snug on my hips.

"How's it going in there? Do we need to send in a rescue team?" Pepper's voice carried through the fitting room door.

"Or a rescue dog?" added Rose.

"Almost ready." I wiggled around in the red wrap dress, rearranging the ties. My wings popped half-open as I hauled my cleavage to its maximum height. "Settle down," I muttered, and they retracted serenely behind me.

"Can I see?" Pepper hopped up and down, her feet the only part of her visible from behind the fitting room door.

"All right." I opened the door.

Rose and Pepper stared.

So did Peanut, who cocked his head to the side.

"Well? What do you think?" I pivoted and ran my hands down the dress. "Too much?"

Fifi walked over and nosed around the hem of the dress.

Pepper whistled, and shook out her hand like she'd touched something hot.

I rolled my eyes. "Is it too much, Pepper?"

"It's just the right amount of too much," Rose put in.

Pepper nodded. "What she said."

I pirouetted in front of the three-way mirror, admiring

how the crimson fabric swirled above my knees. "Ring it up, Fifi."

The poodle sneezed.

I whipped the skirt of the dress out of the way. "Hey, don't sneeze on the merchandise. Not unless you want to give me a discount for dog snot." I retreated to the fitting room and changed, then brought my purchase to the counter for Fifi's owner to ring up.

"After your store credit, that'll be nine dollars and four cents," she said.

Deal of the century. I handed over the cash.

Rose fished in her bag, exposing a row of lipsticks in a bandolier-like holder, while holding Peanut's leash with the other hand. "Take this."

"Thanks." I stashed the lipstick in my purse, then patted Fifi one last time.

Pepper hugged me, then took me by the shoulders and shook me for emphasis. "You promise to tell us all about it afterward, right?"

My stomach fluttered. "Sure. No big deal. Just me, a roomful of art-loving strangers, and a guy I nearly went to the prom with a million years ago."

"Who painted the downtown murals," Rose added.

"Who painted the downtown murals, may or may not be married, and may or may not be the pope."

Pepper shoved her hands in her pockets. "Guess I better get back to the office."

"I better get Peanut back home." Rose took in the slack on Peanut's leash.

"Bye, Peanut. Later, girls." I waved and headed to my car.

It felt strange to return to my half-empty apartment, like having one foot in an old life and one foot in a new one. I hung up the dress in the bathroom to knock out the wrinkles while I took an exorbitantly long, hot shower.

When I met Raphael, we were both in high school, but we didn't run in the same circles. Our paths never would have crossed if it weren't for the fact that we ended up in the school play together.

Our friendship grew quickly in the hothouse environment of the theater. Neither of us got a leading role, so we spent hours in the darkened auditorium during rehearsals, talking about everything and nothing, while the rest of the cast went through the motions onstage. I laughed at his jokes. He tried to imitate my Southern accent—badly. We pretended we were the stars of the play, reading monologues in increasingly ridiculous voices until we both collapsed, giggling, into the folding seats.

When the play finished its run, he asked me to go to prom with him. I accepted.

Days later, his family abruptly moved out of state.

We never went to prom, and I never saw him again.

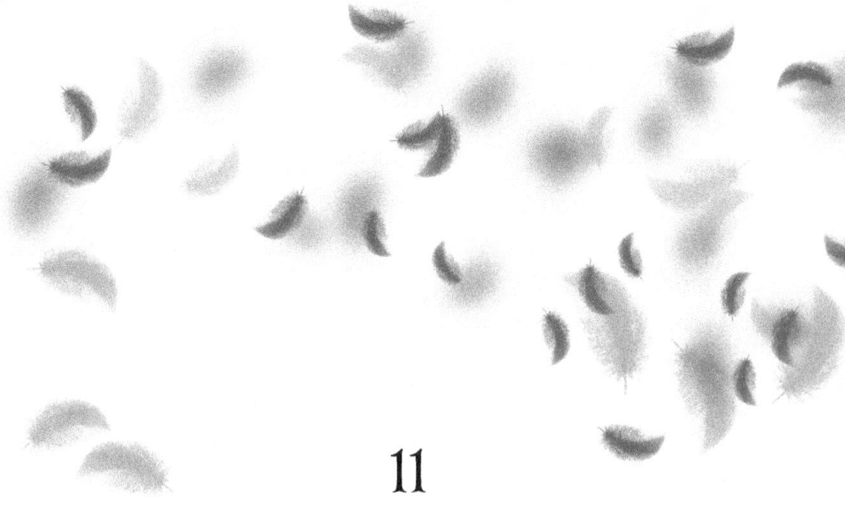

11

Artist's Alley didn't have the prime downtown real estate facing the river. Instead, as its name implied, it was tucked away on a tiny side street with a coffee shop on one side and a homebrewing supply store on the other. Those shops had already closed for the night, lending the street an air of desertion alleviated only by the illumination leaking from the windows of the gallery.

My low-heeled shoes clacked on the sidewalk. I tugged my dress into place and fluffed my hair. My wings remained an eye-popping accessory that would be visible to no one but me.

I didn't need to be nervous—not really. I needed information, that was all. Well, information, and an up-close look at the boy I'd known so long ago.

I pushed open the gallery door.

The crowd included the usual types: adults hungry for any type of culture available in a small town, overly boisterous teenagers eager to fulfill a school requirement, and the hapless few who'd been dragged to the show by friends or family. I fell into none of the above categories. Seeing no one I knew, I pretended to examine the artworks on the walls, while in fact all I could think about were the questions whirling in my head.

They didn't separate themselves neatly, either. Questions about the murals, about my magic, tangled with memories and conjectures about Raphael like an overgrown garden of climbing roses. I stared at an abstract painting filled with blasts of color and realized it perfectly captured the chaos of my inner state.

The refreshments table beckoned. Sparkle Beach art shows didn't command champagne and caviar, but I managed to snag a clear plastic cup of white wine and a pair of chocolate chip cookies straight from the grocery store bakery box.

The cookies tasted too sweet, but I washed each bite down with a sip of wine and made a mental note that the combination actually tasted pretty good.

I examined the artwork as I moved through the gallery. Landscapes of Sparkle Beach filled an entire wall. I coveted a brilliantly colored painting of a royal poinciana tree for my new home, but the price tag kept that desire firmly in the realm of fantasy.

Raphael's canvases burst with bold colors illustrating a mix of representational and abstract designs. Knowing the connection, it was easy to recognize his style from the downtown murals.

When I finished the second cookie, I noticed a dot of chocolate on my finger and surreptitiously licked it off.

Or so I thought.

A dark-haired man stared at me from across the room. If he'd caught me licking my finger, I'd have to hope I'd at least been successful removing the chocolate. I hid my hand behind my back just in case.

He spoke to the people he stood with, obviously excusing himself, and crossed the gallery. He walked with easy confidence and the beginning of a smile playing around his lips. He looked much too young to be halfway between forty and fifty.

My gaze slid from his dark, curly hair, down his neat beard, and stopped at his finely shaped mouth. I reluctantly hauled my eyes north to meet his bemused gaze.

"Excuse me," he said. His warm but clear voice sounded like the low notes of a violin. "You look so familiar. Do we know each other?"

Just as smells bring back memories, so do voices. I felt sixteen all over again. "I think … we went to high school together?" I couldn't repress a smile.

"Oh, my God—Luella!" He broke into a wide grin and threw his arms out. "How long has it been?"

"Since the earth cooled." Very smooth.

He laughed, like I remembered, but deeper and richer with the resonance time can bring. "That is the truth. Do you remember sitting in the back of the auditorium and goofing off back then? We were terrible!"

I tried to stop myself from checking his hand for a ring. I lasted two seconds.

He wasn't wearing a ring. "I remember!" I laughed. "How've you been, Raphael? No one ever heard from you after your family moved."

Raphael looked down and grimaced. "It was so sudden. I lost touch with everybody. No internet back then, you know? By the time it was a thing, everyone had moved on." He met my gaze. "But I'm doing good." He paused, taking me in with a glance. "You look like you're doing fantastic."

Minus the recent firing, the disaster date that burned down my most recent relationship, and the rampant uncontrollable weirdness in my life, sure. "I am. Doing fantastic, that is."

Raphael made a show of looking around the room. "Is there a Mr. Luella I should meet?"

I chuckled. "No. There's no Mr. Luella. The former Mr. Luella and I are divorced."

"I'm sorry to hear that." He sounded simultaneously sincere and pleased.

"I do have a lovely daughter, but she's not here." I gestured with my wine cup. "She's off at college."

"That is amazing. Time flies, doesn't it?" He moved closer.

"And you? Is there a Mrs. Raphael?"

"Nope. Not currently. Although, like yourself, I got a couple of little troublemakers." He smirked. "I shouldn't say 'little' anymore, though. Not if they're old enough to drink."

"It's hard to stop thinking of them that way, isn't it? Lily will always be my baby."

"Damn right." He nodded once, decisively. "What brings you here? You a big fan of the arts?"

"Believe it or not, this is not my usual scene." I paused for a sip of wine. "I was looking for the person who painted the downtown murals."

Raphael pressed his hands to his chest. "That's this guy right here."

The motion drew my attention from his face to his chest and his elegant hands. I blinked and recovered. "The Downtown Merchant Guild told me on the phone. I never imagined it would be the same guy I knew in high school. I figured it was some other Raphael Andalucia." A little white lie to keep him from assuming I'd dressed up for his sake. He didn't need to know that. It would be the funny story I'd tell him after we were married.

Wait—where did *that* thought come from?

He put his hands on his hips. "What a small world. So what did you need to know?"

"Oh my gosh, I don't want to take you away from your event with my questions." Yes, I did, but I had manners. "You should keep on mingling."

His dark brown eyes twinkled in the gallery lights. "There's only one solution to that."

I raised my eyebrows.

"We'll have to go out sometime," he said with an utterly deadpan delivery.

"Too bad the coffee shop next door is closed," I said.

"Coffee? Bah." He waved his hand in an exaggerated motion. "We have so much catching up to do—it'll have to be dinner. What do you say?"

I clamped down on my smile before it turned into a ridiculous grin. "That sounds lovely."

"Great!" He placed a warm hand briefly on the arm I had hidden behind my back. "Before I get back into mingling, I'm going to sneak off and grab a few chocolate chip cookies before they're all gone. I'm a sucker for anything with chocolate." He winked. "Catch you later."

My whole body vibrated like a struck tuning fork as he walked away. He'd *winked* at me. About *chocolate*. I felt my cheeks heat up.

I blessed the air conditioner for kicking on and sending a cool breeze onto my cheeks—until I realized it wasn't the air conditioner. My skirt swirled around my knees as the wind increased. I scanned the room and caught a flash of white and silver along the rear wall of the gallery. The crowd parted long enough for me to spot Zephyr, her tail wagging playfully, looking like she was seconds away from romping across the room. I hustled through the crowd to cut her off before she could raise enough wind to knock the paintings off the wall.

The closer I got, the more my lightweight skirt danced. I tried to subtly hold it down, but it levitated wherever my hands were not. "Zephyr, come!" My voice came out in a strangled whisper. I had no choice but to detour into the hallway at the back of the gallery, hoping I could find either an exit or a bathroom where I could be alone with my adorable yet disruptive canine friend.

Zephyr bounded down the hall beside me.

I bumped the bathroom door open with my hip and slipped inside with Zephyr, firmly locking the door and thanking all my lucky stars that the room was single-occupancy—and that it had been unoccupied.

Zephyr gamboled in the small space, making the toilet paper and paper towels flap in the wind.

"Settle down, girl."

She shook herself all over, then sat.

"Zephyr, baby, you can't blow up my skirt at an art opening. People won't understand."

She cocked her head.

"It doesn't look good if I show up and a big mess gets made, either. I can't afford to cover the damages if all those nice paintings get knocked down."

She shrank to the floor.

My heart cracked. I didn't mean to hurt her feelings. "You're a good dog, Zephyr. We just need to work together, okay?"

She leaped to her feet and paced the tiny room as if looking for an exit. Her body bunched, as if she were coiling in on herself.

"Wait, don't go—" I reached for her, but it was too late.

Zephyr sprang through the wall as if it were insubstantial.

I flung open the bathroom door and ran into the hallway, hoping to catch her.

She was gone.

I slammed my hands into the wall. "Damn it!"

"Are you okay?"

I whirled. "Raphael!" I must have looked like a basket case. I smoothed my dress. "I'm fine. I—uh—just realized I left my phone in the car."

My phone picked that moment to buzz. Loudly.

Confusion wrinkled his brow. His gaze shifted to my purse, and his lips twitched in amusement.

My cheeks burned again. I slowly opened my purse. "What do you know? It was there all along." I tried to laugh lightly.

We faced each other down the dim, narrow hallway.

"That's fortunate." He closed the distance between us slowly and deliberately. "May I give you my number?"

The narrow hallway suddenly felt cozy. The low light reminded me of the back of the auditorium during those long rehearsals. I cleared my throat. "Yes. I'd like that." I retrieved the phone and punched in his number, then slipped the phone back in my purse. "I should go."

"Can I walk you to your car?"

"No, I'll be fine. But thank you."

"The least I can do is see you out." He gestured for me to precede him down the hallway.

We both meant to look away, I think—but we looked up at the same time and our eyes met as I squeezed past. As I walked ahead of him down the hall, I quietly exhaled the breath I'd been holding.

He followed me to the door. "Thank you for coming. I hope we can see each other again soon."

"Me too. It was good to see you." I hesitated, then settled on giving him a friendly goodbye hug.

By mutual agreement, it may have lasted one or two seconds longer than strictly necessary.

My emotions swirled like the humid night air by the time I reached my car. I slid into the driver's seat. My fingers flew over the phone as I composed a text to Rose. *Rose, I need your help with a dog. I don't know what I'm doing and I don't want to scare her away but I also don't want to have my life wrecked by random tornadoes wherever I go.*

I rested my head on the backrest and closed my eyes, probably not the wisest move while sitting in a dark parking lot, but I didn't care.

The phone buzzed. *Would this be that new white dog?*

The one and only, I wrote.

I'm in, she replied.

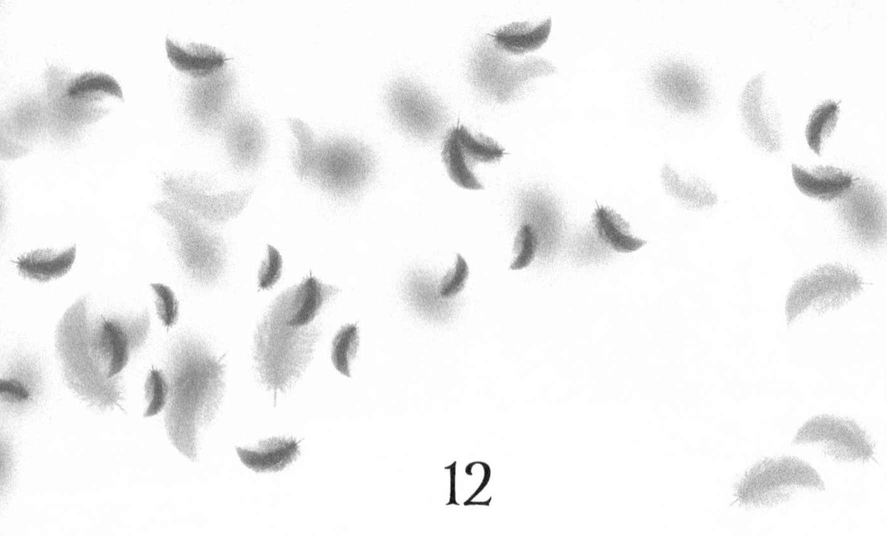

12

I drove to Rose's cabin the next morning, early enough that the sky retained its crystal clarity before the afternoon haze took over. Rose lived about fifteen minutes outside Sparkle Beach city limits, near Black Bear Ridge—a sprawling state forest of tall sand pines and dense palmetto-filled underbrush. The unmarked turnoff led to a dirt road that wound through stands of skinny oak trees.

I took the steps to the front door of the cabin, knocked, and stood waiting under the deep shade of the slanted roof. The knock set a dog barking, the noise echoing from within the house.

The door opened. Rose stood in the entrance wearing a black tank top emblazoned with a moon phase graphic, and black capri-length yoga pants with white letters running down the side seams. It took a second glance to realize they were Ouija board letters. "Come in!" she said.

I wiped my feet on the mat to knock off sand and stepped inside. A doggy scent predominated, cut by the smoky aroma of a recently blown-out candle.

Rose gestured to the sofa. "Have a seat. I'll get us some drinks."

I sat.

A large dog—something like a pit bull, with a Kodiak bear in its ancestry—trotted self-importantly around the room, then flopped by the empty fireplace and laid its large head on its paws.

I looked around for a caramel-colored Chihuahua. "Where's Peanut?"

"Back home," Rose called from the kitchen.

"What's this guy's name?"

"Who?"

"The dog built like a mountain. Dog Mountain." I eyed the massive animal, who snorted and rolled onto his flank.

Rose reappeared with chilled cans of seltzer. She handed one to me, then took a seat by the cold fireplace, next to the dog. "This is Braveheart. He's getting a little training before he goes up for adoption."

"He's a foster?"

Rose nodded, then cracked open her can and took a long drink. "So where's your dog?"

"I don't know."

Her eyebrows shot up. "You don't know?"

"I think I insulted her." I watched the condensation drip from my can of seltzer. "She found me in the art gallery last night—"

"How did that go? You never said."

"I was so flustered I never got around to it. The dog showed up in the middle of the gallery, and the wind started blowing, like before, so I tried to tell her to stop—but she ran away."

"And Raphael?"

"He caught me running after Zephyr. I don't know what he thought, but he must have overlooked my apparent nuttiness, because he gave me his number. He wants to go to dinner sometime."

"Was he like what you remembered from high school?"

"Yes. No. I don't know. It's like I know him, but he's also a stranger."

"Kind of like this magic dog of yours." Rose rubbed Braveheart's back. "Dogs aren't that different from people, you know."

"What do you mean?"

"Dogs make choices based on what they want, and what they're afraid of. Figure out what they want, or what they're afraid of, and you'll understand why they do what they do. Then you'll know how to get them to do what you want."

"That's . . . unnerving, in a way."

She shrugged. "It doesn't have to be negative or controlling. Not if you think of it as aligning yourself with their needs. For example, take Braveheart."

The dog's paw twitched as Rose scratched his basketball-sized head.

"Braveheart came from a home where the owner decided to buy a new dog. A small dog." Her lips pursed in judgment. "He called me in a panic because Braveheart nearly took a chunk out of the new dog, despite never having shown aggression before."

I groped for a nearby pillow and placed it over my lap like a shield.

"I had to explain to him that all dogs nip, under the right—or wrong—circumstances. And that dogs can automatically view smaller animals as prey, unless they're raised together. He'd set up a power imbalance by buying a new dog. Picture this: the small dog nips at Braveheart. No harm done, right?"

I nodded slowly.

"But if Braveheart did the same thing, the smaller dog wouldn't stand a chance. Not because the behavior is abnormal, but because the owner foolishly created a no-win situation."

"How do you fix it?"

"You can't. You look at the situation through Braveheart's point of view. Braveheart's a normal dog who wants to do normal dog things. There's no correcting that."

"The owner got rid of him?"

"It was the safest choice, to protect the smaller dog. Braveheart's a good boy—but he needs to be in a home without smaller animals running around."

"Wow." I removed the pillow, feeling sheepish.

"Or take Peanut. Peanut was afraid of other dogs. And people. So much so that she'd get nervous and start barking like crazy if she got close to anyone. I had to teach her how to not be afraid."

My ears pricked up. "How'd you do that?"

"Remember when I said dogs are like people? At the end of the day, they just want to be loved. Every time Peanut encountered a dog and didn't freak out, I praised her and gave her plenty of affection."

"I'll have to remember that the next time I'm in a relationship and I want to encourage a certain behavior. Like doing the dishes."

Rose chuckled. "Dogs and people, people and dogs. The difference is like this." She held her thumb and forefinger less than an inch apart. "But dogs are obviously superior."

"Obviously. I should put myself in Zephyr's paws, then?"

"Exactly. What does she want? What is she afraid of?"

I thought about it. "She seems … to want to show up for me."

"When?"

Good question. I ticked the answers off, one by one, on my fingers. "When I got fired. When I broke up with Dan. When I went downtown. When I went to the new house. When I got interviewed—no, wait, that was the crow, not Zephyr. When I went to the art gallery to see Raphael."

"Sounds like times when you were nervous. Or excited."

"Or both."

We drank from our cans.

Braveheart snored gently.

"Maybe she wants to protect you," said Rose. "And maybe she's afraid of failure."

"How do I help her?"

"She has to learn to trust you. You have to show her affection and love until her fear subsides."

"I can do that—if I could get her to show up on command."

"She'll show up on command a lot better once she learns to trust you."

I sighed. "Do you see the problem?"

Rose considered. "I don't usually use treats for dog training, but maybe it would help in this case."

I laughed. "Treats? For a magical dog? What would that even be?"

"Does she seem to get pleasure out of anything?"

Memories of Zephyr flitted through my mind. "She seems . . . playful?"

Rose got up. "Let's work with that. What would a magical, windy dog like to play with?"

I racked my brain for things to do with moving air. "A fan. A hairdryer. Feathers? A kite?"

"Pinwheels?"

We both cracked up.

"Oh my gosh, Rose. This is so crazy."

"Hang on—I've got bubbles for when my nieces come to visit." Rose ran down the hall, her bare feet loud on the raised floor of the cabin. She returned with two clear plastic bottles of bubbles, complete with matching wands in the lids. "Here." She handed one to me and joined me on the couch.

"Now what?" I gestured with the bottle. "I blow bubbles and say 'Here, Zephyr'?"

"Got any better ideas?"

I shot her a look and unscrewed the cap. I withdrew the wand with care to avoid spilling bubble liquid on the couch. My first attempt at blowing bubbles failed—the liquid sputtered sideways and formed no bubbles.

"Try blowing slow and steady."

"If you're so good at it, you do it."

"Fine." Rose unscrewed the cap on her bottle. She pursed her lips and blew a perfect stream of rainbow-colored bubbles on the first try.

"Showoff." I tried again. I produced one large bubble, which popped with a tiny splash. I stood so I could support my breath from my diaphragm, like my high school chorus teacher taught me.

Finally, a stream of bubbles floated across the living room and popped on the stones of the fireplace.

"Here, Zephyr. Come out and play, baby." I blew more bubbles. "Come play, girl."

The next set of bubbles zigged and zagged wildly, as if under the influence of a chaotic air current.

I met Rose's gaze with a meaningful look.

She lifted her bubble wand and blew more bubbles in concert with my efforts.

Braveheart snuffled, stretched, and stood. His tail wagged as if he expected a friend.

The bubbles shot in all directions as the breeze in the room increased.

A white and silver blur shot out of the fireplace, bringing a flurry of ash with it.

"Zephyr!" I didn't know whether to put the bubbles down or keep on blowing.

Braveheart blundered around the room, chasing the uncatchable Zephyr.

Zephyr skidded to a halt in front of me, followed closely by Braveheart, who seemed to have instantly fallen in love.

I blew another round of bubbles. "Who's a good girl? Zephyr's a good girl!"

Rose spoke up from the couch. "Can Braveheart see your dog?"

"He definitely can." I kept making bubbles, to Zephyr's obvious delight—she nipped at them happily. "I'm going to try something." I opened my wings and extended them until the tips reached past the ends of the couch.

"Did you notice that they're dripping glitter now?"

I glanced at my wings. Sure enough, tiny silver sparkles lazily floated down from the bottom edges. When I vibrated my wings to create a breeze, sparkles cascaded like salt from a shaker before wafting away.

The breeze sent the bubbles zipping in all directions. Zephyr barked and ran in a circle, chasing them with glee. After the bubbles popped, she trotted to me and licked my hand.

I knelt and set down the bubbles. "Here, girl." I sank my fingers into her thick fur, feeling the subtle tickle of its constant airstream. "Good girl."

"See if you can get her to lower the wind," Rose said.

"Lower it?" I wasn't sure how to do that. I focused on stilling my wings, nullifying the current of air rather than encouraging it. I patted Zephyr's head rhythmically. "Hush, hush," I said, like she was a baby to be soothed.

She blinked at me and the light movement of air in the room stopped.

"Good Zephyr!" I praised her lavishly with words and caresses.

Rose got off the couch and crept closer. “Now try to get her to raise it again.”

I retrieved the bottle and stood. “Bubbles!” A steady breath sent a dozen into the air. I vibrated my wings and sent the bubbles flying.

Zephyr leaped and the wind increased.

“Yay, Zephyr! Go Zephyr!” I added more bubbles and watched them zing around the room. Then I ceased the movement of my wings and dropped to the floor. “Hush, hush,” I cajoled the dog.

She instantly sat and the wind died.

I smoothed my hands over her velvet ears, a warm feeling blossoming in my heart. “I knew we could be a team.”

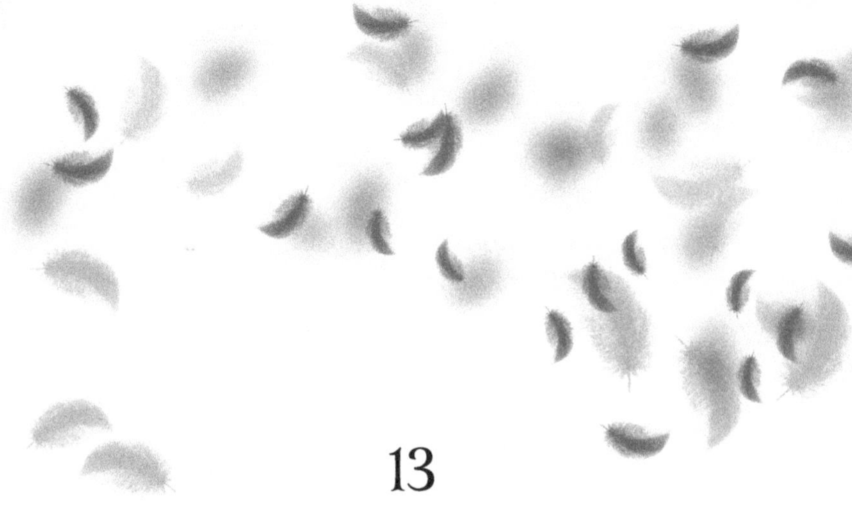

13

The phone rang the next evening while I was desperately trying to find any new job listings within a one hundred mile radius. I bounded up from my chair, accidentally sending my can of soda flying sideways toward the desktop computer.

The can tipped and spilled. The contents crept across the table.

"No, no, no, no, no!" If I ran for paper towels, the soda would reach the computer before I made it back. If I touched the liquid after it had reached the computer, I could electrocute myself. "Damn it!" I did the only thing I could think of.

I whipped off my shirt and dropped it on the encroaching lake of soda, carefully corralling the trickles that tried to escape. "I liked that shirt," I said—then realized the phone was still ringing.

"Double damn it!" Shirtless, I grabbed the phone from the coffee table and picked up, silently thanking the gods of technology that video calling had not become the norm. "Hello?"

"Luella? It's London. How are you?"

Half-naked, flustered, and recently fired, but I didn't say that to my former intern. "Dandy. What's up?"

"I talked to my aunt."

"And?"

"It was *very* interesting."

It wasn't possible to physically reach through the phone and shake her, so I bit my lip and waited for her to continue.

"How about we meet up and I'll tell you all about it?"

She was trying to be helpful, bless her—but she couldn't help craving a live audience for it. "Fine. How about Shelly's Place? You know where that is?"

"Is that the mermaid bar with the old rock music?"

Old rock music! "Classic rock music, yes. That's the one."

"Nine?"

"Sure. See you at nine at Shelly's Place."

She hung up without a word.

"Weird." Maybe Suntan Queen was about to lay off more people. Maybe Queenie had revealed her secret identity as a lizard woman from Mars.

Maybe London just wanted to know where I hid the good pens.

I retrieved a new shirt from my bedroom. I had an idea for blowing off a little steam before the meeting—there was enough time to enjoy the sunset before I had to head over to Shelly's. "Zephyr! Here, girl." My head poked through the collar. "Who wants to go to the beach?" My arms came through the sleeves.

By the time I had the shirt pulled down, I could feel a noticeable breeze. The ceiling fan was off, and the air conditioning wasn't currently blowing. I spread my arms and felt my wings kick into action, increasing the movement in the air. "Zephyr," I called, my voice playful and teasing.

She burst through the bedroom window, her passage rippling the blinds as if the window were open to the evening air.

"Zephyr!" I knelt and caressed her. "Who's the bestest magical dog?" I ruffled her furry head. "You are!"

Zephyr leaped and chased her tail a few times.

I let my wings relax. "You want to ride in the car? Last one's a rotten egg!" I grabbed my purse, locked the door, and ran down the stairs, my footsteps light and quick with Zephyr at my heels.

She beat me to the sidewalk by running through my legs. Literally. Then she jumped through the car window on the passenger side.

I slid into the driver's seat and regarded her as she sat in the passenger seat. "Cheater. No fair when you can run through someone."

Zephyr cocked her head, and her tongue lolled.

"Don't play innocent with me, princess." I shot her a skeptical look and put the car into motion. It would be one of the last times I would have to travel this route. Soon I'd be fully ensconced in my new digs—as soon as I managed to get a moving truck and haul the rest of my stuff over there. It might have to wait for a lull in job searches, magical creatures, and high school crushes, but I'd get it done.

I never knew unemployment could be so busy.

While I mulled these thoughts, I didn't notice Zephyr getting antsy—until she drew back like a spring and launched herself through the windshield. She blew through the air, ran a loop-de-loop around a green light, and zipped ahead of the stop-and-go traffic keeping me at a crawl.

"Really? Is that fair?" I threw one hand up in mock annoyance, but a grin broke out on my face. "Goofy dog."

Zephyr doubled back like she was returning a Frisbee at the park, then ran up the hood of the car.

"All right, you goofball. Don't sit on the windshield and cause an accident." I made kissy faces at her so she'd know I wasn't mad.

This caught the attention of the man in the car next to mine, who rolled down his window and wiggled his eyebrows at me before making a kissy face of his own.

"Oh, for heaven's sake—" I flipped my sun visor down to the side to cut off my view of him as Zephyr leaped away and gamboled playfully in the traffic.

For the rest of the drive, I kept my eyes on the road and my kissy faces to myself.

Zephyr beat me to the beachside parking lot and kicked up a whopping wind, blowing loose sand and small pebbles in all directions.

I grabbed a beach towel out of the back seat and eased out of the car. "Hush, hush," I murmured.

Zephyr sent a few more leaves flying before coming to my side.

Now that we were in public, I couldn't risk patting her too obviously, or it would look to any observer like I was patting thin air. Verbal praise would have to suffice. "Good girl, Zephyr."

We walked over the wooden ramp across the dunes and down to the white sand. I removed my shoes. The dry sand squeaked under my feet as the steady onshore breeze pushed my hair back.

Zephyr took off like a shot, surging across the sand. She didn't stop when she reached the water—she ran across it as if the waves were no less solid than the sandy shore.

I found the high water mark in the sand and spread my towel on the dry side, figuring Zephyr would return when she'd had her fill of walking on water. Truth be told, I felt envious.

But maybe I didn't have to.

If Zephyr could walk over water, why couldn't I? After all, my wings had already saved me from a nasty fall in the kitchen. It might have been instinct that activated them, but surely the mechanism of flight could be accessed under other, less stressful circumstances. At least, I hoped it could.

I imagined myself floating over the waves, the wind in my face and the spray tickling my toes. Any such shenanigans on my part would have to take place under the cover of darkness, since passersby would likely take notice of a flying woman. Zephyr's invisibility granted her freedom to run or fly wherever she pleased.

This time, instead of envy, the thought of Zephyr produced another line of questions. Perhaps if she had the innate ability to go unseen, I could develop it too. Like a mirage—wasn't that a trick of the air?

Possibilities drifted through my mind like clouds across the dimming eastern horizon.

Zephyr finished her romp and trotted across the sand. Her paws left no footprints—no wonder, for she floated above the ground when she walked.

"You touch the ground only when you want to," I observed as she flopped down on the towel next to me.

She watched the crashing waves, content to be still.

Come to think of it, her effects were selective. She could bound through solid objects, or send them flying, as she chose. I hadn't even come close to unraveling her mysteries, but I was sure going to try. I surreptitiously slipped my hand over her shoulder and gave her a scratch.

We sat companionably, side by side, as the sun sank behind us. To the south, the Sparkle Beach lighthouse disappeared in a gathering fog. The shadows of the condo towers lengthened across the sand until the fading light abandoned the water, leaving it the shade of spilled ink.

"Time to go, girl." I stood and shook out the beach towel.

Zephyr bowed into a playful position and sent a blast of air at the towel, perhaps attempting to be helpful—or perhaps taking the opportunity to tease me.

The towel wound around my arm. I chuckled as I unwrapped it. "Very funny. Let's go."

When we arrived at Shelly's, I realized I had no idea what to do with Zephyr. Could I tell her to stay in the car? She seemed unlikely to listen.

I shifted in my seat to face her. "Can you be a good doggy and be hush-hush inside?" I felt like I was talking to Lily, circa age two, when she'd acquiesce happily to my request that she behave herself at the grocery store—only to tear off down an aisle the second we entered the building.

Zephyr raised her paw.

"Does that mean you agree?"

She lowered her paw and sneezed.

I shook my head. This was getting nowhere—fast. "Fine. You can come in. But be good," I admonished, opening the car door.

She rewarded me with a short bark before diving through the windshield.

"Can't you come out the open door like a normal dog?" I muttered.

The loud cry of a crow pierced the air.

"What now?" I slammed the door. In the time it took for my eyes to adjust, a blur of black flew past and landed on the mermaid sign.

The crow turned its head and pointedly looked at me—and at Zephyr.

"Midnight?" I said.

"I didn't say midnight."

I spun around so fast I nearly lost my balance. "London! You startled me."

London approached, her outfit impeccable as always, and several degrees ritzier than Shelly's Place warranted. "Sorry. I heard you talking—I thought maybe you were confused about the time."

"Not confused." I couldn't stop myself from sneaking one last glance in the crow's direction.

London drew her phone like a gunslinger and snapped a picture of the mermaid. "Cool sign."

I bit my tongue before I could ask if she could see the crow sitting on it. "Shall we?" I gestured for her to precede me.

Zephyr's gaze tracked London as my former trainee walked by.

I followed London into Shelly's. The glowing Christmas lights and loud music promised good times, but this meeting wasn't exactly a party. I concentrated on summoning a neutral expression as we took our seats. It wouldn't do to get my hopes up or down.

Zephyr curled up under the table. I felt a touch of her hairdryer-esque fur, but it appeared she'd turned it down to low speed, so to speak.

London sat gingerly and picked up the menu. "What's good?" Her attempt at a friendly tone clashed with her awkward body language.

I had the feeling she'd feel more at home with a plate of sushi or a trendy brunch. "The triple play is nice." I sounded inane. We'd never socialized outside of work, and it showed.

London dropped her menu with a dramatic flourish.

I laid my menu aside. "Are you okay?"

She leaned closer. "I think my aunt is up to something."

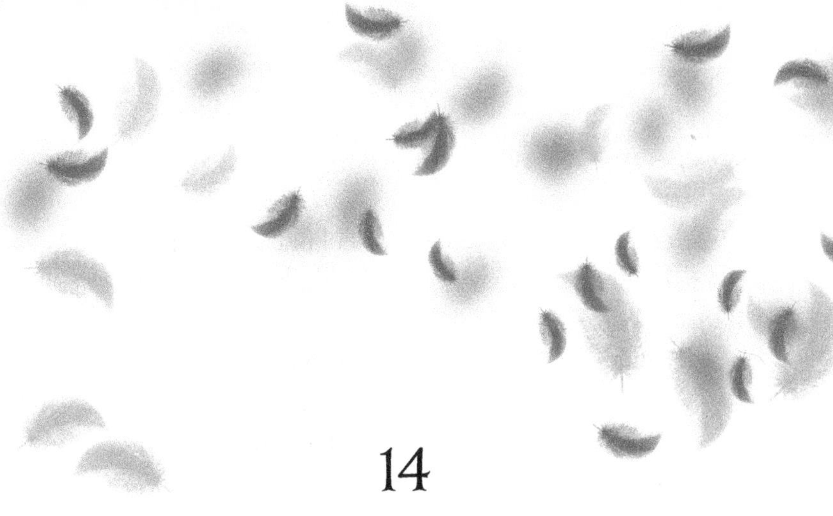

14

After the server took our order, I summoned an understanding tone that had worked well with Lily in the past. “Why don’t you tell me all about it?”

London reached across the table and pressed my hand. “Promise me something.” The words came out in a rush. “You can’t get mad at me—not until you’ve heard everything I have to say.”

“Okay.” I tried to keep a straight face. She was certainly making a meal of this.

“After you got—after you left, I went to talk to Queenie.”

“I remember you said you were going to talk to her. You were going to use your influence, as I recall.”

“I did! I asked if she would reconsider firing you.”

“And?”

“And she said it was none of my business.”

“So why are we here?” I gestured to our surroundings.

"Because that's not all I asked." She paused to sip from her drink.

Unlike when we were on the phone, this time I could have reached across the table and shaken her. It was very hard not to.

"Remember, you promised not to get mad—"

"I remember. Just… get on with it."

"Since trying to get your job back was a dead end, I tried something else."

I raised my eyebrows.

"I asked for your job."

"You *what*?"

She fluttered her hands. "I told you not to get mad!"

With great effort, I made my voice level. "I thought you were trying to help me."

"I was. I am. You have to let me finish."

"Then finish."

"When I told her she should give your old job to me, she said"—she switched to an impression of Queenie's manner of speech—"'Darling, whatever are you thinking? Asking for her job when her chair is hardly cool? Really, darling, it's too much.'" She flipped her hands in a diva-ish gesture reminiscent of her aunt.

I smiled at the thought of Queenie putting the brakes on her niece's ambition. Then I sat back in my chair and regarded London. "So she told you to back off. So what?"

London took another sip of her drink, clearly pleased with herself. "So I did a little checking down in human resources. Not only is she not hiring for that job—but your name is still on everything to do with that position.

I made a noise of disbelief. "They just haven't taken it off yet."

She shook her head vehemently. "No. Everyone expects me to be as useless as the rest of the family—other than Aunt Queenie—but I know those procedures backwards and forwards. Remember? I shadowed HR before I shadowed you. They're not hiring for that job. It's like you were never fired."

"I was there, London. I remember it well."

London pressed her lips together and gave me a hard look, an expression I hadn't seen before. "I'm telling you: she's up to something."

I laughed. "She's busy running Suntan Queen. What possible sane reason could she have for firing me, or not firing me, or whatever she might be doing?"

London drummed her fingers. "I don't know. I tried to ask my dad about it at the obligatory Russell family barbecue at her house, over the weekend, but he didn't know anything about it." London laughed with a bitter edge. "Aunt Queenie would drive her convertible into the ocean before she dropped one word of information on my dad. They can't stand each other."

The server delivered a triple play platter, pausing the conversation.

"Your family barbecues must be a real hoot."

She rolled her eyes. "You have no idea. Everyone wants a piece of Suntan Queen, so they show up and play nice. They don't mean any of it, though. My dad used to recruit me to steal the Suntan Queen books when I was in elementary school."

My jaw dropped. The Russells were even crazier than I thought. "He couldn't get them himself?"

"Aunt Queenie wouldn't let him touch them. Didn't trust him." She nonchalantly drowned a chicken finger in honey mustard sauce. "I snuck them out, delivered them to Dad, then returned them before she missed them. He paid me in Oreos. I thought it was a fun game."

"Wow." The Russells could give the Borgias a run for their money. I nudged Zephyr gently with my foot, to let her know she hadn't been forgotten.

She swished her tail against my leg.

I used the excuse of stuffing my mouth with fried cheese to mull over what London had said. If there was any chance, no matter how remote, of Queenie rehiring me, I had to take it. Whatever Machiavellian game she might be playing, I wanted my job back. I wanted to finish accumulating my years and retire with dignity down the road.

Perhaps I had been unknowingly exposed to a chemical at the Suntan Queen plant. Maybe Queenie fired me to get me out of the way until a solution could be found to keep the company safe from lawsuits. Or she thought I'd be so grateful to be rehired that I'd forego suing Suntan Queen into the ground. Each scenario I thought of became more absurd than the last, and none of it made any sense.

London's gaze drifted to the Christmas lights before returning to make eye contact. "Some weird lady showed up during the barbecue, too, but she wasn't a guest."

"What weird lady?" I was grasping at straws. "Can you describe her a little more?"

"She looked like one of those politicians you see on TV. Hair sprayed down like a helmet. Matching suit jacket and knee-length skirt. Conservative heels."

"Age?"

"Older."

"Older than what? You? Me? Dirt?"

London appeared to be at a loss for words.

"I won't be insulted. No matter what comparison you make." I might, but I wouldn't let it show.

"She's older than you. Around Aunt Queenie's age."

"Maybe they're friends."

"They were arguing. Something about 'the plan.' The second they saw me, they stopped talking and the woman left."

I felt Zephyr raise her head under the table, as if she'd heard something of interest. *Down, girl.*

Having reached the limits of London's inside information, we segued to lighter topics. After we polished off the remainder of the triple play platter, she insisted on paying the check—and promised to pass along anything else she heard.

The only thing she asked in return was that I help her take a flattering picture in front of the mermaid sign so she could post it to her personal social media feed.

As I drove over the bridge connecting the peninsula and the mainland, the streetlights cast flickering shadows that whipped across the car. This time, Zephyr rode quietly, and when we returned to the apartment complex, she ran off and disappeared into the night.

Inside the apartment, I crawled into bed and surveyed the empty walls. I'd already taken the wall decorations—family photos, a framed Disney poster or two, and a small collection of souvenir landscape prints—to the shotgun house on Seabreeze Lane. The things that represented my life had migrated from one location to another, leaving the apartment more sterile and featureless than ever.

I picked up my phone from the nightstand and peered at Raphael's phone number. I'd had my share of dates and boyfriends, but I didn't claim to be fully up on all the unwritten guidelines for how long you should wait to text or call someone. I could have gotten advice from Lily, who would have found the whole situation immensely entertaining—she viewed my dating life like a not-to-be-missed reality show, when in fact it seemed to have more in common with C-SPAN.

I rolled onto my stomach and my wings unfurled slightly, as if they had a mind of their own and were trying to peek over my shoulder.

I wasn't going to send him a text now, of course. I was going to compose a draft. I'd send it after I'd mulled it over for a few days.

Or weeks.

Or years.

Hey, I wrote.

Brilliant opening, if I said so myself. Or maybe I should personalize it. *Hey. It's Luella.*

Better. That way he wouldn't think I was a spammer or a scammer.

Or *Hey. It's Luella. I think you're hot.* I cracked myself up. No way in hell.

An errant breeze caught a corner of the blanket and slid it across the phone.

A timestamp appeared under the sent message.

A wordless cry—something between a shriek and a groan—came out of my mouth. The sound bounced off the bare walls. "No! Unsend! Delete? Retract?" My fingers punched the screen in increasing desperation. "Please . . . "

Three dots appeared under my message, indicating that someone was typing a response.

"Kill me now." I buried my head in the pillow.

The phone buzzed.

I couldn't bear to look. I cringed and held the phone up.

Hey. It's Raphael.

"That's it, I'm going to die." I put the phone down and returned my face to the pillow.

The phone buzzed again. I picked it up.

I think you're hot, too.

"Wha—" I stared at the screen.

The dots reappeared. He was typing another message.

When the phone buzzed again, I nearly dropped it.

Now that we have that out of the way, when can I take you to dinner?

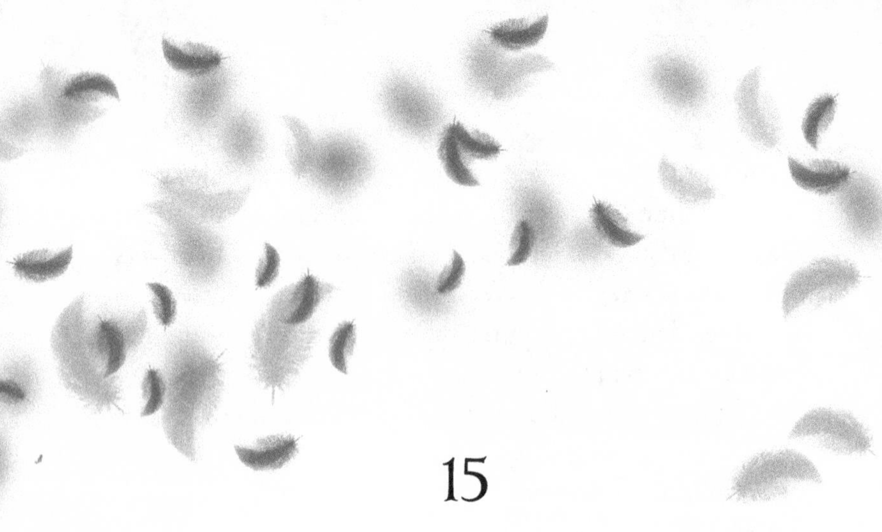

15

Moving day snuck up on me. Thankfully, Pepper and Rose had volunteered to help. Mama insisted on helping out, too—but only if she got to drive the moving truck. Zephyr amused herself during the commotion by racing around in circles, not letting silly things like walls and traffic stop her from a good old-fashioned frolic.

"Mama, watch out for that car—" I shut my eyes and felt suddenly closer to God.

Mama braked sharply. "Quiet, girl. I've been driving since before you were a twinkle in your father's eye."

The contents of the moving truck slid loudly in the trailer, then stopped with a crash that shook the cab.

"At this rate we might as well open the hatch and let it all fly out. There won't be anything left in one piece by the time we get to the house."

"Ain't my fault some fool changed lanes without putting on his turn signal." Mama took both hands off the wheel to adjust her sunglasses.

We arrived at the shotgun house and found the girls waiting on the front porch. Zephyr bounded happily across the tiny lawn.

Pepper waved enthusiastically. "Hey, Mama!"

Mama considered Pepper and Rose her honorary children. She embraced Pepper, then turned to Rose. "Rose, when're you going to stop wearing all that black and put on some color?"

A ghost of a smile flitted across Rose's face. "Next week, Mama. I promise."

It was a running gag with the two of them.

"Y'all want to have some lemonade before we unload the truck?" I unlocked the door and ushered the three of them in.

Mama stopped in the living room with her hands on her hips. "Well, isn't this real pretty?"

"Oh, wow," said Pepper.

Rose wandered down the hall. "You got a pool out here?"

"Just a little bitty one. But big enough to take a dip."

Mama and Pepper followed Rose down the hall. They crowded around the back door to peer out the window.

Zephyr ran straight through the lot of them and disappeared outside.

I got the lemonade out of the refrigerator and filled up glasses with ice. By the time they'd satisfied their curiosity by opening every door, closet, and cabinet in the house, I had their drinks ready. "Guess we'll sit on the floor."

Mama remained standing by the bar. "If I sit on the floor, Luella, you all might need a forklift to get me back up again."

Rose slid down the wall to sit cross-legged on the floor.

Pepper sat on the floor and stretched in between sips of lemonade.

"I got some news from London."

Mama narrowed her eyes and set her glass on the bar with a *thunk*. "Do tell."

"She said Queenie wouldn't put her in my vacant position. She thinks—"

"She thinks!" Mama scoffed.

I shot her a pointed look over the interruption and continued. "She thinks Queenie is keeping the job open for some reason. Maybe Queenie wanted me out of the way temporarily. Maybe she's waiting for the right time to bring me back, once whatever it is has been taken care of."

Mama rolled her eyes. "London has more money than sense."

"At least she's trying to be helpful."

"You don't think she was actually trying to take your job?" asked Rose.

"I don't think so. She doesn't want a job—she wants to run the place."

"All right, Luella, if you say so," said Mama. "But if she crosses you, you know what to do. Take her out. Like you did with that useless boyfriend—what was his name again?" She cocked her head.

"You know what his name was—"

"Dan," said Rose.

"Dan the Man," added Pepper.

"Dan the Useless Man," countered Mama with a cackle.

Pepper laughed so hard she choked on her lemonade.

Once they wound each other up, they didn't stop.

"Anyway—"

Pepper sat up abruptly. "Did you tell Mama about Raphael?"

My first thought was to throw something at Pepper, maybe a glass of lemonade. Instead, I caught her gaze with my best imitation of Rose's basilisk stare.

It bounced off Pepper harmlessly. Clearly, I didn't have Rose's technique.

"Who's Raphael?" Mama drew his name out with long, insinuating syllables.

"We went to high school together. He invited me to dinner." I hoped the conversation would end there.

No such luck.

Mama's face took on a quizzical look. "What for?"

"What do you mean, 'What for'? Can't someone ask me to dinner?"

"You know I don't mean that, girl. I mean how did he happen to find you and give you the invitation?"

I quickly categorized possible tidbits of information into things-Mama-could-know and things-Mama-couldn't-know. "I went to an art show. He was there."

"What'd you go to an art show for? Are you getting some culture?" She said it without judgment, referring to culture as if it were something you could pick up at the drugstore.

Rose and Pepper looked back and forth between Mama and me with wide eyes. They knew the full story. I trusted

Rose to keep her mouth shut, and I hoped Pepper had realized her mistake and would do the same.

"Pepper, Rose, and I took pictures in front of the murals downtown, and then I heard the artist who did the murals was going to have a show. I thought it might be neat to check it out."

Mama's face froze while I spoke. It was like watching a rippled lake solidify in fast motion. "The mural artist?"

"Yeah, why?" Judging from the looks on their faces, even Pepper and Rose thought Mama was acting oddly.

Mama's face re-animated with shocking speed. "No reason. Let's get you unpacked!" She looked down and fished in the pockets of her denim cutoffs, then withdrew the keys with a jangling sound. "I'll get the truck opened up." She exited the house and let the door bang shut behind her.

The three of us looked at each other.

Pepper got up and set her empty glass on the bar. "What was that about?"

Rose joined Pepper. "Did she know Raphael?"

"No, I don't think so. We never went on that prom date, so she never had any cause to meet him."

Rose pursed her lips in thought, but said nothing.

We unloaded the truck as quickly as possible in the stifling heat, stopping occasionally to cool off in the house before getting back to the sweaty business of moving boxes and furniture. The house took on the look of my life as it filled with my belongings.

With the task of moving complete, I threw a pan of cookies in the oven to bake so we could salve our fatigue with sugar. Mama, Rose, and Pepper settled on the newly placed furniture.

While the cookies were cooling, someone knocked on the front door. I hustled to the door and opened it.

Red stood on the porch. She went on tiptoe to peek over my shoulder. "You got company?"

I started to close the door slowly. "Yes, my friends and my mother are here."

"Smells really good." Her eyes widened hopefully.

Mama's voice floated from inside. "Who's at the door, Luella?"

"A neighbor girl," I called.

"Well, let her in before you let all the cold air out."

I stepped aside.

Red beamed, then crossed the threshold.

"Mama, this is Red. Red, Mama. And those are my friends, Pepper and Rose."

Mama eyed her up and down. "Aren't you a little sweetheart?" A smile creased her face. "You know my Luella?"

Red shyly looked at the floor. "Yes, ma'am."

This was the teenager who brazenly drank vodka in my pool and had the nerve to sass me about it—wringing her hands in apparent meekness and addressing my mother with utmost respect.

The whole world had flipped upside down.

I retreated to the kitchen and silently fanned the cookies with my wings to make them cool faster. When they firmed up, I piled them on a plate and passed them to my guests.

Pepper and Rose took one each.

Red took two, one for each hand.

Mama kept the plate with the remaining cookies.

"You gonna eat all of those, Mama?"

"I reckon," she said placidly. "You live around here, Miss Red?"

"Yes, ma'am. Down the lane."

"You ought to drop by for a swim sometime. Luella wouldn't mind, would you, honey?" Her eyes twinkled with mischief, making her look like a silver-haired old pixie in cutoff shorts.

Troublemaker. I stuffed a cookie in my mouth so I wasn't tempted to respond.

"These are so yummy, Miss Luella."

Oh, now I was *Miss* Luella? That beat all. What magic had Mama worked on her? "Thank you, Red. I used to make these for my daughter."

"Is that her?" She unselfconsciously wiped her fingers on her shirt and picked up a picture frame.

"That's my Lily."

"She don't live with you no more?"

"She's at college now. NYU." I couldn't keep the pride out of my voice.

"Wow." Red studied the photo with genuine admiration before placing it back on the bar. "Did you go to college?"

I glanced at Mama before speaking. "No, I went to work at Suntan Queen right out of high school."

Mama piped up. "Luella was smart enough to go to college."

Neither of us would say our regrets out loud, but the truth was there hadn't been enough money for me to go to college. My grades were good—but not good enough to get a scholarship like Lily's.

Rose addressed Red. "Are you going to go to college?"

"I don't know," she replied cheerfully. "I expect I will someday. Maybe I'll be a doctor or something."

"Dr. Red," said Mama.

Zephyr breezed in from down the hallway and went straight to Mama. She sniffed at Mama's feet, turned in a circle, and settled calmly on the floor next to her.

Despite knowing Zephyr was invisible to everyone but Rose, Pepper, and myself, I felt irrationally sure that Mama would feel Zephyr's airy fur against her foot. Any second now—

Mama caught me staring. "Something wrong, Luella?"

I dragged my gaze away from Zephyr. "Just admiring your shoes. Are they new?"

She slid her hand down her calf, mere inches from Zephyr's pointed ears. "These old things? I think I got these at the consignment store."

My eyes widened as Zephyr turned her head and licked my mother's hand.

Mama didn't flinch, react, or do anything at all to show that she perceived what was happening—but that pixie-ish twinkle was back in her eyes.

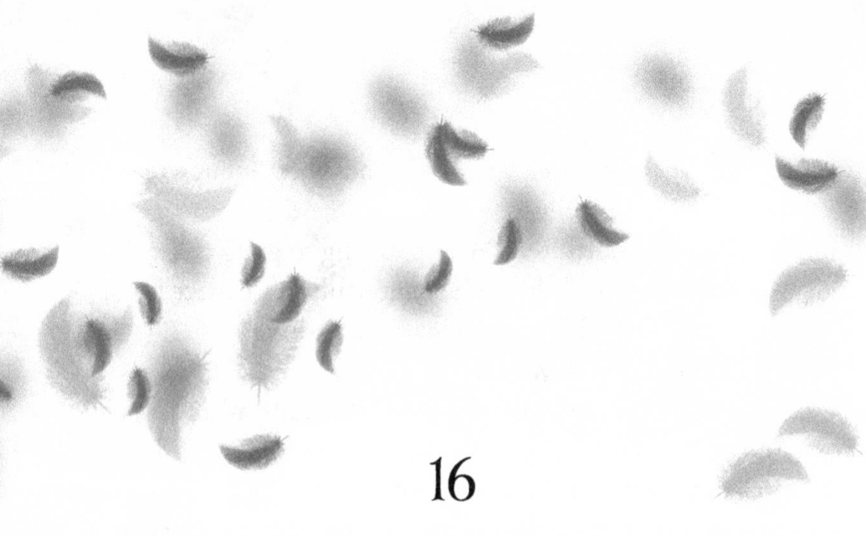

16

I entered Thai Fi through a cobblestone courtyard with a three-tiered fountain that cascaded water from level to level. The cool interior of the restaurant featured elegant mood lighting and Thai pop music at a low volume. My eyes adjusted slowly from the evening sunlight as I peered around a large display of blooming orchids in search of Raphael.

He'd offered to pick me up for our date, but I chose to drive myself. Call me pragmatic, call me unromantic—but after the titanic date disaster at La Tierra y el Mar, I wanted to have my own way home just in case.

It's not quite fair to have to impress someone a second time when you already went all-out on meeting number one. I'd used maximum firepower with my flaming red dress from Fifi's, and I couldn't afford to blow more money on clothing when I was saving everything, including the gold coin, for the expenses Lily's scholarship didn't cover.

I'd settled on wearing a pair of capri pants and a short-sleeved linen top. Dressy but not too dressy. Whoever said capri pants were unflattering could go jump in a lake. My calves needed to breathe in the relentless summer heat and humidity.

"Luella?"

When I caught sight of my date, I almost wolf-whistled. "Raphael!"

He'd ditched the slightly scruffy artist look in favor of elegantly creased dark slacks and—Lord have mercy—was that a red silk shirt?

My fingers itched to find out for sure.

"Good to see you again," he said. The scent of him—something like sandalwood—delicately entwined with the aroma of spicy curry coming from the kitchen as we shared a brief embrace.

It was definitely a silk shirt.

"You look wonderful," he said as we took our seats in a booth.

"Likewise." I didn't trust myself to elaborate. I thought I was calm, but my heart sped up as we made eye contact across the table.

He looked away with a self-deprecating chuckle. "This shouldn't be so hard."

I laughed with relief. "Right? We know each other already. We shouldn't be nervous."

Raphael looked me in the eyes. "And yet—"

"And yet it's been a long time." I laid my hands in my lap to keep my fidgeting out of view. "I've always wanted to know: Why did your family move, anyway? I heard some weird rumors after you left."

"Are you ready for this?"

"Lay it on me."

"A sinkhole opened up in our front yard."

My mouth fell open. "A sinkhole? The rumor was true?"

"The house cracked right down to the foundation. We had to move immediately. My parents decided they were through with Florida forever."

"That must have been hard for you."

"It left me with regrets." He grabbed a menu and pretended to study it carefully. "So, stranger—what's good? The pad thai? The pineapple curry? The—oh no, if I try to pronounce that I'll make a fool of myself." He hid his face with one hand.

"Let me see." I reached for his menu to angle it in my direction.

A brief tug-of-war ensued.

"Don't. My humiliation will be complete."

"Nonsense. Which one?" I found the menu item under his fingertip. "The tom yum goong? Seems pretty straightforward."

He hung his head. "My humiliation is now complete."

I let him have a slow, teasing smile as I leaned in. "Think about it this way: Now that the worst has already happened, you can relax."

Raphael dropped the menu to the table and looked at me with undisguised delight. "You're absolutely right. I forgot what a genius you are."

"Never forget that." I returned to scanning my own menu. Everything looked good. "My daughter and I used to come here all the time. They have a special gluten-free menu, so she was able to eat safely."

"Is she allergic?"

"Celiac."

"Ah." He nodded. "That's tough."

"I think I want the pad thai. And the spring rolls." I slid the menu aside.

He flipped his menu over. "Is dessert good?"

"Not bad, but it's better at Sparkle Beach Creamery down the way."

He inhaled and shook his hand as if he'd touched something hot. "Now you're tempting me, you shameless woman."

"No more than I tempt myself. Save room."

The server took our order and retreated.

By the time a fragrant platter of spring rolls arrived, we were well into a discussion of marriage, children, and divorce—the conversational trifecta of middle age. I confessed my recent firing as we dipped our spring rolls in sweet chili sauce.

"I can't believe they fired you," Raphael mused.

"Me neither." I bit into a spring roll.

"You'll find something soon, though. There's always a demand for technology skills."

"Maybe, but it's a young person's game these days. Everyone wants a fresh face—and a college degree to go with it." I gestured with the spring roll to make the point.

"Who says you're not young?"

I rolled my eyes. "Flatterer."

"You could go back to school. Get yourself a college degree."

"No money. Everything I have is going to Lily. This is her shot at success."

He nodded thoughtfully.

I set down my iced tea. "What about you? Tell me about your art job."

"More of a hobby than a job."

"No way—you do beautiful work!"

"Flatterer." He retrieved another spring roll, then leaned forward like he was about to impart a secret. "Don't tell anyone, but I'm actually a lawyer."

"A lawyer?"

"Not the fancy kind—well, not anymore. I left that behind when I couldn't sweep my ethics under the rug anymore. Now I work at a legal aid office."

"Would you rather be an artist?"

"Obviously! But art doesn't pay. Law does."

The server placed an oval platter of pad thai in front of me, and a bowl of massaman curry in front of Raphael. Conversation ceased as we dug in.

It spoke to his character that he'd opted for representing the powerless over collecting a fat paycheck, and I couldn't help but find his artistic side attractive, too. Not to mention his easy smile and sense of humor.

I broke the silence. "My Mama says a quiet meal is a sign of good food."

Raphael grinned and dabbed a stray dot of curry from his lips. "Your mama is right."

"You want to try a bite of mine?"

"You bet I do."

I twirled some rice noodles on my fork, making sure to pick up sauce and garnishes, then held it out.

He leaned slightly over the table and closed his full lips over the forkful, finishing the bite before speaking. "Mm. That is divine. Try mine?"

I nodded.

He carefully spooned up rice and curry, lifted it across the space between us, then pulled his hand back slightly. "Be careful. It's spicy—"

"I can handle it." I drew his hand across the table so the spoon could reach my mouth. The curry burned, but in a pleasant way. I released his hand. "Just the right amount of hot."

His eyebrow lifted. He set down the spoon and rubbed his hand, almost absentmindedly, where I had touched it. "Perhaps we should cool down with ice cream?"

A man after my own heart. A flirtatious tone sneaked into my voice before I could restrain myself. "Yes, please."

When the check hit the table, Raphael deftly retrieved it before I could even react.

I reached for my purse. "I don't mind splitting the bill, Raphael. I'm a modern woman."

Raphael nonchalantly pulled out his wallet. "I know you are. And I'm buying this modern woman dinner. And ice cream. And more ice cream, if it will convince you to continue spending time with me."

I laughed. "In exchange for unlimited ice cream? You have yourself a deal, mister."

"Good." He nodded once, with evident satisfaction, and tended to the bill.

"Excuse me." I slid out of the booth. "I'm going to the ladies room, but I'll meet you in the courtyard." I retreated to the restroom to powder my nose and gather my thoughts.

As I checked my appearance in the mirror, I considered how best to approach the subject of the mysterious hidden mural without sounding like some sort of nutty conspiracy theorist. We would pass the rose mural on the way to Sparkle Beach Creamery. Perhaps the subject would arise naturally—or as naturally as I could slip it into the conversation.

My course of action determined, I took a small container of bubble liquid out of my purse. Although Zephyr would usually come at my call, I wanted to make it a sure thing. I blew a stream and murmured her name.

The bubbles floated and popped one by one.

Thank goodness the restroom had a single stall—I had the place to myself—but if I didn't get out soon, Raphael would think I'd fallen in.

I engaged my wings and blew more bubbles, the airstream sending them zipping in all directions. "Zephyr?"

Her magic answered mine, adding a crosswind to the already blustery room, and she plunged straight through an outside wall and into the tiny restroom, eyes shining and tail wagging.

I bent and ruffled her silver-white fur. "I feel like Superman changing in a phone booth."

She sat and regarded me with her head tilted.

I wasn't too sure about her knowledge of pop culture references, so I changed the subject out of politeness. "Do you want to come meet my new friend? We're going to see if we can find out where my wings come from."

At that, she actually barked.

"I'm glad we're on the same page." I ran my hands over her soft, pointed ears. "Who's the best girl? You are!"

We exited together and found Raphael waiting in the courtyard, where the last light of the setting sun withdrew like a tide of gold as the day turned into night.

Zephyr paused when she caught sight of him, then bounded forward and stood before him with her tail wagging. I tried not to stare—to Raphael, it would have looked like my eyes were focused on empty air around the level of his knees—but it was unusual to see her so immediately friendly, except for the incident with Mama.

"Ready?" He smiled so perfectly I heard a noise in my head like a sparkle sound effect in a commercial. *Ting!*

I suppressed a laugh. "I'm always ready."

We set out on foot for Sparkle Beach Creamery.

"So, tell me about the downtown murals." I congratulated myself on my segue as we strolled past the large, tattoo-style rose mural. "My friend Rose likes this one best. For obvious reasons. Did you have a lot of leeway in choosing what to paint?"

He chuckled. "A little. I had to run everything past the Downtown Merchant Guild first. The lady in charge was very . . . exacting."

"Did she stop you from painting nude mermaids or something?"

"Nude mermen, actually. It was probably for the best. Those chest hairs would have been a bear to paint."

"And you did all the paintings, right?"

He counted them off on his fingers. "The rose, the cupcake, the lighthouse, and the rainbow mural. That's the lot of them."

No mention of magical wings that zap you and stick to your back. "Did you have any others in mind?"

"Other than the nude mermen?"

"You know what I mean—designs you didn't get to do." It was a real irony that I was enjoying myself immensely yet getting absolutely nowhere with answering any questions about my wings.

"Oh, I dream up new ones all the time."

Downtown rolled up the sidewalks at night. With no cars on the road, it was easy to cross the street. The buildings around us faded into darkness where the shops had closed for the day.

I had my eye on the beckoning light of the ice cream shop down the street when I heard an uncharacteristic noise from Zephyr, who had kept pace with us as we walked.

She stopped on the sidewalk and whined.

I stopped, too, but there was no way to communicate with her in front of Raphael. I had to pretend her anxiety was my own. "I think I heard something."

Raphael stopped and looked around.

Zephyr paced from side to side, then turned to look behind us. Her body tensed. She lowered herself into a defensive crouch.

I followed her gaze and peered into the shadows.

Zephyr let out a low, rumbling growl, like the sound of thunder on a continuous loop. The wind rose and whistled down the empty street, carrying leaves in its wake.

Someone was following us. He stood a short distance away, his face hidden within the depths of a hood attached to a jacket, saying nothing.

Watching us.

No one in their right mind would have been wearing a jacket in Florida in August.

Raphael touched my arm, his gaze fixed on the intruder. "Luella? We should probably walk faster now."

We turned together and walked at a quickened pace.

I divided my attention between the sidewalk in front of me so I didn't trip and the stranger who kept on coming, his footsteps a dull echo of our own. In the shadows of the night, the surrounding buildings no longer seemed quaint and old-fashioned—they loomed like man-made cliffs, penning us in.

Zephyr dashed forward and back, torn between staying close to me and growling at the man behind us.

Hundreds of feet lay between us and safety. I glanced over my shoulder at the sinister figure. Even if we ran, the man would catch up to us long before we reached the ice cream shop and other people.

I refused to be run to earth like a scared rabbit.

"Raphael, stop." I rounded on the man following us and raised my voice to its strongest, most diaphragm-supported timbre. My chorus teacher would have been proud. "What do you want?"

"What are you doing?" Raphael murmured. When I didn't answer, he didn't question further—but he took up a protective stance slightly in front of me.

Zephyr crouched beside me, showing white fangs I'd never noticed before.

The man stopped a stone's throw away from us.

My hand went involuntarily to my mouth. *His eyes.* Though his face was lost in darkness, his irises flickered with silver light.

Zephyr barked furiously. The wind increased to a howl.

Raphael took a step forward. "Luella, run—"

"No!" I tensed. My wings blew open and shook like sheets of corrugated iron, with a thunderous sound to match, at least to my ears. I raised my voice even more and addressed the hooded man. "*What do you want?*" The words startled even me as they blasted across the distance like a shock wave.

His eyes closed and reopened. Tiny silver flames trickled down his cheeks like lit match heads. "Luella . . . "

That voice—

Zephyr sprang forward and ran in circles around the man. The motion blurred her form until she no longer resembled a dog.

She looked like a localized tornado.

The man didn't appear to notice her—at first. Then the flames in his eyes spluttered like candles under a bell jar. His hands went to his throat.

The air! Zephyr wasn't increasing the wind—she was taking it away. Every lap in her frenzied run drained the air from the vicinity of the man she circled.

The fire in his eyes winked into blackness, plunging the contours of his face into total darkness.

If Zephyr took his air away, would he faint?

Could he die?

She was trying to protect me the only way she knew how, but I couldn't risk hurting someone—fiery eyes or not—if I could stop it. I didn't have the luxury to care what Raphael heard or saw, not with someone's life on the line. "Zephyr!"

The man dropped to his knees and his hood fell back, revealing his face.

A face I'd last seen across a table at La Tierra y el Mar.

"Dan!" I rushed forward. Why had Dan followed us? Why the hell had his eyes filled with flames?

His eyes rolled back as he lost consciousness.

There was no time to think.

I kneeled in front of Dan and held my arms out to the blur that was Zephyr. "Zephyr," I murmured soothingly. "Hush-hush, baby. Hush-hush. It's okay. I'm safe. You can stop now."

The blur slowed and the tornado resolved into her canine form.

Dan crumpled face-first to the sidewalk.

I felt a cooling puff as air collapsed into the vacuum Zephyr had created. My wings curled up along my back, and the ambient wind died. I rolled Dan over.

His chest rose and fell.

He was alive.

And I knew I was in more trouble than I'd ever been in my life.

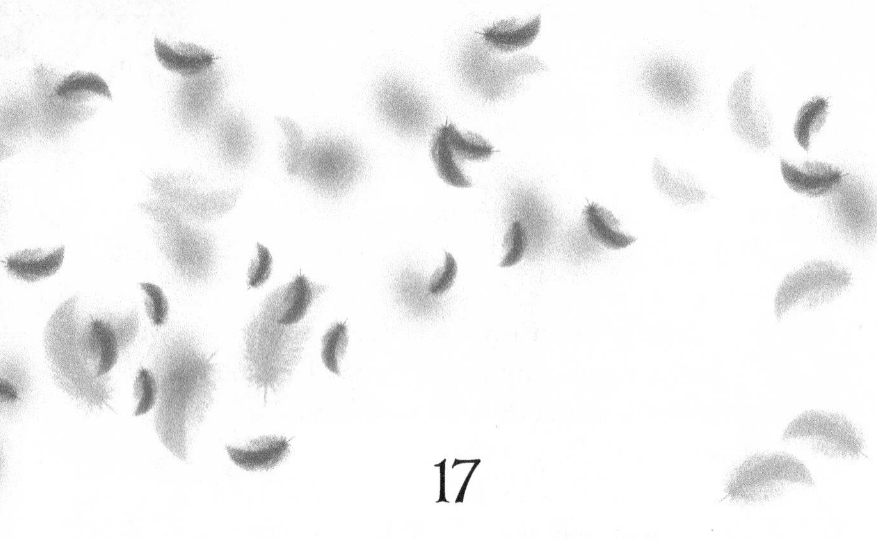

17

I looked over my shoulder to check on Raphael, who I'd lost sight of during the commotion, in time to watch him drop to the ground in a mirror image of Dan's collapse. "Raphael!"

Why did I have to be the only one left conscious?

I looked back and forth between the two unconscious men. I decided to wake Raphael first, for backup, in case Dan decided to repeat his flame-eyed performance. "Raphael, wake up!" I shook his shoulder. Strangely, the sidewalk had deep cracks radiating out from where he'd fallen.

He inhaled a sharp gasp of air as his eyelids fluttered open. "Luella?" He raised himself to a sitting position, then scrambled backwards hastily when he caught sight of Dan sprawled on the concrete. "Him! Those eyes! I've seen those—" His gaze pivoted to me. He stood unsteadily and pointed in my direction. "The wings! From the wall!

Oh, my God—it wasn't a dream." He rubbed his face with both hands.

"What do you mean, the wings?" So far Rose and Pepper were the only other people who could see my wings. Was he referring to the mural?

"Oh, my God." He repeated the phrase three times, speaking through his hands, running the words together so quickly they sounded like a single word: *ohmygod ohmygod ohmygod.*

I seized his shoulders. "Raphael. Snap out of it. What wings?"

He lowered his hands and composure returned to his countenance. "I'm sorry I freaked out, but this … " He spoke with the air of someone imparting bad news. "Luella … you have wings. And there's some kind of weird dog here." He eyed Zephyr dubiously.

Zephyr cocked her head like *Who are you calling weird?*

I rolled my eyes. "No kidding. The question is—how can you see them? Never mind. We'll figure that out later." I turned to Dan, who was making small whimpering noises as he came around. "And what on earth happened to my ex-boyfriend?"

Raphael's eyes widened. He pointed at Dan. "This guy? This is the boyfriend who—"

"Yeah, that one. Listen, Raphael—don't mention the wings or the dog or the flaming eyes unless Dan mentions them first, okay?"

"You got it."

I patted Dan's shoulder. I also checked the ground beneath him for cracks. There were none. "Wake up, Dan."

Dan groaned.

"Come on, Dan."

"Luella?" He sounded like he'd been on an extended bender.

"Dan, have you been drinking?" It didn't explain the flaming eyes, but it might go a short distance toward explaining why my normally mild-mannered ex-boyfriend had taken it into his head to follow me and my date around.

"Oh, my head… " He groaned, then sat upright with great effort. "Where am I?"

"Downtown. Why were you following us?"

"Following you?" Dan rubbed his face. "I can't remember."

Annoyance made menace creep into my voice. "Try."

"It's all blurry." He reached for my hand.

I took it, thinking he wanted help to stand up.

Instead, he pressed it to his cheek and closed his eyes. "About the other night." He looked sad and sorry, sprawled on the ground with his hair in disarray.

Then he nuzzled my hand.

I snatched my hand away. "Dan, this is no time to be maudlin. Pull yourself together."

Raphael shot me an amused look and offered his hand to Dan, presumably so I didn't have to.

Dan blinked at Raphael with obvious irritation. "Who's this guy?"

"Dan, Raphael. Raphael, Dan. Now that we're all friends, perhaps you could tell me why you were following us around?"

Dan waved away Raphael's offer of assistance. He stood, then brushed off his khaki trousers. "I don't remember," he replied, with a peevish glance at Raphael. "But I'm sure there's a rational explanation."

I stood awkwardly between my date, my ex-boyfriend, and my magical dog. "Anyone for ice cream?"

They both looked at me as if I'd lost my mind.

"It's better than standing around on a dark street," I added.

Raphael laughed. "Why not? Ice cream cures anything." He gallantly held out his arm.

Lord, but he was attractive! Quick to recover and game for dealing with anything: danger, magic, or even an ex-boyfriend.

Dan narrowed his eyes. "I'm sure it does." He, too, held out his arm.

I looped my arms through theirs, and we walked on.

Zephyr bounded ahead, seemingly reassured that I had the situation well in hand.

The warm lights of Sparkle Beach Creamery beckoned. Inside, the scent of freshly baked waffle cones filled the air, and the polished brass, ornate wood trim, and tiny hexagonal black-and-white floor tiles in geometric patterns all drew the eye.

I peered into the ice cream case. "Pistachio, chocolate, vanilla, strawberry, caramel cashew, mint chocolate chip. How do I choose?"

Raphael read the menu board. "What's the Kitchen Sink?"

I glanced up. "That's the big one. Every flavor in one big stainless steel bowl."

Dan hung back with his hands in his pockets.

"What do you say, Luella? You in?" Raphael's expression turned a little bit wicked.

"I'm in."

"One Kitchen Sink, please," Raphael said to the person behind the counter. He struck a heroic pose. "If we die, we die happy."

Dan ordered a single scoop of vanilla in a cup.

We seated ourselves around a table in a quiet corner, in red cafe chairs with heart-shaped metal twists forming the backrests. Zephyr sat on the floor between Raphael and me.

A cozy *tête-à-tête*—plus one ex-boyfriend and the magical dog who'd just tried to strangle him.

Totally normal.

If this was my circus, I was going to have to be the ringmaster. "Dan." I pointed a spoonful of caramel cashew at Dan.

My former boyfriend paused mid-bite over his vanilla scoop.

"You followed us down a dark street. Why?"

Dan leveled an unsubtle glare at Raphael. "I wasn't following *him*."

"You do remember!"

"No! I mean, kind of. I remember—" He stopped. Embarrassment crept over his face "Does he have to be here?"

"I'm not ending my date just because you decided to chase us down a dark street."

"Fine. I wasn't lying when I said I didn't remember. I don't. It's all blurry. I was at home, and I was thinking about . . ."

"Yes?"

He cleared his throat and looked down at the table. "It doesn't matter." His posture remained as stiff as his words.

"Someone knocked at the door. I opened it. There was a woman standing there—"

I dropped my spoon into the Kitchen Sink with a clatter. "A woman? What woman?"

"I don't know! Then I had this strong urge to go find you, and it gets all fuzzy."

"You know that sounds stalker-ish, right?"

"Luella, I swear I didn't mean to do anything like that."

I raised a skeptical eyebrow.

Dan pushed his cup away. "Look, my cards are on the table. I regret what I said to you at dinner. It was stupid, all right? Happy now?" He shot me an aggrieved look. "But I'm not stalking you."

I glanced down at Zephyr, who looked back at me innocently. I patted her in a subtle way so Dan wouldn't notice the movement. "Thank you for your honesty. If you remember anything else, will you please call me?"

Dan and Raphael shot each other mutually suspicious looks. "Sure," said Dan.

I blinked at him, waiting for him to take the hint.

"I should go," he muttered.

"Bye, Dan," I said.

"Bye, Dan," echoed Raphael.

We both doubled over with laughter as soon as he was gone.

I dabbed at my eyes with a napkin. "All right. Your turn. What happened to you? Why did you pass out?"

Raphael had another bite of ice cream, then reluctantly set down his spoon. "When I first saw that guy following us, I didn't notice anything unusual. I thought he was a mugger or something. But when his eyes got weird, I started to blank out."

"Blank out?" I asked.

"Everything got quiet except for this loud buzzing sound in my ears. Then my vision faded from the outside in." His hands framed his face, demonstrating tunnel vision. "Something about his eyes triggered a memory. I remembered painting in the dark. Everything was black: the sky, the walls, the paint. I had to create this intricate pattern." He traced the top of my shoulder with a fingertip. "And now you're wearing it."

His touch sent goosebumps down my arms. I lowered my voice and leaned closer. "Raphael, I have to ask—are you magical?"

He grinned. "I like to think I am."

I nudged him. "I'm serious."

He shook his head. "Not that I know of. Until now, that is. Now that I can see your"—he switched to a whisper—"wings."

"How is it that you can see them?" I rubbed my forehead. Why Raphael and not Dan? A memory of the cracks in the sidewalk popped into my mind.

Raphael leaned his chin in his hand and displayed a carbon copy of the flirtatious smile he'd used in high school. "I don't know, but this was fun. We should get together again, so you can ask me some more questions."

I placed my hand on his arm, enjoying the sensation of his warm skin under my fingers. "Next time, we'll go somewhere we won't be interrupted."

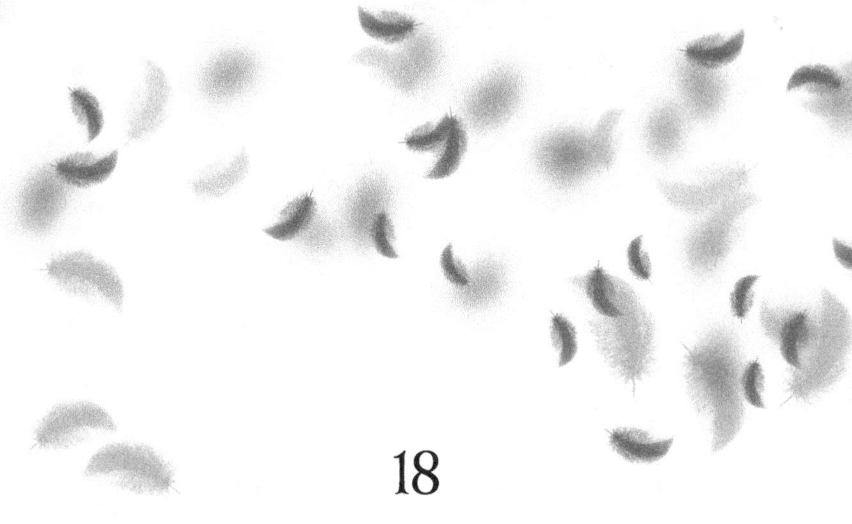

18

After getting fully settled at the shotgun house, I decided to follow up on the Ultimate Crate interview since it was the only nibble I'd gotten so far. Perhaps Alex had only forgotten to call me back and offer me the job.

I dialed the number.

It didn't ring. It beeped a loud series of tones, then played a recorded voice: "We're sorry. The number you have dialed has been disconnected." *Click.*

Weird.

I tried again, figuring I'd misdialed.

"We're sorry. The number you have dialed has been disconnected." *Click.*

Maybe Alex got a new phone number. I found an email address on the Ultimate Crate website and composed a brief message to Alex. *Thank you for taking the time to interview me for the social media position. It was a pleasure speaking—and stretching—with you. I look forward to hearing from you soon.*

I sent the message.

Sixty seconds later, my inbox pinged with a new email. My hopes rose at the unusually fast reply—until I opened the message.

> *Mail Delivery Failed. A message that you sent could not be delivered to one or more of its recipients. This is a permanent error. The following address(es) failed: support@ultimatecrate.com.*

As a longtime webmaster—long before the term itself became somewhat obsolete—I knew what that meant. With growing dread, I typed the Ultimate Crate web address into my browser.

The page didn't appear. Instead, I got an error message on a white background: *This site can't be reached. Server IP address not found.*

I pulled up the Ultimate Crate social media profiles. On every page, I found error messages instead of the familiar Ultimate Crate logo and aspirational fitness graphics: *Page not found. User does not exist.*

I leaned back in my chair and stared at the screen. No phone. No website. No email. No social media. Ultimate Crate had more or less vanished off the face of the digital planet.

Clearly I wouldn't be getting a job from Ultimate Crate. I sighed and nearly closed my browser—until I had a sudden thought. I searched for "Ultimate Crate" not to find their official accounts, but to find any related fan accounts.

Bingo. The Unofficial Ultimate Crate Fan Club for Serious Craters.

I joined the group and scrolled the recent activity. My screen filled with the desperate posts and comments of customers who'd paid their subscription fees—some in the hundreds of dollars—and never received any boxes.

Had Ultimate Crate taken the money and run?

Didn't Alex care that there were real people on the other end of those subscriptions?

Anger sharpened my movements as I clicked and scrolled, looking for more details. It appeared my misgivings before the interview were not unfounded. Customers had messaged and emailed to no avail after paying their subscription fees and receiving nothing.

Alex must have thought he could milk the subscriptions a little while longer if he kept the social media scrubbed of complaints.

A grim smile tightened my lips. Alex didn't know who he was dealing with when he interviewed me. He didn't think I'd follow up—or if I did, that I wouldn't care what Ultimate Crate had done. Maybe he thought he'd disappeared without a trace, leaving his internet customers behind, but I knew exactly where he was and I wasn't going to let him get away with scamming a bunch of innocent people.

Righteous anger put me in the mood for a good, old-fashioned confrontation.

I snatched my purse from the bar, slipped on my shoes, and was out the door faster than a New York minute—where I nearly tripped over Red, who had parked herself on the front porch.

"Hey, Miss Luella! Where you going in such a hurry?"

"Can't talk now, Red. Got to take care of something real quick." I dodged her and went down the steps.

"All right," she said. "Watch out for that crow."

I pulled up short. "What crow?"

She pointed. "The one sitting on your mirror."

I approached the driver's side of the car and rummaged in my purse for the keys.

The bird cocked its head at the jangling sound of the keys before flying away in a huffy flutter of black wings.

"Great," I muttered as I opened the door. "Let's all get in on the act. Dan, Red, Raphael—how about the pope? Is he too busy to get involved?" I dropped heavily into the seat and fired up the engine.

The trip downtown took less time than usual, probably because I put too much pedal to the metal. I parked crookedly but didn't bother to correct—I left it where it was and speed-walked to the Ultimate Crate office.

The door was locked. I banged on it.

No one answered. I peered through the glass.

The lights were off and most of the furniture was gone, save for a few heavy-looking pieces like a reception desk and a file cabinet.

I sat on the raised concrete planter to consider my options. Alex and Ultimate Crate had practically disappeared overnight. Without a working phone number or email address, Alex might as well be on the moon. I didn't even know his last name.

Obviously, I couldn't get into the building without smashing a window—

Or maybe I could.

I closed my eyes and concentrated. "Zephyr," I murmured. "Come out and play."

Zephyr came bounding down the sidewalk like she'd been awaiting my call around a corner.

"Good girl!" I couldn't make too much of a fuss, lest I attract attention from passersby, but I could talk quietly without drawing too much notice. It was time to start thinking creatively when it came to my powers. "Zephyr, baby—can you go in there?"

She walked obediently toward the building.

"Wait for me!" I walked to the door and stood next to Zephyr.

She looked at me with her ice-blue eyes.

The next part depended on her following more complex instructions. "Can you put your paws on the door? Open it?" I gestured with my hands to demonstrate pushing on the bar on the inside of the door. She'd have to be insubstantial as air to pass through the door—but solid as a real dog to push on the lever that would open it. Would she understand?

Zephyr walked right through the door and into the reception area. She sniffed her way around the room, then made her way back to the door. She stood on her hind legs and put her front paws on the horizontal handle.

The second her weight triggered the latch mechanism from the inside, I pulled the door handle on the outside—and the door opened. I stepped inside as if I belonged there, letting the door click shut behind me. "Good job, girl. The last time I pulled that trick, I had to use a wire coat hanger. I have to say, I like this method better." My words echoed in the empty room now that there were no soft furnishings to absorb the sound. "Let's have a look around, shall we?"

We walked down the narrow hallway to the office where I'd been interviewed.

I knocked on the closed door—even while breaking and entering, I couldn't shake the manners I'd been raised with—then pushed it open.

It squeaked loudly.

The chairs were gone. The desk remained, bare of all but a few stray paper clips and pens.

I pulled open the drawers while Zephyr sniffed around the perimeter of the room.

She whined and pawed at the narrow gap between the desk and the wall.

I knelt next to her and spotted a thin sheaf of paper caught in the gap. "Must have fallen off the desk." I pulled it out and rifled through the papers. A full-color Downtown Merchant Guild brochure lay on top. Underneath the brochure, I found a meeting calendar, followed by a printed membership certificate for Ultimate Crate. At least it gave me one more place to look for the Ultimate Crate founder.

I returned the stack to where I'd found it. A cursory inspection of the rest of the office revealed nothing else. The rooms had been well and truly cleaned out of anything that could be carried away with ease. I'd ridden a wave of anger all the way here, and now I found the tide receding with no one to confront.

We exited the same way we came in, and I walked as if I were in a dream, letting my feet take me where they would. I ended up crossing the street to the promenade along the river. The fronds of the palm trees whipped in the river breeze as dark clouds drifted to obscure the late morning sun.

The promising job interview had ended up a complete wash.

The value of the gold coin I'd happily deposited in my account would be spent in a short time on Lily's expenses. My small amount of savings would be similarly dispatched in a short while. The unemployment program would only provide enough to pay for groceries and utilities, making it a temporary Band-Aid, but not a solution to any of my money woes.

Zephyr dashed off the promenade and ran across the river whitecaps, her fluffy tail waving like a flag in the wind.

I was back at square one—but I couldn't give up. Lily depended on me.

My head spun and the world felt like it had tipped slightly sideways... and then I realized it *had* tipped slightly sideways.

Because I was floating.

In midair.

In broad daylight.

In front of anyone who cared to look.

My wings glittered at their full length, shedding dainty glimmers of silver into the air beneath them. At least they were invisible to passersby—my desire to keep flying warred with my need not to get caught doing anything unusual in public. A glance in every direction confirmed no one was close enough to notice that my feet didn't touch the ground. I reveled in the sensation as I swayed in the force of the updrafts holding me aloft.

Zephyr must have noticed, for she dashed back to my side and ran merry circles around my feet, barking joyously.

I threw my head back and laughed. "I did it, Zephyr!"

The distant wail of a police siren brought me abruptly back to earth. I winced as I landed a little too hard. My knees and ankles didn't appreciate the shock. "Ow." I leaned on the riverside guardrail and massaged my knee joints as my wings silently retracted. "Well, that was fun while it lasted."

My purse vibrated.

I plunged my hand into the interior and fished out my phone. A glance at the screen revealed the caller. "Pepper?"

"Luella, you have to get over here now."

"Pepper, what's going on? Are you okay? Where are you?"

"My house. I'm okay, but—come over. Please!" She hung up.

I shoved my phone in my purse and made a beeline to my car, figuring Zephyr would follow when she felt like it.

Pepper lived in a brand new subdivision called Happy Harbor, located at the north end of mainland Sparkle Beach. A miniature version of the Sparkle Beach lighthouse rose from the landscaped planter at the entrance to the neighborhood. The sign on the lighthouse said "No Soliciting" in smaller letters under the words "Happy Harbor." I turned in and hit the brakes before the steep speed bump.

A lady walking her dog gave me the stink eye as I drove past.

Happy Harbor, indeed. More like nosy neighbors measuring your lawn with a ruler. I bet their homeowner's association meetings were a real hoot. Sometimes I wondered how Pepper put up with it. It didn't fit with her free-spirited vibe.

I walked up the path through the carefully maintained lawn and lifted the shiny brass knocker on one of the double doors.

Pepper must have been watching, for she whipped the door open and dragged me inside before I could even let it fall.

"Whoa, girl." I stumbled over the threshold. "Hold your horses!"

"You hold them!" she squawked as she charged into the house.

"You're not making sense." I looked around. "Where is everyone?"

"Kids—camp. Peter—office." She paced barefoot on the plush carpet, then she stopped on a dime and pointed at me. "This is your fault, you know."

"My fault?"

"You had to go and get yourself a magic dog. And now it's rubbing off. Like a—like a *virus*." She clutched the pearl on her leather necklace and tugged at it fretfully.

"Pepper, what are you talking about? You're not making any sense."

Pepper's eyes narrowed. "Come here." She opened the sliding glass door separating the expansive living room from the pool area. "Watch this." She drew back her hand like she was about to throw a baseball, then thrust it forward in the direction of the sparkling pool.

A cataract of water erupted from the deep end, sending fat droplets of water into the air to fall with a pattering sound on the surrounding deck.

I looked from Pepper to the pool and back again. "How'd you do that?"

"How do you *think* I did it?" She pulled back both hands and pushed them at the pool.

A double splash shot upwards and drenched a nearby potted plant.

"Whoa! That's awesome!"

"No, it isn't! It's awesome when it's someone else. It's awesome when you don't already have enough to deal with in your life." Pepper slammed the sliding door shut and dropped onto the couch, punching a tasteful throw pillow for good measure.

"Be careful how you throw those hands around. You might explode your sink or something."

"Good. I hope it explodes." She stared daggers at the kitchen.

I carefully took a seat next to her on the couch. "You don't mean that. You have a lovely house."

"Screw the house," she muttered.

"Pepper, look—I'm scared, too."

"I'm not scared."

I detected a whiff of protesting too much, but I let it slide. "Dan chased me and my date through the streets of downtown with literal fire in his eyes. I don't understand any of this."

She sank into the couch, letting her eyes close. "What am I supposed to do with this? I'm not Wonder Woman."

"Yes, you are."

"No, I'm not."

"Shut up, Pepper. Yes, you are. You're already a great person, a great mom—what's a little magic on top of that?"

Pepper made a disbelieving noise.

"I mean, I lost my job, I dumped my boyfriend, I gained some sort of magical powers, and the one interview I managed to get turned out to be a dud."

"Wait—what happened to Challenge Container?"

"Ultimate Crate. It folded. Poof. Gone. Took all their customers' money with them, too."

"Damn." She elongated the word until it came out more like *dayum*.

"It's hard. *Change* is hard." I grabbed her shoulder and shook it. "But we'll survive. And your new magic can only help."

"Oh, yeah? How's that?"

My mind raced for a good answer. "It'll make you an even better surfer!"

Her eyebrows lifted.

"And you'll win every splash fight!"

Pepper laughed. "Stop, you're making it worse."

"Honestly, I don't know what to tell you." I leaned back. "I wonder what I'm supposed to do with this newfound power. And my adorable yet mysterious magic dog. And I still don't understand what happened with Raphael and the wall and Dan's weird hypnosis, or whatever that was.

But we get up each day and we keep going, right? Because that's what we do."

Pepper opened her mouth to reply, but her ringtone—Dick Dale's Misirlou—interrupted.

We looked at each other as the opening riff played, the twanging sounds of the guitar foreboding in the quiet room. The hair on my arms rose, and not because of the ice-cold air conditioning.

She lifted the phone and broke eye contact to check the caller ID. "It's Rose."

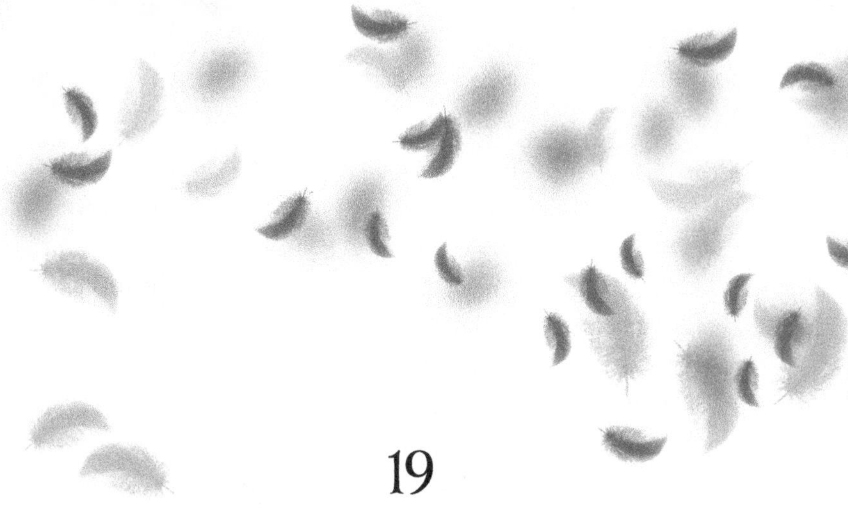

19

Black smoke poured from the chimney of Rose's cabin as we pulled up in Pepper's SUV. We dashed to the front door. Pepper got there first and pushed the door open.

More smoke billowed from inside the house.

"Rose? Where are you?" Pepper tugged her t-shirt collar over her nose and entered.

I did the same and followed. "Rose!"

Rose coughed. "I'm by the fireplace—but don't come any closer! Can you open some windows?"

I briefly wondered why Rose hadn't already opened them. I had almost turned away when I heard a loud noise and saw a bright flash of light. "What in the world—"

Fire filled the fireplace, rolling upward in a scorching wave. Rose held her hands toward the blackened stones.

"Was that *you*?" The words came out through my shirt muffled, but full of alarm.

Rose collapsed from a kneeling position to resting on all fours. "It's like the worst stomach virus ever—except with fire coming out of your hands."

Pepper froze, staring at the fireplace. "Holy mother of—"

I gave her shoulder a quick pat. "Pepper, get the bedroom windows. I'll get the bathroom and kitchen."

Rose coughed again. "Hurry."

We flung open the windows and ran back.

Rose turned her face from the fireplace and looked at me.

My heart skipped a beat. "Oh, my God—Rose, your eyes!"

Pinpoints of silver light glinted in her dark brown irises.

"What about them?" A look of confusion passed over her face. "Get Braveheart. I took him outside when this came on, but it's too hot for a dog to be outside right now. He can't stay out there much longer."

My feet moved before conscious thought took place, as if my body obeyed before my mind agreed. My thoughts caught up as I opened the back door and found Braveheart leashed to a post a short distance from the house. Of course I'd wanted to ensure the dog's safety, but why had I felt almost compelled to follow Rose's command?

I brought Braveheart in on his leash. "Rose, try not to make any demands, okay?"

"Why?" Her voice crackled, low and hoarse.

"Trust me on this one."

She hung her head, clearly exhausted. "When will this stop?"

Pepper and I sat on the couch. I held Braveheart's leash to make sure he didn't run to Rose and get singed. I'd never seen Rose so undone. She usually had more composure than Pepper and I put together. "Tell me about the feeling. You said you felt this coming on."

She squeezed her eyes closed. "It's like a need to sneeze. Or vomit. Sorry—I know that's gross."

Pepper glanced at me before speaking. "It wanted to come out?"

I nodded. "Rose, stay with me on this. Remember when we summoned Zephyr with bubbles? Remember telling me about paying attention to what a dog wants, and what they're afraid of?"

Rose nodded without speaking, looking for all the world like someone who was trying not to be sick.

"What does this power want?"

She dropped into a crouch with her head resting on the floor. Several seconds passed before she spoke. "Like Pepper said. It wants . . . to come out."

"And what is it afraid of?"

The only sound inside the room was Rose's labored breath and Braveheart's tail thumping on the floor. Outside, the summer crickets whirred.

"Come on, Rose. You've got this," said Pepper.

Rose lifted her head. "It's afraid . . . of being stifled. Of being"—she rolled her head and shoulders in a stretching motion—"snuffed out."

I leaned forward. "Talk to it. Talk to it like you would talk to one of the dogs."

Rose laughed weakly.

"Do it."

"Okay, okay." She wiped her eyes and sat up straighter. "Listen, fire—I won't stifle you. I won't put you out. You don't have to be afraid."

"You're a good fire," I prompted.

A uncharacteristically hysterical giggle escaped Rose's lips before her composure reasserted itself. "You're a good fire. A powerful fire."

"Pat it," said Pepper.

Rose looked at her like Pepper had lost her mind.

"No, really! Show affection. Like you do with your dogs."

Rose sat on her heels before the fireplace and closed her eyes. Her hands shaped the air before her like a potter shaping a vase.

Instead of a fiery explosion, tiny silver flames danced on her fingertips.

"Good fire," she murmured. "Nice fire." She opened her eyes and gazed at her fingers in wonder. One finger at a time, she slowly closed her hands into fists, extinguishing the flames. When they were out, she stood and wobbled over to the couch.

We jumped up to make room, then helped her lie down with her feet up.

I released Braveheart from the leash.

Pepper tucked a pillow under Rose's head. "You okay, girl?"

"Dandy." Rose chuckled. "I sound like Luella."

"Can you get her a seltzer?" I asked Pepper.

Pepper scurried to the kitchen and returned with a cold can of seltzer. She popped the top and handed the can to Rose.

Rose sipped, then turned her head to look at me. "Why did you tell me not to boss you around?"

"Your eyes—they started to look like Raphael's, and Dan's. When you told me to go get Braveheart, it was like your words bypassed my brain and went straight to my feet."

"You think I did to you what someone did to Raphael and Dan?"

I shrugged. "No other explanation I can think of."

"Holy cow," said Pepper. She made a pass in the air with her hand, then spoke in a bad British accent. "These are not the droids you're looking for."

"Except this isn't Star Wars, and Rose isn't Obi-Wan Kenobi."

"Yet." A crooked half-smile lifted a corner of Rose's lips. "Luella's full of air, I'm burning up—"

"And I'm all wet," finished Pepper.

Rose raised herself to a sitting position. "What do you mean?"

"I didn't get to tell you when you called."

"Tell me what?"

"Luella, can you get me a bowl of water?"

I went to the kitchen, retrieved a cereal bowl and filled it with water at the kitchen sink, then returned to the living room and handed it to Pepper.

She set it on the hearth and backed up across the room. "Watch this." She flung her hand toward the bowl.

Water shot into the fireplace and dripped down the blackened walls.

"Whoa," said Rose. "Water, fire, and air." Her lips pursed as she considered something. "Where's my dog?"

"Right there." I pointed to Braveheart, who lay sprawled on the floor.

"Not that one. Like yours."

"Yeah, where are our fun magical animals? I want one, too." Pepper pouted like she'd been denied dessert.

I threw my hands up. "How should I know? This is all new to me. There's no *So You Have Magical Powers* book out there to tell me what to do next."

"That would be a good book," Pepper mused. She toyed thoughtfully with her leather necklace and its shining black pearl, then glanced at her watch. "Oh, my God—the kids! I have to pick them up."

"I'll come with you." I took a step toward the door, then stopped. "But we can't leave Rose alone."

"Do you want to stay with her?" asked Pepper. "I can come get you later. Or Rose can take you home if she feels up to it."

I looked in Rose's direction. "Rose?"

Rose examined her hands and spoke in a quiet voice. "Do you think I could come with you?"

I looked at Pepper. "Pepper?"

"You're not going to barf fire or something with the kids in the car? Because that would be hard to explain."

"It's under control."

Pepper raised one eyebrow.

"I promise."

"Fine. Ride-or-die besties, mount up!" Pepper whipped out her keys and headed out the door.

Rose and I followed. I helped her into the front seat, figuring it was better than the back seat if she was feeling queasy.

Pepper maneuvered the SUV down the dirt road. The live oaks gave way to slash pine forest as we pulled onto the paved highway toward Sparkle Beach. "Anyone got any bright ideas about why the three of us are suddenly superpowered?"

I shook my head. "I *flew* today. I still can't get over it."

Rose turned to look at me. "When?"

"When what?"

"When did you fly?"

"Late this morning. On the Riverwalk, after I went to Ultimate Crate and found it deserted."

"Pepper, did this start for you today?" I asked.

Pepper gripped the leather-wrapped steering wheel as we sped toward the Sparkle Beach city limits. "Yes."

Rose held her hands out, rolling her wrists and splaying her fingers like an orchestra conductor about to perform.

Pepper glanced over. "Rose, you're making me nervous. Please don't set the dashboard on fire."

She dropped her hands in her lap. "It can't be a coincidence."

I stared out the window as the trees flashed by. "Why us?"

"Why not?" said Rose.

"Why not? Because now is not a great time to have to figure all this out." Pepper flipped her sun visor down with more force than necessary.

Rose made a skeptical noise. "When would be a good time to figure it out?"

We passed the Sparkle Beach city limits sign, emblazoned with the lighthouse logo and surrounded by a semi-circle of palm trees.

It was like I had a puzzle to solve, but only a handful of the pieces.

Rose glanced over her shoulder and caught my expression as I racked my brain. "Something wrong?"

I shook my head. "Nothing."

She pierced me with a disbelieving stare.

"Don't you look at me with your flaming eyes, woman."

Rose smirked. "I could try to command you to squawk like a chicken."

"Don't you dare," said Pepper. "How would I explain that to the kids?"

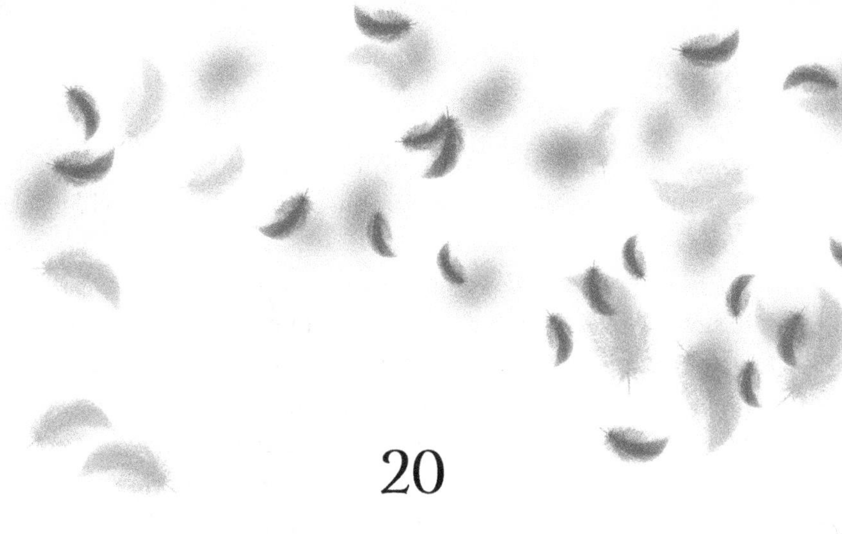

20

We pulled into the parent pickup lane at Sparkle Beach Elementary, home of the summer recreation program.

Pepper triggered the locks open as her boys came running up: Rocky, the older one, with short hair, thick glasses, and an open but serious face; and Kevin, the younger one with puppy dog eyes and tousled locks.

Rocky pulled the door open and pushed his younger brother into the car like a sheepdog guiding a wayward sheep into the fold.

Kevin tumbled merrily into the middle seat and pushed his dark hair out of his face. "Mom! Can we go to Highway to Grill?"

Rocky clambered in behind him and shut the door. "Highway to Grill is way better than McDonald's. Can we go, Mom?"

Kevin bounced up and down, barely restrained by the seat belt. "Did you know hamburgers cause worldwide defenestration—"

Rocky waved his arms with the air of someone who has explained a concept a thousand times and has, at long last, finally lost patience. "*Deforestation*, not defenestration. Defenestration means throwing someone out a window. Deforestation means cutting or burning down trees."

Unbothered by his brother's correction, Kevin shouted, "Get it right or pay the price!" at no one in particular.

"Boys, say hello to Luella and Rose." Pepper pulled out of the parking lot and headed toward Happy Harbor.

"Hello, Luella and Rose!" they said in unison.

Rose and I exchanged glances. Pepper's boys were energetic, to say the least.

Rocky leaned forward. "So, can we?"

Pepper shook herself as if trying to get her scattered thoughts in line. "Can we what?"

"Can we go to Highway to Grill?"

She glanced in the rear view mirror at Rocky. "Aren't you worried about deforestation?"

"I'll plant a tree!" shouted Kevin. "Two trees! One for each cheeseburger."

Rose covered her mouth to hide a laugh.

"Fine, two trees." Pepper reached across the center console and patted Rose. "We could all use a cheeseburger or two."

Highway to Grill stood alongside the main road into Sparkle Beach, in an original 1960s building that had been lovingly restored and re-restored over the years, including the sign: a hamburger patty branded with tire marks, over a road surrounded by flames and stretching into the infinite distance.

Our order was long, complicated, and involved no less than three attempts to explain that Rocky wanted pickles but no onions, and Kevin wanted onions but no pickles. By the time we received our paper bags filled with piping hot food, the impatient person in the car behind us had honked more than once.

Gripping an iced coffee in her left hand, Pepper swerved one-handedly into a nearby parking space. "Car picnic," she declared.

I unwrapped my slightly flattened cheeseburger and took a bite. I alternated bites of cheeseburger with bites of french fry until our meal was interrupted by a knock at Pepper's window.

The man who knocked motioned with one hand for Pepper to roll down her window. In his other hand, he gripped a large cup with condensation beading on the sides.

I figured he wanted to point out a tire that was low on air.

Pepper rolled down the window. "Can I help you?"

"Did you know you're parked over the line?" He stepped back and gestured angrily toward the ground.

"Oops. Sorry about that." Pepper took a hearty bite of her cheeseburger with supreme unconcern, as if to say, *Who are you to criticize my parking?* She reached for the window controls.

He made a noise of disgust. "Women drivers."

Pepper froze, and her voice wound up to pure fury in just two words. "Excuse me?"

He waved a dismissive hand and turned to walk away.

Pepper fumbled for her seat belt release.

Rose grabbed at her. "Pepper, no! Ignore him. He's just some crank."

"I'll give him what for! 'Women drivers' my—"

I leaned forward. "Pepper, he's crazy. Let it go."

Pepper subsided and left her seatbelt on, so I thought it was over.

It wasn't.

"I'm not going to let my kids see someone treat me like that." She put her hands on the door and leaned out so her voice would carry. "Listen here, you semi-sentient pile of walking garbage! This is the twenty-first century! You don't talk to women like that, you hear me? Hey! I'm talking to you, you festering dung heap!"

He turned around. A nasty, rage-filled expression distorted his face as he took heavy, deliberate steps in the direction of our vehicle.

Pepper hit the automatic window button to roll up her window. "Time to go, guys!" She dropped her cheeseburger in a cup holder and threw the SUV into reverse, turning the wheel as she backed out, leaving the passenger side of the car—and Rose's window—facing the rude man.

"Pepper, wait! I can deal with him." Rose rolled down her window and flexed her fingers.

Pepper slammed the brakes.

The man charged the car, directly at Rose.

"Rose, what are you—" I didn't finish in time.

Rose stared bullets at him and shouted, "The best way to cool off is to pour it down your pants!"

The man's mouth went slack. He pulled at his waistband and dumped the entire contents of the cup—a vividly green milkshake—into his trousers.

In the bright midday light, it was hard to see the change in his eyes, but I knew what I was looking for. That silvery glint wasn't coming from the sun.

"Whoa!" said the boys.

"'Whoa' is right," said Pepper. She hit the gas. The car lurched forward, carrying us out of the parking lot and away from the milkshake-soaked man.

Rose fumbled in her purse and slammed her sunglasses into place.

I had no doubt—if she took them off, there would be flickers of silver flame in her eyes.

Kevin punched his fist into the air. "That was awesome!"

"You showed him!" Rocky's eyes shone behind his thick lenses as he stared admiringly at Rose. "How'd you do that?"

"Rose is a dog trainer. She's good at giving commands," Pepper said.

You had to admire Pepper's on-the-spot improvisation. "Right," I chimed in. "It's a knack. Isn't that right, Rose?"

Rose didn't speak. She balled her hands into fists like someone prone to being carsick who was trying to hold back the inevitable.

Judging by the look on Rose's face, we didn't have much time before she put on a repeat performance of the eruption in her cabin. At least we had managed to put a couple of blocks between ourselves and Mr. Pile of Walking Garbage. "Find a place to pull over, Pepper," I said.

"What? Why?"

"I think Rose has *food poisoning*." I prayed she would catch my drift.

Pepper skidded the SUV to the side of the road.

I climbed over Kevin and Rocky—ignoring their excited cries of "Is she going to barf?"—then I jumped out, pulled Rose's door open, and dragged her out of the car, slamming the door as soon as we were clear.

She collapsed to the ground on all fours, pressing her hands into the dirt.

I held her hair back.

Hiss. The dirt smoked beneath her hands as flames shot into the ground and extinguished themselves.

"I'm sorry," she croaked. "I shouldn't have done that."

"Hush. It's fine. He deserved it. Hang on and it'll pass." I looked over my shoulder at the car windows. Pepper had somehow managed to entice the boys away from the windows on our side of the car, but I had no idea if their inquisitive faces would soon be pressed against the glass, watching smoke puff from Rose's hands.

Like Pepper said, it would be hard to explain.

I extended my wings and did my best to disperse the smoke, then I murmured Zephyr's name.

She appeared without any transition, as if she hadn't come running, but had been nearby—and invisible—all along.

"How do you do that?" I cocked my head as I studied her adorable face. "Never mind. We'll talk later. Come here, girl."

Zephyr padded over obediently.

"Can you lie on Rose's hands, please? We need to block the air from feeding the fire. No air for the fire. Got it?"

Zephyr settled her furry body over Rose's hands.

"Feels like a handheld vacuum," said Rose. She groaned. "Here comes another one."

This time, the flames merely fizzled, and only a wisp of smoke escaped.

Rose exhaled. "I think it's passing."

"Did that help?"

"I think so. The urge is leaving."

"If you're sure, we can get back in the car." I helped her stand.

Zephyr backpedaled out of the way.

Rose brushed the dirt from her hands, then nodded to indicate my wings as they swirled neatly away behind my back. "This is going to take getting used to."

"Understatement of the year." I held her arm as she slid into the front passenger's seat.

Pepper's eyes widened until the whites could be seen around her irises. "Are you okay?"

"Bad hamburger," Rose replied, settling in the seat and buckling up. "All good now."

"Are you sure?"

"She's fine," I said. I shut Rose's door and knelt out of sight to thank Zephyr with a hug and an affectionate ruffle of her ears. Then I opened the rear passenger door and motioned for Kevin and Rocky to scoot across the bench seat so I wouldn't have to climb over them again.

Kevin's eyes widened like his mother's. "Mom, am I going to barf, too?"

"No, honey. Your burger was fine." Pepper glanced at Rose, then caught my gaze in her rearview mirror. "But I think Mommy and Luella and Rose are going to need to have a little talk about *food poisoning* when we get home."

As we pulled away, I glanced behind to watch Zephyr dash off, presumably to do whatever it was she did for fun when she wasn't with me: chasing clouds, skimming white-caps, or setting leaves aflutter.

We passed the Happy Harbor miniature lighthouse and returned to Pepper's house without further incident.

Pepper declared an extra ration of screen time for the boys, who whooped with delight and promptly disappeared to play video games—which was exactly what Pepper had intended. She turned to me. "Outside. Now."

"It's a hundred degrees outside—"

"Then cool off with your magical wing power. We need to talk where the boys can't sneak up on us." Pepper slid open the door to the pool area.

Rose and I followed.

Thankfully, half of the pool area was shaded by an over-hang. We took seats on the wicker furniture, steps away from the inviting shimmer of the turquoise pool.

Pepper spoke first. "This has gotten crazy. We need to figure all this out, pronto. What if I lose control like Rose did? What if I flood the whole house or something?"

Rose put her back up. "I didn't lose control—"

"What do you call spewing fire in broad daylight by the side of the road?"

"Hang on." I had to interrupt before tempers got out of hand. A best friend throwdown was the last thing any of us needed. "Dial it back. I thought you were excited when you first saw Zephyr."

Pepper huffed. "Of course I was! It was cool. It wasn't like I had a bunch of craziness blowing up my life." She paused and reconsidered her turn of phrase. "No offense. I don't mean you're crazy."

I sighed. "I know. And it is crazy. In the sense of being wild and unpredictable, I mean."

Rose looked at her hands and frowned. "What I don't get is why my powers are more erratic than yours, Luella."

"I had trouble getting Zephyr to mind, remember? And I still can't always control these wings—not well enough to do anything other than push the air around."

Rose looked at Pepper. "Why aren't Pepper's powers uncontrollable?"

I turned my gaze in Pepper's direction and raised my eyebrows. "Any ideas?"

Pepper looked down at the floor and frowned.

"Pepper?"

Still looking at the floor, she mumbled something indistinct.

I leaned in to hear her better. "Say again?"

Pepper jerked her head up. "I said, because I've been practicing!"

I gasped. "What do you mean, you've been practicing? You acted like this was the first time you've had anything happen!"

"I lied," she muttered.

Rose fixed Pepper with a look. "Pepper, how long have you had powers?"

Pepper's face took on a sheepish expression. "Since the day after Luella got fired."

My jaw dropped. "What?"

"I noticed the next morning when I went surfing. Everything was different. The water—I don't know how to put it—the water carried me around like I was some kind of princess."

"What else can you do?" said Rose.

"Well, I can surf better than usual."

Rose rolled her eyes. "That's all you've tried?"

"I didn't want it to get out of hand! I wanted to have a little fun, that's all. A little fun of my very own."

I softened my tone. "Why didn't you tell me?"

Pepper looked down again. "I figured it was temporary, like the wings were at first. And I didn't want to get you all excited about it, if it was just going to go away. Then I was—uh—goofing around in the shower, trying to send some water sideways and rinse some suds off the wall . . . and I exploded the showerhead."

Rose and I burst out laughing.

Pepper made a face like a grumpy cat. "Laugh it up, you two."

I wiped a tear of laughter from the corner of my eye. "I'm sorry. This is all a bit much."

Pepper buried her face in an outdoor pillow emblazoned with a parrot, then let out a muffled howl of frustration.

"It'll be okay. It's a lot to get used to." I tugged the pillow away from Pepper. "But if we work together, it doesn't have to be so scary."

Pepper grabbed the pillow and smacked me in the leg with it. "Really? Silver fire in your ex-boyfriend's eyes?

Mysterious weirdos hypnotizing grown men into a stupor? Fire billowing out of Rose's hands? I call that scary."

Rose raised her eyebrows. "Are you calling me a mysterious weirdo?"

"You are a mysterious weirdo, Rose—but no, I was referring to whoever put the voodoo on Dan and Raphael."

"Stop talking and let me think." I squeezed my eyes shut, working out the connections. "Rose convinced Mr. Pile of Walking Garbage to pour his milkshake down his pants. Someone convinced Dan to follow me. Someone also convinced Raphael to paint the wing mural."

"I didn't hypnotize Dan and Raphael—"

I opened my eyes. "I know you didn't, Rose. What I mean is: We're not the only ones with powers. And whoever they are, they may or may not have our best interests at heart."

"Has Raphael remembered anything else since your date?" asked Rose.

Pepper interrupted before I could answer. "You need to put that guy in a chair under a hot light and jog his memory."

I smiled at the thought. "What if I put him in a pool instead?"

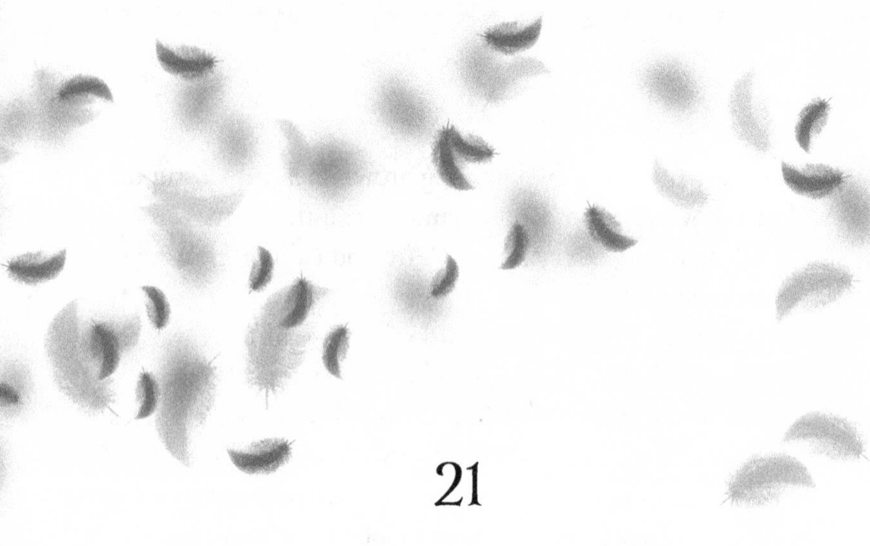

21

I tugged my bathing suit into place and adjusted the industrial strength chest reinforcement. The dark purple fabric flattered my curves and the metal accents added enough flash to look pretty rather than gaudy. I fluffed the short skirt to arrange the best drape and admired the view, front and back, in the mirror.

Considering that if I were a wedding anniversary, I'd be sapphire—I didn't look half bad. It certainly didn't hurt my self-image to have a pair of honest-to-goodness wings on my back, dripping silver glitter like raindrops off a palm frond.

I slipped into a thick terry cloth robe and tied the belt securely, then went to the kitchen and made a platter of ham and turkey sandwiches. You couldn't pump someone for information and not have a little snack on hand. It wouldn't be polite.

I hummed as I covered the platter with plastic wrap and slid it into the refrigerator. The door almost closed itself before I arrested the motion with my hand. I retrieved a clear container of strawberries and ran them under the faucet, rinsing them clean. After I removed the stems, they looked like edible rubies.

A knock interrupted my preparations.

I tucked the strawberries away with the sandwiches, straightened my robe, and hastened to open the door. "Raphael!"

He stood on the porch, grinning, sunglasses on, his dark, curly hair ruffled by the humid sea breeze, a gigantic watermelon cradled in his arms.

I stepped aside to make room. "Come on in."

"Where should I put this?"

"On the bar is fine." I joined him. The watermelon was cool to the touch. "Did you get a refrigerated one?"

He removed his sunglasses and tucked them into the pocket of his Hawaiian shirt. "What, you think I would bring you a warm watermelon? On a day like this?"

An ice cold watermelon, Raphael in a bathing suit, and a pool for two. My troubles flapped right out of my head like butterflies on the wing. I cleared my throat, attempting to recall whatever it was I was supposed to be discussing. "I made sandwiches. And there's strawberries, too."

Raphael peeked into the refrigerator. "You are amazing." He closed it and pivoted around the kitchen, pointing at various cabinets and drawers. "Where would I find a knife?"

"Right here." I retrieved my chef's knife and laid it on the cutting board.

"Perfect." He hauled the watermelon over and set to work. He proffered the first slice with a flourish. "Ladies first."

"Oh—thank you!" I received the slice and took a bite, self-conscious of the dripping juice.

He continued cutting slices with deft movements.

"You seem pretty good with that," I said.

"I cook a little."

"Do you really? I bake."

"No kidding? That's awesome." He cleared the cut slices onto a plate to make room. "What do you bake?"

"Gluten-free stuff. That's what I learned so Lily could enjoy as many normal foods as possible."

Raphael set down the knife and leaned against the counter. "Favorite recipe?"

"Rugelach."

He rolled his eyes heavenward. "Save me! I love rugelach. You'll have to teach me your recipe some time."

I found his enthusiasm mighty appealing, so I took another bite of watermelon to cover the infatuated look I was sure had spread over my face.

"Why don't we take this party outside?" He lifted the platter of watermelon slices.

I picked up the plate of strawberries and carefully stacked it on the sandwiches.

He opened the back door for me, and I took the steps down to the tiny back patio. I'd already placed a small folding table within reach of the pool, so I set the plates on the table and stepped back to allow Raphael to set down the platter of watermelon. When my gaze met his, his eyes were boyish all over again. I couldn't have told you whether we were high school kids, or fortysomething adults.

We were just Raphael and Luella.

Raphael removed his sunglasses from his pocket and put them on again. His fingers deftly unbuttoned the Hawaiian shirt, exposing his chest to the Florida sun.

I shrugged off the robe like standing there in a bathing suit was no big deal at all. The light sweat that broke out on my forehead stayed in place—it was too humid for it to evaporate. I could only hope that it gave me a dewy glow.

I could tell from his expression that he was debating whether it would be better to compliment me or leave his thoughts unsaid. I smirked as I climbed into the pool, until the cold water nearly knocked the breath out of my body. "Go ahead. I can take it."

"Take what?" His innocent act was adorable.

"Whatever you were going to say." I shifted to the other side of the pool, leaving room for him to get in.

He slipped into the water. "I was going to say"—he reached for two strawberries, then settled back comfortably—"that you look like a goddess."

I felt the color crawl into my cheeks, hot and tingling.

Raphael raised an eyebrow. "You all right, there?"

I pressed my wet hands against my face, half expecting to hear a hissing sound as I touched my cheeks. "A little warmer out here than I expected."

He smiled to himself as he examined a strawberry. "Perfectly ripe." He held it out to me. "Strawberry?"

Our fingers touched as I took it.

If this kept going, I'd have scrambled eggs for brains in no time. I swore I'd stop flirting and start asking questions.

Well, maybe a little flirting.

"Tell me about the wings mural. I want to make sure I got every detail." I bit into the strawberry, letting its summery aroma fill my senses.

"The mural." He placed one arm around the edge of the pool, holding himself steady as he took a bite from the strawberry in his other hand. "I didn't remember a thing until our little escapade downtown. All I remembered before that was waking up one day and wondering why I smelled like paint and why I felt like I'd run a marathon."

"Got it. Go on."

"When we ran into that guy—"

"Dan." The way he said it—*that guy*—showed exactly what he thought of Dan.

"Dan, right. You remember his eyes, right?"

"Who could forget?"

"When I looked into his eyes, it was like . . . unlocking a file cabinet. You know how there's an audible *clunk* as the locking bar shifts? That's when it started coming back."

"Do you remember everything now?"

"Not every detail, but it's much clearer now."

"Tell me everything you remember."

"I was at home. Late evening. Dark. Probably watching *Property Brothers* or something."

I shuddered. "I hate that show. But I can't stop watching it."

"See? You know what I'm talking about." He shifted and leaned closer, lowering his voice. "Someone knocked on the door."

I couldn't help noticing his lips had been stained slightly

red by the strawberry. I dragged my gaze up to his eyes and tried to concentrate.

He continued the story. "I opened it. Someone was standing there—a woman, I'm sure of, but everything else is a blur."

"A woman? Like with Dan?"

"Her voice sounded slow and strange, like it was underwater. All of a sudden, I felt like it was a really good idea to go finish painting the downtown murals."

"Finish? You'd already finished, though, right?"

"Exactly! But the feeling—it was so natural, like it was an extension of wanting to do the murals in the first place."

"You didn't feel an urge to fight it?"

"Why would I?" He blinked, as if realizing how close we were to each other. His lips parted and his gaze slipped down to my shoulder. "Have I mentioned that your wings make you look even more stunning?"

A light shiver passed over my skin. "Do you remember who originally hired you to do the murals?"

"The head of the Downtown Merchant Guild." He sounded distracted, and his gaze lingered, tracing the line of my shoulders like he was creating a mental schematic for a sculpture.

I eased closer, ducking lower in the water to intercept his gaze with my own. "I know that, Raphael. What was her name?"

"Mel—something." He drifted toward me.

Our gazes locked. We circled each other in slow motion, tracing a double spiral that drew us to the center.

"Mrs. Millefleur," he murmured.

"What?" My feet slipped on the bottom of the pool. I floundered for purchase and water flew in every direction.

Raphael steadied me, drawing me into a comfortable embrace that kept me from dunking my own head in the water. "Is that bad?"

The warmth of his embrace threatened to drive away all coherent thought, but I pulled myself together. Bracing my hands against his chest helped. Then again, perhaps it didn't. "You're sure? Mrs. Millefleur?"

His face registered confusion. "Well, yeah. She's the head of the Downtown Merchant Guild. Probably owns half of River Street."

I allowed myself the pleasure of floating in his arms—I was only human—before returning to the matter at hand. "I have to go."

"What? No . . . we haven't finished the fruit." His charming brown eyes and his teasing voice nearly broke my resolve.

"I have to. I have a hunch about this."

He sighed, then nodded. "If you must, you must. Can I help? Do you need me to do anything?"

"No—wait—on second thought, yes." I hauled myself out of the water and grabbed my towel. "Can you help me make a logo and four dozen cookies?"

It was time for me to join the Downtown Merchant Guild.

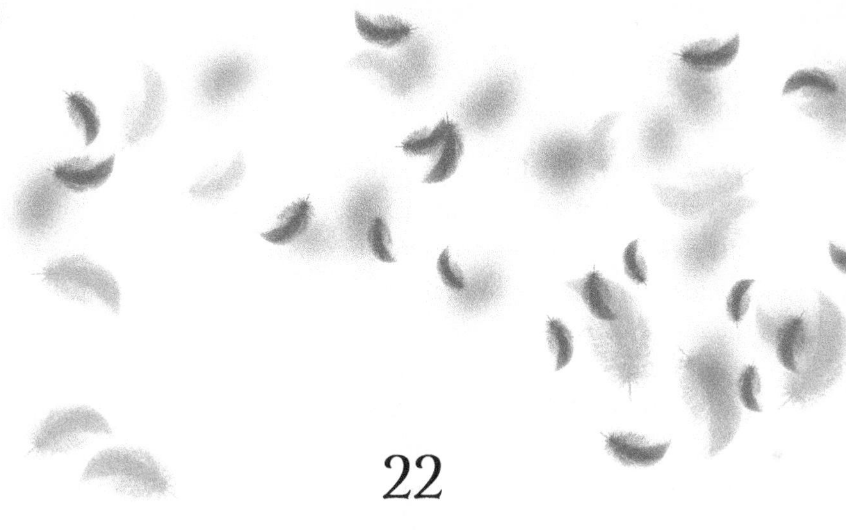

22

The next morning, I decked myself in my business casual best. The cookies had been neatly packed in individual cellophane bags. All I had left to do was attach the business cards I'd had run off at a copy shop the night before.

"Luella's Gluten-Free Goodies," I read aloud, admiring the fanciful pink script and the colorful sweet treats emblazoned across the card. I threaded a length of thin satin ribbon through a hole in each card and tied them to the cellophane bags, then loaded them into a box and carried it out to the car.

The Downtown Merchant Guild held their weekly meeting in a restored theater off River Street, not too far from Artists' Alley, Sparkle Beach Creamery, and Thai Fi.

As I approached the sign-in table in the lobby, I heard a girlish giggle that struck a chord in my memory. It sounded like the receptionist who answered my questions on the phone. I'd pictured her in a prim little cardigan—but she was actually wearing a purple velour tracksuit and matching glasses with purple-tinted lenses. "Good morning, I'm Luella Campbell. I think we spoke on the phone—about the mural artist?"

"Why, yes, dear." She leaned across the table and patted my hand. "I'm Gladys. Welcome to the DMG." She winked conspiratorially. "That's what we call the Downtown Merchant Guild. Kind of a mouthful, isn't it?"

Was it the light, or did her hair have a purple tint as well? "I was thinking about joining to promote my new business." I tilted the box to display the cookies.

She tugged at the edge of the box for a better view. "Don't those look delicious?"

"Would you like to try them?"

"Don't mind if I do." Nimble fingers plucked a package from the box. She set it down and collated several papers and brochures into a stack, much like the one I'd found at Ultimate Crate. "Would you prefer to join as an individual or as a business entity?"

I had no idea. "Business?"

Gladys selected one last paper to add to the stack. "You fill these out and bring them back after the meeting."

"Thanks. Oh, by the way—you wouldn't happen to know where I could find Mrs. Millefleur, would you? Is she speaking today?"

Gladys shook her head. "She's still on vacation, as far as I know."

"Does she vacation a lot?"

Her sharp gaze reassessed me. "Why? Did you need something in particular?"

"I . . . was wondering if she knew the guild member from Ultimate Crate." That seemed safe enough. Better than confessing my desire to interrogate Mrs. Millefleur about the downtown murals, which might sound a little odd.

"You don't need Mrs. Millefleur for that. I could look up a member for you in a trice." She snapped her fingers. "Wait a minute—Ultimate Crate? Isn't that the fitness dude?" She stood and peeked through the doors into the theater, then returned to the table. "He's already inside."

Mrs. Millefleur might have been AWOL, but my other quarry was only steps away. I thanked Gladys and hurried across the lobby.

Before entering the theater, I examined it. There were two possible exits: a door halfway between the stage and the lobby, and the doors leading directly to the lobby. I'd have to corner Alex away from those if possible.

He stood in the center aisle, making conversation with a small knot of businesspeople. He was wearing the same type of athletic clothing he'd been wearing before, and he flexed his bicep to emphasize some point he'd been making.

I threaded through the crowd in the center aisle.

Alex, Founder and CEO of the vanishing Ultimate Crate, looked up and spotted me. A pained smile stretched into a rictus as he attempted to excuse himself from whoever he was talking to. He dodged the other members and headed in the direction of the side exit.

No way I was letting my quarry go that easily—but the box of goodies was slowing me down. I dropped it on the stage and jogged after him.

He glanced over his shoulder, then pushed open the door and slipped outside.

I caught the door as it swung closed. The exit led to a sidewalk bordering a grassy field between the buildings.

Alex was booking it down the sidewalk, and he had a good head start.

"Alex, wait!" If he decided to kick it into high gear, there would be no way I could keep up. Even if I could suddenly control my ability to fly, I couldn't start flying down the street in broad daylight.

Maybe I couldn't—but my furry magical friend could. "Zephyr," I huffed as I ran after Alex.

The dog appeared and loped along beside me, seemingly thrilled at this new game, whatever it was.

"Zephyr, see that man?"

Zephyr barked.

"When I say go, knock him on the grass. Gently!" My chest burned, but I kept going. I waited to give the command until Alex passed a rose hedge—I didn't want to injure him, only stop him. "Go!"

Zephyr sped into a blur, then leaped like the playful dog she was, embodying a blast of wind that whipped the roses and sent Alex stumbling into the field.

He landed on his rear end in the grass, giving me enough time to hustle and catch up.

I leaned over him. "Alex." I had to catch my breath

before saying more. "Why were you running? I only wanted to talk to you."

Alex looked at me as if he'd just noticed I was trying to get his attention. "Luella! I was just stepping outside for a quick run. Part of my training. Fitness is a lifestyle with no finish line, am I right?"

I'm not sure who he thought that line would work on, but it wasn't me. "Really? Nothing to do with the fact that you shut down Ultimate Crate without giving your customers their money back?"

His smile remained, but his eyes became guarded.

Bingo.

"Let's talk, shall we?" I sat on the grass. Zephyr, unseen by Alex, settled next to me. "You kept collecting Ultimate Crate subscription money from people even though you knew you weren't going to fulfill the orders, didn't you?"

"That's not exactly how it went—"

"Enlighten me."

"I wasn't trying to steal from anybody, honest. I didn't mean to do it. I thought I had it under control, but it got away from me." He gestured sharply, as if showing off a new workout move.

"Do you still have the money you collected?" I watched his face.

His gaze shot to the side before he answered. "No . . ."

Liar. "Try again."

"Well, some of it."

"Did you think you were going to ride into the sunset and start over?" I rolled my eyes. "Here's the deal. You're going to pay those people back. Or I take all the information I have and turn it over to the proper authorities, and I put my social media skills to work on spreading the word far and wide that you are a—"

He raised his hands. "Whoa, there! No need for that."

"I certainly hope not. Because I'll also tell the Downtown Merchant Guild what you've been up to, and I bet they won't be too happy about it, either. That would put a real crimp into whatever venture you decide to start up next. Now give me your contact info. Your *real* contact info. No funny business. Mess with me—or all those nice people you stole from—and I will make sure you regret it." I readied my phone to add the information.

He meekly recited an email address and phone number.

"See, that wasn't so hard, was it?" I stood. "I'll be in touch—and I'll be watching."

I left the ex-CEO in the grass and returned to the theater to retrieve my box of treats, figuring I could hand out the rest—but in the time it had taken to chase down Alex, the box had been picked clean.

On my way out, I stopped to examine the gilt-framed portraits of the theater donors, each with their own shiny gold nameplate. I'd never paid much attention to the Sparkle Beach muckety-mucks—not my crowd—but the third portrait down the row caught my eye.

Hildegarde Millefleur.

Her proud nose seemed to jut in three dimensions from the picture. A strand of white pearls graced her neck over a sedate shell and jacket combination. Her coiffed hair looked like it wouldn't budge even in a high wind.

She was the image of an upstanding—even stuffy—citizen, except for one unusual accessory: a stunning fire opal enhancer pendant at the center of her string of pearls.

"What are you up to?" I wondered aloud. Intuition trickled through me like a tiny current of electricity. On impulse, I raised my phone, took a photo of the portrait, and sent it to London with a message: *Is this who you saw with your aunt?*

I returned to my car and dropped the empty box in the trunk. As I closed the trunk, the phone buzzed insistently from my back pocket.

London's texts came in one after another. *Yes. How did you know? Who is she?*

I whooped aloud right there in the car.

Mama thought Mrs. Millefleur was in Mallorca, but thanks to London, I knew the truth—Mrs. Millefleur was right here in Sparkle Beach, and odds were good that Queenie knew exactly where she could be found.

Never mind, I wrote. *Is Queenie still going to rent out Fifi's Secondhand Salon to get ready for the Sun Parade this year?*

London's reply came instantly. *As usual.*

I thanked her and shoved the phone in my purse.

I had a plan.

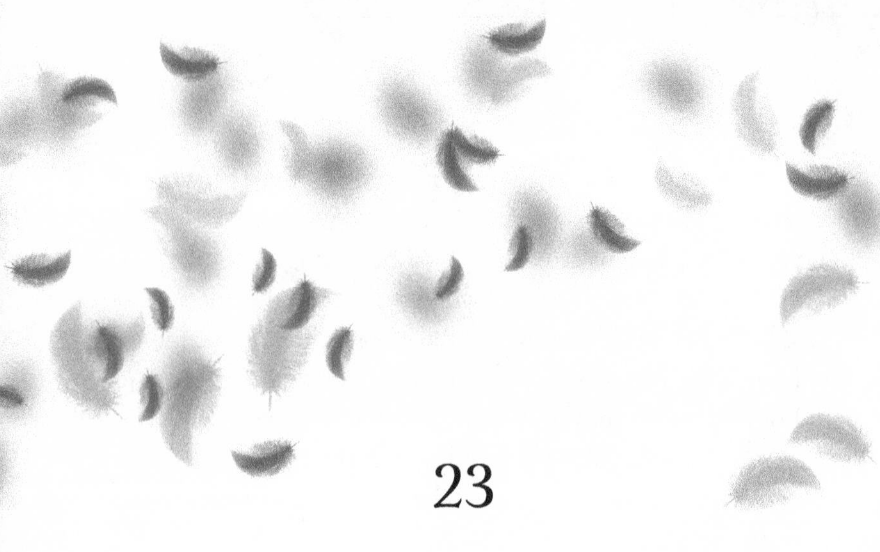

23

I invited Pepper and Rose over to practice our magic together, not unlike teenagers at a slumber party who experiment on each other with makeup, nail polish, and curlers—except we'd be middle-aged women experimenting with air, water, and fire.

Before they arrived, I cast one last look around the living room of the shotgun house. Everything was in place. I'd stacked up every towel I owned, filled as many containers as I could find with water, and placed not one but two fully-charged fire extinguishers within easy reach.

"Zephyr!" I clapped my hands.

Zephyr appeared out of nowhere like she had done on the side of the road, a fine mist dissipating into the air as she became visible.

I knelt and hugged her. "Good girl. Someday you'll have to show me how to do that trick."

She wagged her tail.

The front door opened.

"Your door was unlocked," said Pepper.

I stood. "I'm becoming my mother, apparently."

Rose followed Pepper inside and shut the door. "Looks like you're all set up."

"Can you think of anything else we might need?"

Rose raised an eyebrow. "A manual?"

"We'll wing it." Pepper paused. "Get it? Wing it?" She flapped her arms at me.

I unfurled my wings with a magician's flourish and managed to lift myself a few inches off the floor before I dropped with a loud *thump*. At least I'd gotten better at landing.

Pepper threw both arms in the air like I'd made a touchdown. "And the crowd goes wild!"

Zephyr barked, caught up in Pepper's excitement.

Rose examined the leftover business cards on the bar. "Did you get any nibbles?"

"Dropping the box of goodies on the stage at the Downtown Merchant Guild turned out to be the smartest business move I could have made. From the number of calls and texts I got afterward, everyone and their uncle must know someone who avoids gluten."

Rose scooped up a handful of cards. "Can I take some to give out?"

"Help yourself."

Pepper looked up from patting Zephyr. "I can help you set up an simple accounting program so you can keep track of your expenses. Maybe you'll hit it big!"

"I doubt I'll be retiring anytime soon, but any income source is welcome while I'm still looking for a job."

"You should get Raphael to make some more graphics. You know—for business reasons." Rose fanned herself with the cards.

Pepper snorted. "Yeah, *business* reasons."

"All right, all right. Settle down. I'm trying to take it slow after the Dan debacle."

"Sure you are," said Pepper.

Pepper and Rose looked at each other and doubled over laughing.

I cleared my throat. "I believe we were here to practice, not discuss my love life?"

They put on straight faces.

"Thank you. I call the meeting of the … what are we going to call ourselves, anyway?"

Pepper waved her hand like a kid in school. "Oh, oh, I know! The Downtown Magic Association!"

"We're not downtown, Pepper."

"Darn."

"Witches," Rose mused. "We're witches, right?"

We looked at each other.

"I think so. I mean, it's not like we have anyone else to ask about all this, so it stands to reason we can call ourselves witches if we want to."

"We're not just witches." Pepper leaped to her feet. "We're ride-or-die witches!"

Rose stood and splayed her hands, igniting fire on the tip of each finger. "I call this meeting of the Ride-or-Die Witches to order."

Pepper and I applauded.

Rose took a bow and sat.

"Thank you, Rose. You can shut off the fire before you ignite the couch, though."

Rose looked down at her hands. "Oops." She balled them into fists and the flames disappeared.

"Much better. I can't afford to buy a new couch right now. Now that you've demonstrated your fire, why don't you try your other skill? Hypnotize me."

"What, now?"

"No time like the present."

"What should I hypnotize you to do?"

"I shouldn't know what it is ahead of time—that's not a fair test. Pepper, you think of something and whisper it to Rose. That way I won't know what's coming."

Pepper whispered something in Rose's ear.

Rose rolled her wrists and flexed her fingers. She held my gaze as she spoke. "Luella, act like a chicken." Her eyes sparked with silver light.

I burst out laughing.

Pepper frowned. "It didn't work."

"It's not something Luella was thinking about doing on her own," said Rose. "And it's not related to anything she wants right now. It might not work if it doesn't make sense, on some level, to the subject."

"So why did Mr. Pile of Walking Garbage dump his drink down his pants?"

"It was a hot day. He bought a drink to cool off. Rose gave him a slightly different way of using a drink to cool off." I regarded Rose with a critical eye. "Rose, do you feel like you need to blow off steam? Or blow off fire, as it were?"

She shook her head.

"All right. Let's try again."

Pepper whispered to Rose.

Rose spoke.

It was—as Raphael had described— like someone cut a film reel. I perceived a loss in time, but found myself sitting on the couch as before.

Except Rose held a glass of water in her hand.

"Where'd you get that?"

Rose held it aloft. "This? From you."

"I never—"

"You always offer us drinks when we come over," said Pepper. "So I told her to make you get a drink for her."

I combed through my memory. Pepper's description conjured dreamlike fragments of the sink, a glass, and a stream of water. "This is downright weird. Did I wake up on my own?"

"No, I woke you."

"I wonder if I would have come out of it eventually."

"Maybe it's a power issue," said Rose. "How strong you are determines how long someone stays under."

"What about making someone do what they don't want to do? Could that be a power issue?" asked Pepper.

Rose let out a dark chuckle. "Yeah, a power issue—and a moral issue."

Pepper cackled and curved her fingers into claws. "Look at me! I'm evil. Evil!" She sounded like her high-spirited younger son. "Try me next."

Rose pursed her lips in thought. She stared intently at Pepper.

Pepper bounced in her seat.

Silver fire flashed in Rose's eyes. "Pepper, go surfing."

Pepper stood. She crossed the room, clearly intent on opening the front door.

I dove for the front door and blocked it. "Rose, what were you thinking? She's going to try to go to the beach!"

Pepper turned and calmly headed for the rear of the house.

Zephyr dashed back and forth as if we were playing an exciting new game.

I grabbed the glass of water Rose had abandoned on the coffee table and dashed the contents of the glass in Pepper's face.

"What the—" Pepper spat. She looked down at her wet clothes with dismay.

I retrieved a towel and patted Pepper with it. "You were on your way to the beach."

"I—what?" Pepper took the towel and wiped her dripping face.

"Rose told you to go surfing."

Pepper rounded on Rose. "You didn't stop to think what might happen?"

I stepped between them. "Hey, we made a discovery!"

They stared at me.

"We discovered you can snap someone out of the trance with a glass of water. See? Now we have a new way to wake someone up."

"I prefer breakfast in bed, thank you very much." Pepper continued drying off.

"How about you, Pepper? What do you want to practice?"

Pepper gestured with the towel. "I'm not sure you're really set up for it. I mean, you have a pool, but anyone could be watching out there. Besides, so far all I've been able to do is splash water around. We need a beach. Or a spring. Or at least a more private pool."

"Shall we table the discussion of water magic for the next meeting of the Ride-or-Die Witches?" Rose had procured a pad of a paper. She held a pen poised to write.

"Are you taking notes?" I shot her an incredulous look. "Put that away. What if someone found it?"

"I'd say we were making Halloween plans."

I opened my mouth to nix the idea, but reconsidered. "Fair enough."

Rose smiled triumphantly and began filling the page with her elegant cursive handwriting.

Pepper stretched. "Are we going to have regular meetings?"

Rose pointed her pen like a magic wand. "'When shall we three meet again? In thunder, lightning, or in rain?'" She gave the phrases a peculiar lilt, as if she were quoting something.

When shall we three meet again?

"Rose, what's that from?"

"It's the first line of Macbeth. The scene with the witches. Why?"

"The witches . . . " I massaged my temples in an attempt to bring back the memory. "I saw those words somewhere."

At Mama's house.

On the back of Mama's photo.

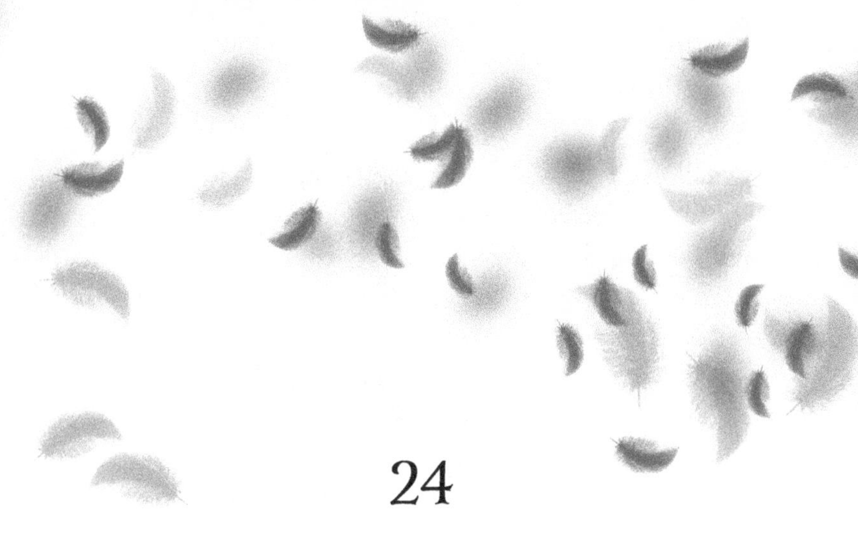

24

The day of the Sun Parade, I woke up drenched in sweat before dawn. In the quiet darkness, punctuated only by the tentative chirps of the earliest birds, I called to Zephyr.

She leaped through the bedroom window, her white and silver fur aglow against the backdrop of the sky.

I sat up halfway, flung back the covers, and patted the bed.

Zephyr jumped in, and I let her fan-like breeze evaporate the sweat while I stretched my stiff limbs. Slightly more limber—and much less sweaty—I rolled over and retrieved my phone from the nightstand. An idle scroll through my messages brought me to the cheerful back-and-forth with Raphael that had accumulated since our get-together in the pool. I smiled at the selfie he'd sent where he was wearing a Hawaiian shirt and holding a giant watermelon.

I closed the messages and pulled up my bank account. The tumbleweeds weren't blowing through it yet, but they were coming closer every day.

Zephyr nudged me with her head, as if sensing my distress.

"It'll be all right, girl. We'll find a way." I patted her head and ran a hand down her flank. Maybe if I convinced her, I could convince myself.

I swung my legs down and my feet touched the cool wood floor. Since the sweat had evaporated, I'd gone from hot to cold in a matter of minutes. I slid my arms into a thick robe and wrapped up tight before going to the front of the house.

The first light of dawn crept in from the living room window facing east. The growing illumination threw a familiar avian shape on the windowsill into silhouette.

"Midnight." I nodded acknowledgment, like one professional to another. "Are you coming with me to see Queenie?"

The crow lifted its beak.

"By the way, I never got to thank you for the coin. So, thanks."

Midnight let out a double croak that might have passed for *You're welcome*. Then he flew away into the gray dawn.

I started the coffee pot and hopped in the shower, grateful I wasn't in danger of having the showerhead explode. The water pushed through my hair, washing away shampoo—and any hesitation I might have had. I knew what I wanted.

Answers.

The Sun Parade provided the perfect opportunity. The parade capped the multi-day Sun Festival, a celebration of all things sun-related that commemorated the summer and kicked off the fall season of events. Queenie rented out Fifi's Secondhand Salon every year to provide a centralized location for the Suntan Queen float riders to get ready. There would be no warren of offices to navigate, no secretaries or underlings to block my way—just a salon full of people in spangly costumes and high-powered hairspray.

Freshly showered and dressed, I added a dash of real cream to my coffee and sat by the window to watch for my ride.

Since parking tended to be scarce downtown during the festival, Pepper, Rose, and I carpooled in Pepper's SUV. This time, Rose let me have the front seat.

"Hey—shotgun house, shotgun seat!" Pepper laughed at her own pun. "Get it?"

In the back seat, Rose smoothed her black hair into a tight ponytail. "You know what you're going to say to Queenie?"

"I'm ready."

Due to the traffic, we ended up having to park a block away and walk to Fifi's.

I pushed open the door.

Float riders streamed from room to room in varying states of undress. They crowded the mirrors, painting on exaggerated eyeliner and lip colors. Feather boas, flower crowns, and sequined masks covered every available surface as each person tried on accessories to find the perfect look.

"Good Lord," said Pepper.

Rose picked up a red and black mask and trailed her fingers over the gems.

"Anyone see Queenie?"

Pepper grabbed a stray sea-green boa and tossed it over her shoulders. "How would you know which one she was?"

"Good point." I squeezed through the hallway and angled toward the salon side of the building.

The steady whir of the bonnet hair dryers increased in volume as we got closer.

Queenie sat under one the dryers, paging through a magazine.

"Excuse me," I said. "Queenie?" I waved to get her attention.

Her eyes widened as she looked up at me. She threw aside the magazine, turned off the bonnet, and raised it to reveal auburn hair of a color not found in nature. Combined with her elegant eye makeup, the effect was striking. She stood and strode forward. "Darling!" She threw her arms around me.

I froze. Whatever I might have expected, this wasn't it. I took a deep breath, which was a mistake, as my lungs filled with a cloud of Queenie's perfume. I coughed.

She stepped back and held me at arm's length. "I'm *so* sorry, darling. This must have been terrible, just terrible!" She let go of me, turned to Rose and Pepper, and opened her arms wide . "And you've brought the others. How simply marvelous!"

Pepper and Rose looked at each other.

"The others?" said Pepper.

"Don't you know? Of course you do, my darlings, or you wouldn't be here." She tugged at my sleeve, pulling me away from the hair dryers and into a small tea room in the back of the salon. "Sit down, my darlings, sit down." She shut the doors, then busied herself at a side table that held an electric kettle and a china tea set.

I lowered myself into a candy-striped upholstered chair. Rose and Pepper followed suit. "Um, Queenie—I don't quite follow. You fired me, remember?"

"Of course I did, darling! And I'm *so* sorry. What you must have felt—oh! I can't imagine." Queenie pressed a hand to her bosom.

"You're sorry… that you fired me?" My head buzzed.

"I *had* to, you know. They *made* me do it." She shook her head as if we were discussing slightly naughty children, then she patted my knee. "But all's well that ends well, isn't it?"

I was officially lost. Judging by the expressions on my friends' faces, they felt the same. "Someone made you fire me? Was it the lawyers? Did I get exposed to a chemical?"

Queenie laughed and clapped her hands. "Lawyers, darling? How funny! Although really, I shouldn't lay the blame on the others. It was my suggestion, I admit."

I had to keep a hold on my temper. I didn't find being fired particularly amusing. "You suggested it? To whom? Queenie, why did you fire me?"

She stared at me. "You don't know? She didn't tell you?"

"Who didn't tell me?"

"Your mother."

My hands went cold. "What do you mean?"

Queenie paced in the tiny room. "Oh, no, this won't do, this won't do at all. It isn't my place—"

I intercepted her and gently took her hands. "Queenie, please tell me what's going on."

"But darling—"

I held her gaze. "Please."

"All right, my love. If you insist. But you simply must sit down." She perched on her own seat and waited for me to sit. "Luella, dear—have you noticed anything unusual happening lately?"

I laughed. How could I even describe what had happened?

"Then you know, don't you? You know what you are?"

I hesitated. Did she know? "What do you mean?"

"You don't trust me. That's understandable." She snapped her fingers. "I'll give you a reason to trust me, my dears. Watch this." She flexed the fingers of one hand, then made a gathering gesture that ended in a slow pull like she was hauling in a rope.

Pepper squinted. "I don't see any—"

Then we all saw it.

A neat stream of tea coiled out of the spout of the china teapot. It snaked around the tea room, glinting in the golden light from the wall sconces. The tea coiled around Queenie's fingers, avoiding her many rings, and funneled back into the spout without losing a drop.

"You're a witch," said Rose, her eyes wide.

Queenie gave a single, regal nod.

"But what does this have to do with—"

"Your mother?" Queenie arched a perfectly shaped eyebrow. "Where did you think your magic came from?"

My jaw dropped. "My mother? My mother's not a witch."

When shall we three meet again?

"Oh. Oh, my." I pressed my hand to my mouth. "There were three—"

"Now you're catching on, darling."

"But I came here to ask about Mama's acquaintance, Mrs. Millefleur—" I pictured the features of the third girl in the photo superimposed on the portrait in the theater. "Mrs. Millefleur is a *witch*? But she's the head of the Downtown Merchant Guild!" Whatever moorings I had left had been cut.

Queenie regarded me with amusement. "We all have lives, darling. I run a sunscreen factory. Mrs. Millefleur is a landowner and a philanthropist."

"She's not in Mallorca, is she?"

"Of course not. We had to work together, we three, to make this happen."

"Is that why you fired me? To make this happen?"

"We had to shake you up to get the magic to take." She leaned over and patted my knee again. "It was all a ruse. Now that your magic has manifested and settled, you can have your job back."

Tears filled my eyes. I wouldn't fail Lily after all. I would have enough money to float her through college, to help her buy safe food—to give her every opportunity I'd always planned to give her. It wasn't all falling apart; it was only the beginning.

Rose and Pepper hugged me. Tears of relief spilled down my face. "I want to talk to Mama." The words came out wobbly.

"No tears, darling. We have a parade to put on." She waved a hand and the tears floated away from my cheeks like raindrops suspended in midair before falling.

I dried my eyes with my shirtsleeves. "But I have so many questions..."

"Of course you do. But first, we'll celebrate. You'll ride with me as my guests of honor." She opened the door of the tea room and addressed the members of her coterie who had lingered in the salon. "Darlings, we have three more. Bring me a red robe, a sea-green robe, and a blue robe, and all the accessories you can carry." She shut the door again and faced me. "Now, tell your mother to come to the parade."

I fumbled for my phone. "I don't know if she's home—"

Queenie closed her hand over mine. "Not like that, darling." She patted my cheek. "You share the same magic. *Air* magic. What is sound, but moving air? Concentrate, speak, and imagine the air vibrating near your mother."

"All I have to do is talk?" I cleared my throat. "Mama?"

Nothing happened.

Queenie gave me an encouraging smile. "Think only of her. Think of her very essence. Send the words to her on little silver wings." She fluttered her hands.

Silence fell as Queenie, Pepper, and Rose watched me.

"Mama." I saw her in my mind, gray-haired and sparkly-eyed, surrounded by silver butterflies carrying my words. "Come to the parade."

Her reply whispered in my ear, soft as a breeze: *I'm on my way, baby.*

A sound halfway between a sob and a laugh escaped my lips. "She heard me! She's coming!"

"Of course she did. Now hurry—we can't be late for the parade." Queenie shooed us out of the tea room.

Women swathed in feathers, glitter, and sequins, swarmed around us.

Queenie clapped her hands to quiet the chattering crowd of ladies. She pointed to Rose. "This one in red like a forest fire." She pointed to me. "This one in blue, the color of the Florida sky on an autumn afternoon." She winked at Pepper. "And this one in sea-green, like the breaking waves in the Atlantic." She retreated and allowed the other women to close in.

With the speed of a backstage quick-change, they draped me in a sky blue robe with many folds, like a Greek chiton, secured with a silver belt and a series of ties that allowed my shoulders to peek through.

They steered me to a chair, brushed my cheeks with rouge, and painted my lips. Other hands pinned my hair up into a twist. They turned me to face the mirror so I could see myself as they lowered a glittering mask over my eyes. My hand traced its outline of swirls.

Pepper, nearly unrecognizable in yards of shimmering sea-green, squeaked in the chair next to me as she evaded a hand wielding a lip liner. "Hey! Watch it! You're going to poke out an eye." She used her hands to ward off the make-up. "Just give me the mask, people." She leaned toward me. "I don't wear all that stuff and I'm not going to start now." She followed up this statement with a firm nod.

On the other side of me, Rose stood and regarded herself in the mirror, from the trailing hem of her red garment to the ruby-colored mask studded with tiny orange gems. Her black hair had been pinned with red and orange flowers. Every inch of her costume spoke fire.

Queenie stepped forward. While we'd been dressed and masked, she'd completed her own preparations. Her costume matched Pepper's in color, but differed in cut—a slit exposed her leg from the top of her thigh to the pointed tip of her matching heels. A satin pageant sash emblazoned with "Suntan Queen" draped her from shoulder to hip. Instead of a mask, she wore a tall rhinestone crown.

The gaggle of women retreated.

Pepper stood and faced Queenie. She took in the resemblance and cocked her head. "Does this mean you're my fairy godmother?" A hopeful expression lit up her masked face. "Do you surf?"

Queenie laughed. "Oh, darling. Have you *seen* my logo?"

Rose hadn't stopped looking at herself in the mirror. She caught the reflection of Queenie's gaze. "When will I meet Mrs. Millefleur?"

A clouded expression passed over Queenie's face and swiftly disappeared, to be replaced by a pageant-winning smile. "Soon, I'm sure. She's a very busy woman, what with all her charities . . . " She swept out of the room.

We followed Queenie out the back door to find the parade float waiting. The colorful paillettes cast bright dots of light in all directions. The Suntan Queen logo and the Sparkle Beach lighthouse logo flanked a central seating area with stepped risers for the float riders.

Queenie mounted the steps to the float platform. She chose a seat on the highest riser and sat with care, arranging the folds of her costume.

I climbed up and took a seat next to her.

With the four of us in place, the other parade participants filled the lower risers like a brilliantly plumaged honor guard.

The float rolled forward. We took a slow turn onto River Street, heading south. The view from the float extended across a wide lawn to the Riverwalk on the left, with the downtown buildings all in a row on our right. People crowded the parade route and milled around the lawn, visiting the festival booths.

Puffy clouds blunted the rays of the sun, but the heat and humidity still made me sweat. I tried to be subtle as I plucked at the gown to circulate cooler air under the fabric.

Queenie glanced at my furtive movements. "Darling, what's the point of having powers if you're not going to use them?"

"Oh! Right." My wings easily generated enough of a breeze to blow back a stray lock of hair—and evaporate my sweat.

Pepper lifted her face to the wind, then tossed her hair like a diva. "I feel like I'm in a Pantene commercial."

As we drew closer to the reviewing stand, a lone motorcyclist deftly evaded the unattended barriers at the far end of River Street and zipped in our direction.

Rose leaned forward and shaded her eyes. "Luella, isn't that—"

My heart pounded. "Mama."

Mama leaned the bike against the reviewing stand, then took off her helmet. She raised her hand in what looked like a wave of greeting—until the clouds above us skidded faster across the sky. A great wind tossed our costumes and undid our hairdos.

Mama made a sweeping gesture and the wind died. She settled into a cocky stance, with her hands on her hips, while she waited for us to complete the route.

The view blurred into a wash of color and light. "You never told me," I whispered. I carefully nudged the tears away before Queenie noticed. I burned with the desire to leap down from the float and run to Mama. Instead, I fidgeted as the parade rounded the final corner and pulled into a parking lot that would serve as a holding area for the floats.

The instant our float stopped moving, I pulled off the mask, gathered my costume, and hurried down the stairs. I pushed through the milling crowd and jogged past the parked floats to reach the reviewing stand. "Mama?"

Our eyes met. Our strides matched as we closed the distance between us.

She threw her arms around me and I melted into them, just as I had when I was a little girl.

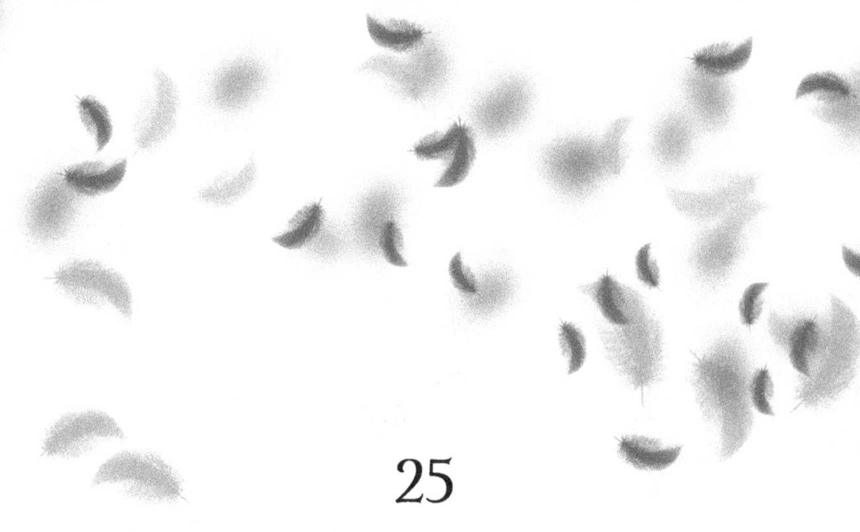

25

After the parade dignitaries vacated the reviewing stand, Mama and I claimed it for ourselves. We sat side by side on the edge of the covered platform, our legs swinging in and out of the shade in syncopated rhythm. Queenie, Rose, and Pepper had wandered off, still in costume, to find a funnel cake truck among the festival vendors.

A crow landed below our dangling feet.

"Is that yours?" I asked.

"Yup," said Mama.

The crow solemnly regarded both of us.

"I've been calling him Midnight."

Mama made a face.

"Don't make a face at me. What do *you* call him?"

"Crow."

"That's it? Just Crow?"

"Just Crow." Her voice rasped as if a laugh were about to escape.

I stared into the distance and watched the seagulls wheel over the river. "How long have you known?"

"About the magic? Since I was a girl."

"You kept it from me all this time? Did Daddy know?"

"He knew."

"Why didn't you tell me?"

"I was trying to protect you. I didn't want people deciding I was crazy, or that they needed to lock me in a room and turn me into a science experiment. I've seen the movies."

"But all those years … " I flashed back to my own childhood. Had she kept me cool on hot summer days? Did she build castles in the clouds to make me smile?

She shrugged. "Well, now you know."

"Queenie said my magic came from you."

Mama glanced down at Crow—or Midnight—who hopped backwards on his clawed feet. "Yes, it did."

"And? I feel like there's something you're not telling me. She said I needed to talk to you, not her."

Mama chuckled. "Of course she did. She knew you'd be mad that we made you think you'd lost your job."

"Did you really have to do that?"

"What else could we do that would really shake you up without hurting you? Getting you to think you'd been fired was the best thing we could come up with." She wrung her hands. "I'm getting old, girl. What do you think happens when I die?"

"You're not going to die—"

"Maybe not today, maybe not tomorrow, but sure as shootin' I will someday. What happens to this then?" She squeezed her hands into fists and opened them, releasing a stiff breeze that blew the dust from the road in front of us. "Everything I've learned. Everything I've done. Gone."

If she was trying to use maternal guilt on me, it worked. I seized her hands and turned her toward me. "No, Mama, no. Don't say that. It won't. I promise."

Mama released one hand and tucked a stray lock of hair behind my ear. "I know, baby. And I'm sorry I put you through thinking you lost your job."

"I forgive you." I hugged her so hard I nearly tipped both of us off the platform.

"Whoa, girl, you're about to knock me on my rear end." Mama let go and straightened up. "We had it all planned out, Queenie and Mrs. Millefleur and me. We waited till we knew you were fired. Then we cast our spell. We sent my powers to you and hoped they'd stick."

"Wait a minute—if I took your powers, how come you're still blowing things around?"

"That's the funny part. I thought I was just handing them off. Like a basket of corn muffins at the dinner table. But no, you managed to grow your own. I kept my magic—and this deadbeat bird." She jerked her chin at Midnight. "Ain't that right, you good-for-nothing crow?"

The crow fluttered up and settled on her shoulder, unfazed by the insults.

I leaned back on my hands. "But what happened to Rose and Pepper? Did Queenie and Mrs. Millefleur share their powers?"

"That's a bit complicated. Queenie and Mrs. Millefleur weren't planning on passing along any of their powers. Somehow, when you connected to me, and your own magic, you linked Pepper to Queenie and Rose to Mrs. Millefleur."

I blinked as I tried to wrap my mind around what I'd done.

"Queenie says her powers are as good as ever—but Mrs. Millefleur says she can't do what she used to do."

"She lost her powers?"

"So she said."

"Maybe I could try to give them back."

Mama's face crinkled as she considered the question. "Might end up worse off. You don't know what you're doing—no offense—and you might end up setting the whole town on fire."

Midnight flew down to the ground.

"Still, I wish I knew how to fix it. I didn't mean to take any of her powers away."

"You got a good heart, Luella—I'm sure we'll figure something out. Give it time."

"How did all three of you end up with magical powers?"

"I don't rightly know. Best I can figure, somebody passed off their powers without letting us know what was coming. We put two and two together in high school one night when there was a big party on the beach. I spotted Queenie using her magic in the water. Queenie caught Hilda—that's Mrs. Millefleur—helping start the bonfire."

"What about the photo? The one you pretended to have 'old-timer's disease' about?"

Mama chuckled. "Took that about a week after we met. We were so pleased to have found each other. Never told another soul, not till your Daddy."

I tried to fit Daddy into this new mental picture. "What did he say?"

"Your Daddy was the kindest, gentlest man who ever walked this earth. He said—and I'll never forget this—'Your gift is part of who you are, and how could I not love every part of you?'"

"I miss Daddy."

"Lord, so do I." Mama shifted and climbed to her feet on the platform. "We better get a move on before Rose and Pepper eat up all the funnel cakes." She offered me a hand.

I took it. Her grip had the strength of years behind it—she pulled me up with ease. "Thanks." I had a million more questions, but I was also eager to reunite with my friends and Queenie.

We followed our noses to the funnel cake food truck.

"Hey, Mama," said Pepper around a mouthful of fried dough. Powdered sugar dotted her costume.

"Hey, girl." Mama hugged her and Rose in turn, being careful not to bump their sugar-covered funnel cakes. "What do y'all think about going someplace with air conditioning? It's too dang hot to be outside."

Queenie gestured grandly. "Why don't we bring dessert back to Fifi's? It's ours for the whole day."

I bought funnel cakes for Mama and myself, and we retraced the parade route to Fifi's.

The door jangled with bells as it opened.

"Anybody home?" I said.

The cold air swirled with the humid outdoor breeze as we filed inside. We settled in the swiveling salon chairs, our reflections infinitely multiplied in the mirrors lining the walls.

The two older women looked at each other. "Where do we start?" said Queenie.

"What do you call yourselves?" said Rose.

"We're the Ride-or-Die Witches," added Pepper.

Queenie covered her face with her hand in mock horror. "Oh, darlings—how vulgar!"

"Didn't you ever come up with a name for yourselves, Mama?"

Mama snorted. "No. Doesn't matter what you call yourselves. You could be the Ladies' Magical Cotillion or the Traveling Sorcerous Hootenannies. Don't make a bit of difference."

Rose finished her funnel cake and set aside the sugar-covered paper plate. "Tell us about your magic. What can you do?"

"I can bring the wind, and I can stop it. I can make my voice heard far away, although that's not as much use anymore now everybody and their dog has a cell phone. And I can see what my crow sees."

I made a mental note of that particular skill.

"Can you fly?" asked Rose.

"Nope. Never got the knack. That's why we made a special effort to give Luella some wings, in hopes she would pick it up."

I started to ask about the wings, but Queenie interrupted.

"The interesting thing, darlings, is that magic is unique to each person. Luella, you have air magic, and so does she"—Queenie gestured at Mama—"but it's different for each of you. Just as Pepper's water magic will be different from mine."

Pepper rubbed her hands together. "Can you ride a dolphin?"

"Hardly, my dear. I can manipulate water in various ways. I can sense living things, because they're made of water. And creatures of the water respond to my call."

"Cool," said Pepper.

From the faraway look on her face, I could tell she was picturing riding a wave surrounded by leaping dolphins.

"I can sense people, too," added Mama. "Living things have to breathe, so they're always moving the air around—and if I'm paying attention, I notice it. Sometimes, I can even tell what people are thinking."

"What am I thinking *right now*?" Pepper bounced in her chair.

"Sit still, girl."

Pepper settled meekly in her chair.

Mama's eyes narrowed as she concentrated. "You're thinking . . . something about a funnel cake. I couldn't get it all."

Pepper slapped her own knee. "How'd you do that?"

"You're always thinking of funnel cakes, Pepper," said Rose.

Pepper stuck her tongue out at Rose.

"How did you do that, Mama?"

"When you think, sometimes you vocalize a bit without realizing it. I can pick it up if I'm paying attention and if it's clear enough." Mama nodded at Queenie. "She can tell when your heart's beating faster."

"Blood is thicker than water, they say—but it's still mostly water," said Queenie.

Pepper shivered. "I hate blood."

Rose steepled her fingers. "What about Mrs. Millefleur?"

"Mrs. Millefleur had a way with fire, as you would expect," Mama replied. "She could sense living things by heat. She also had a knack for hypnotism. How many times did she tell us, Queenie—"

"Oh, yes." Queenie put on a patrician air and quoted Mrs. Millefleur: "'Thoughts are the fire of the mind.'"

I clapped my hands as the realization hit me. "It was Mrs. Millefleur who hired Raphael to paint the regular murals—and then hypnotized him to paint the hidden one!"

Mama gave me a sidelong look. "I didn't know you two were going to ... get acquainted. That wasn't part of the plan. Although I will say I didn't shed any tears over the other one. What was his name again?"

"Dan," Rose and Pepper chorused.

"Right." Mama winked. "Never can remember."

I was about to ask Mama why the plan included hypnotizing Dan, too, but my phone buzzed. I pulled it out and peered at the newest notification. "Speak of the devil—it's Raphael. He says he wants to take me on the 'Sunset and Moonrise' tour of the lighthouse tonight, if I'm free."

A chorus of oohs erupted.

"Say yes!" said Pepper.

"That's two hundred steps to the top," said Rose.

Mama clutched her knees. "Lord have mercy on your joints!"

"I thought that tour was only on weekdays." Queenie shook her head, dismissing the thought. "Never mind. Tell him you want champagne."

"I'll need the champagne to recover from the steps," I muttered.

To Raphael, I typed: *Sounds great. Bring champagne.*

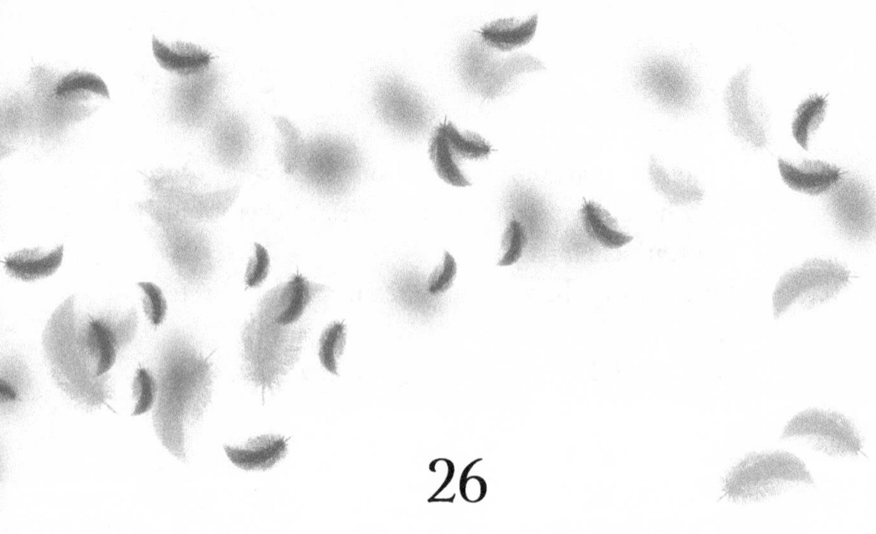

26

The red brick lighthouse loomed over the palmettos and the twisted oaks, its outbuildings at neat angles like improvements on a Monopoly space. I crossed the plaza and took note of the setting sun—the golden quality of the light indicated less than an hour remaining before full dark.

I expected to find the tour group huddled at the base of the lighthouse. No one was there, so I whipped out my phone and scrolled through Raphael's messages to make sure I had the right place and time.

I did.

I tucked the phone away and walked around the base of the lighthouse. They'd have to forgive me for ignoring the "Don't Walk on the Grass" signs. When a complete circuit revealed no tour guide, no tour-related signs, and no Raphael, I put my hands on my hips and stared up at the top of the lighthouse, as if it might reveal some secret.

The phone—which I had just put away—buzzed. I retrieved it.

Under my exchange with Raphael, a new message appeared. *Come up.*

I scoffed. Walking up two hundred stairs alone was not my idea of a fun date. *Why didn't you wait?* I hesitated, then sent one more message. *What kind of date is this?*

A date with destiny.

I frowned. *Raphael, you have thirty seconds to explain yourself.*

I meant it. I counted.

Fifteen seconds later, a new message arrived. *This isn't Raphael.*

I fumbled the phone and nearly dropped it on the sidewalk. *Raphael, this isn't funny.*

You are correct. It's not. Several fast heartbeats later: *And this still isn't Raphael.*

I mashed the keys, making and correcting typos every few letters as I replied in haste. *What do you want?*

Come up and you'll find out.

I didn't like the sound of that all. *Why should I?*

Because if you don't come up, Raphael will come down. A pause emphasized the implied threat. *Now leave the phone on the ground and start climbing.*

"Damn it!" I pressed my free hand to my forehead. "Think, Luella!"

Phone down NOW.

I growled and set the phone on the grass. I pushed the door at the bottom of the lighthouse open, setting off a harsh creak that echoed in the stuffy air inside the building. I put my hand on the guardrail and climbed.

"Zephyr," I whispered.

She appeared on the stairs above me, her coat aglow in the darkening tower.

"Looks like you're one step ahead of me." She bounded down the stairs between us, and I patted her head. Together, surely nothing could harm us.

I continued climbing. My knees protested. I gritted my teeth and kept going. I hated the thought of reaching the top exhausted. I stopped and leaned against the wall. It wouldn't do to delay for long, but a moment's rest was unavoidable. "Think, Luella," I repeated.

What about sending my voice to Mama? I'd done it at Fifi's, hadn't I?

I concentrated on the image of her face, on making a connection across the miles that lay between us. We were mother and daughter, connected as we would never be connected to anyone else on Earth.

"Mama." I spoke clearly, my voice bouncing off the walls and returning to me. "I need you to come to the lighthouse. Raphael is in danger. Bring help." I paused. "I love you." The air vibrated around me.

Her reply whispered in my ear. *I'm coming, baby. What's going on?*

"I don't know. Queenie was right—there's no tour tonight. Someone's holding Raphael hostage at the top of the lighthouse. I have to go now."

Got it. The cavalry is on the way.

I looked up the stairs as they spiraled into the heights. How could I save my strength for the fight ahead?

If only I didn't have to climb the rest of the way...

"Zephyr, I'm not real solid on this whole flying business." I knelt and smoothed the fur on her back, and she laid her muzzle on my shoulder. "Think you can give me a boost?" I poured my concentration into my wings until they shimmered into full radiance at their maximum wingspan. My feet left the ground, but by less than an inch. "A little more," I murmured.

Zephyr barked and shook herself. Whatever she did, it was enough to allow me to float over the stairs as if I were riding an invisible escalator.

"Much better." I had second thoughts immediately, however, as I realized that hovering would bring me to the top even faster. Butterflies kicked up a powerful fuss in my stomach. I'd have been lying to myself if I claimed I wasn't afraid.

The light in the windows faded with every minute. The view down the center of the stairs, all the way to the ground floor, dizzied me.

At the top, the stairs ended at a wooden door with a faceted glass doorknob.

"Ready, Zephyr?" I whispered. No need to alert whoever was on the other side. I planned to blast them with whatever I could muster, grab Raphael, and run hell-for-leather back the way we came.

I turned the knob, my hand slipping on the glass from the sweat that coated my palm, and eased the door open.

We passed through the deserted lantern room and through a second door to the outside catwalk.

Raphael leaned against the waist-high catwalk railing. He held a bottle of champagne and two glasses in a loose grip. Strangely, he didn't move or speak.

"Raphael?"

His eyes. Silver. Swirling with fire.

I hesitated to rush to him, lest he overbalance and tip himself over the guardrail. I'd need to get him away from the edge—carefully—then perhaps I could splash him with champagne to break the spell.

"You made it." A woman's voice carried from around the curve of the catwalk. Her heels clicked in a businesslike fashion as she approached. Sensible pumps, below-the-knee skirt, matching suit jacket. Pearls with a single fire opal. Dark eyes that weighed and assessed. Hair so firmly styled it looked carved from stone. She smiled, showing perfect teeth, and cocked her head like a hawk observing a mouse. "Hello, Luella."

Zephyr pressed against my leg and growled.

"Mrs. Millefleur?" Uncertainty raced through me. Wasn't she Mama's friend? And Queenie's, too? And a paragon of the Sparkle Beach community? I glanced around, looking for the perpetrator of Raphael's hypnosis—and the threatening messages. "What's going on?"

"I've been following your progress, you know. Very impressive. You have a strength that hasn't been seen in a generation."

"Thanks, but we should really be waking up Raphael and getting back down—"

"I don't think so. After all, he serves a purpose. Like Dan."

"Dan?" The gap in Mama and Queenie's story sprang to mind—they'd never mentioned hypnotizing Dan. "That was you."

Her lips quirked with amusement. "Most things in this town are because of me."

"Why did you hypnotize Dan?"

Mrs. Millefleur laughed, a light, musical sound that fell evenly down the musical scale. "To see what you could do, of course."

"I didn't know what I was doing—I could have killed him!" I glanced at Raphael, barely daring to take my eyes off her. He remained motionless.

"But you didn't, did you? You discovered your strength, and the will to use it."

"You're nuttier than a five-pound fruitcake. You can't push people around like that."

"Why not? Your mother and Queenie manipulated you to get you to manifest your powers."

"That's different!"

"Is it? I don't think so. A difference of degree, perhaps, but not of substance."

"You didn't have to drag Raphael up here to get my attention, you know. You could have called me on the phone like a normal person."

"But it concentrates the mind wonderfully, doesn't it? Look at you. You're practically vibrating with magic." She eyed me with avid interest.

My skin crawled. I wanted off that lighthouse and far away from her as soon as possible. "What do you want?"

Mrs. Millefleur sighed, as if I'd interrupted a pleasant conversation. "So impatient." She moved to Raphael.

"Leave him alone. I'm warning you!"

"You're warning me?"

"Mama said you weren't as powerful as you were before."

"I'm not. But I think—if you were properly motivated—you'd be powerful enough to give back what you took."

I rallied with more bravery than I felt. "You seem to be doing all right with what you have." I gestured to a virtually inert Raphael.

"Oh, Luella. You have no idea what's coming." She clucked as though I were a child. Her hands clenched into fists and her voice became low and tight. "Every element must be in place." Her gaze flicked to Raphael and back to me.

My mind ran through options that had nothing to do with giving her back her powers. Could I knock her down? Drain the air around her until she fainted like Dan?

She must have read the look in my eyes. "Don't even think of trying something foolish."

A crow silently landed on the railing behind her.

"I don't know how to give your powers back. I can't!" I held my hands out, half in pleading, half in preparation to make a grab at Raphael—hoping the gesture would also distract her from noticing that Midnight had snuck up behind her.

"You think you can't." Her eyes darkened as the sun disappeared behind the horizon. "You don't know what you're capable of—until you're pushed."

In one swift movement, she seized Raphael's ankle and flipped him over the railing.

The champagne and the flutes left his hands and turned end over end in slow motion through the air. My memory flicked to the sensation of falling off the high step of the kitchen stool.

I heard my mother's voice: *Fly, Luella!*

Fear left me, and in its place, a calm breeze lifted my spirit.

I dove over the railing.

Zephyr and Midnight dove with me.

My wings exploded into brightness as we plunged after Raphael. I flew hard, angling downward as the ground rocketed upward—praying I wasn't simply hastening my own death—then I slid beneath him and threw my arms around him, straining to catch the air with my wings.

They grew so bright they dazzled my vision.

I hoped they weren't the last thing I would see.

Dirt blasted into the air as we struck a soft surface not unlike the interior of the bouncy castle I'd rented many years ago on my daughter's birthday. It eased beneath me, deflating softly, until my back sank into the churned dirt with Raphael's weight heavy upon me. His head rested on my shoulder, and his breath tickled my neck.

Zephyr peered over the edge of the depression, her tongue lolling, a remarkably pleased expression on her doggy face. Midnight wheeled in the air above.

"Raphael?" I patted his back. "Raphael? You're squashing me." Since his face nestled in the space between my neck and shoulder, I couldn't tell if he'd woken from his hypnotized state.

"I'm sorry," he croaked. "I'm just recovering from almost dying." He lifted his head and rolled to the side, where he lay panting in the dirt next to me. He turned his head and gave me an off-kilter grin. "We have to stop meeting like this."

I laughed so hard I gasped for breath.

He staggered as he stood, then offered me a hand.

We climbed out of the crater together. I surveyed the damage to the lawn and attempted to remove some of the dirt from my clothing.

Raphael put his hands on his hips and looked around. "Where'd that champagne get to?"

We found it a few feet from the edge of the hollowed out ground—smashed, fizzing, and draining forlornly into the sod.

Kind of like we would have been if my wings hadn't worked.

I looked to the entrance of the lighthouse. "We have to stop Mrs. Millefleur—"

The low snarl of a motorcycle engine interrupted me as the beam of a single headlight swung across the plaza. The bike hopped the curb and drove straight to the lighthouse. A lone figure dismounted. "Cavalry's here!"

I'd have known that voice anywhere.

"Mama!" I ran across the grass to meet her.

She gave me a quick hug with a businesslike pat on the back. "Called in the troops. Should be here any minute. You all right?" She held me by the shoulders and assessed me with a look. "You look all right." She glanced at Raphael. "Nice to see you again, son."

Raphael made a face like he was trying to place where he'd seen her before.

"I'm Luella's mama. She's got my magic." Mama slapped me on the back and gave Raphael a saucy wink. "You helped, though."

"She means the wings," I said.

"The wings!" Raphael clapped his forehead. "You were there for that?"

"I was." Mama noticed the depression in the ground and walked the short distance to examine it.

Raphael raised his voice to carry to where she stood. "Maybe we could have a little talk sometime about not hypnotizing me anymore?"

I hid a smile at his hopeful tone.

"Sure, sonny," Mama replied. She knelt by the edge and touched the ground. "We got bigger fish to fry, though."

More headlights swept across the plaza. Car doors slammed, one after the other.

Queenie, Pepper, and Rose ran up.

"What'd we miss?" said Pepper.

"We shared a nice bottle of champagne—and a near-death experience."

"If by sharing you mean it fell off a lighthouse and smashed into a zillion pieces, yes, that's accurate," Raphael added.

Queenie turned to the lighthouse. "What's Hilda doing here?"

Mrs. Millefleur had appeared at the entrance to the lighthouse. I expected her to run away when she spotted us.

She didn't. She closed the lighthouse door as calmly as you please and waited like a monarch for us to approach.

I hurried over with the rest of our group hot on my heels. "This is who threw Raphael off the top of the lighthouse!"

All eyes turned to Raphael, who looked embarrassed, before returning to Mrs. Millefleur.

A smile of quiet satisfaction curved her lips.

Mama crossed her arms over her chest. "Mrs. Millefleur, what do you have to say for yourself?"

Mrs. Millefleur looked at Raphael. "He's unhurt." She proffered his phone, which he took with two fingers like it might be contaminated. She turned her attention to me. "The important thing is that Luella has learned to fly."

"Are you crazy? You tried to kill him! You flipped him right over the edge of the railing. What if I couldn't fly that well? What if we fell?"

Mrs. Millefleur was unruffled. "You didn't."

"I'm calling the police," I said.

Her musical laugh pierced the night. "Go ahead. Tell them I hypnotized your friend and threw him off the top of the lighthouse." She pressed a hand to her chest in mock disbelief. "Me? Sparkle Beach's most prominent philanthropist and business community leader?"

A white Lincoln Town Car pulled up along the plaza curb and kept its engine running. A uniformed chauffeur emerged and opened one of the passenger doors.

"Excuse me, won't you? That's my ride." She nodded to me. "Goodbye, Luella. Such a pleasure to meet you at last. Shame you couldn't give me back the rest of my powers, but perhaps in time . . . " She pivoted to Rose. "Au revoir, Rose. I imagine we'll be seeing each other again very soon." She walked away, her heels clicking smartly on the paved sidewalk.

"Anyone want to stop her?" Raphael said with a casual air.

No one moved.

Rose frowned. "That's who I'm supposed to learn magic from?"

We watched the Lincoln Town Car pull away.

Mama dusted her hands. "Somebody's a few bricks short of a load."

"That's it? That's all you have to say?"

"I don't need to talk about revenge, girl." She met my gaze. "I just get it done."

I shivered at the cold look in Mama's eyes.

"Come on, Queenie," she said. Her cold look evaporated like dry ice. "I got to show you something."

I left Raphael to be peppered with questions by my friends while I followed Mama and Queenie to the edge of the hole in the ground.

"See this? It ain't natural. Something threw all this dirt around and knocked a hole clean through the sod."

"Isn't that where my air magic hit the ground?"

Queenie shook her head. "No, darling. This is the work of someone with earth magic. They may not have known what they were doing, but they clearly have enough power to shovel a lot of dirt—fast."

The two elder witches looked at each other, then at Raphael.

He must have felt their gazes, for he turned and gave a friendly wave.

Mama put her arm around my shoulder. "How much do you know about this boy, anyway?"

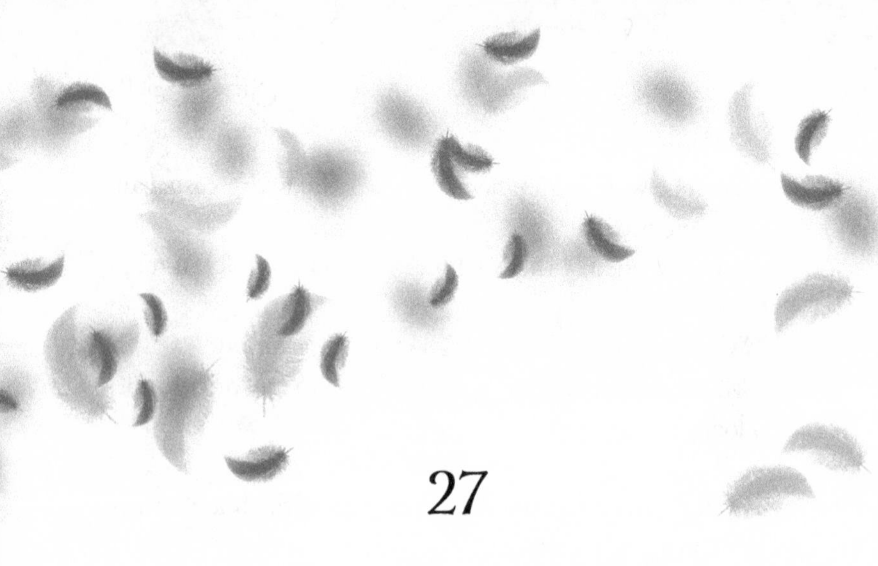

27

All the elements were in place for a perfect evening get-together at the shotgun house. Rose and Pepper minded the grill in the driveway while Mama and I handled the kitchen prep. Queenie and Raphael took on the task of fitting chairs and folding tables into the space in the backyard not taken up by the miniature pool.

I winced as I sliced onions for the burgers and hot dogs, and not because the juice was making me tear up. I wiped my hands, rolled up my sleeve, and examined the tender area on my upper arm.

Mama chuckled. "Hurts, don't it? I remember my first tattoo. Whoo-ee!" She leaned over and traced the ink on my arm. "Looks like it's healing nicely."

The front door banged open. Rose and Pepper crossed the living room and entered the kitchen.

"You looking at Luella's tattoo?" Pepper rolled up her sleeve. "Check this out." The tattoo she displayed, although not her first, was as new as mine.

Mama peered at Pepper's arm. "Am I mistaken, or is that a chili pepper with sunglasses riding a surfboard?"

Pepper glowed with joy. "It sure is!"

"I got mine upgraded." Rose rolled up her sleeve. Her rose tattoo sprouted new leaves of flame.

"I think mine is the cutest. Zephyr! Come here so everybody can see the resemblance."

Zephyr, who had been peacefully observing the party preparations from her perch on the couch, obediently trotted to the kitchen.

"That's so sweet," said Mama as she compared the real thing to the tattoo on my arm of a dog atop fluffy clouds. "How'd you tell the tattoo artist what the dog should look like?"

"Raphael sketched her for me."

The back door banged, and Queenie entered the room, followed by Raphael.

"Darlings, the seating arrangements have been made," she said.

"What are we looking at?" Raphael leaned into our mutual admiration society. "The tattoos? When do I get one?"

The rest of us laughed.

I elbowed him. "Are you going to get the words, too?"

He read aloud from my arm: "Ride-or-Die Witches." He pressed a hand to his chest. "I'm a modern guy. I got no problem being a Ride-or-Die Witch."

Mama poked him. “First you gotta prove your worth.” She cackled and turned away to pick up a tray of hot dogs. “You can start by taking these out to the grill.”

“I *relish* the chance.” He wiggled his eyebrows up and down, then winked at me.

I shot him a secret smile, then handed a tray of burger patties to Rose.

Queenie and Pepper gathered the bags of buns.

We made a happy parade as we walked through the living room and out the front door to gather around the grill parked in the driveway. The coals glowed cheerfully, and the meats sizzled as they hit the hot grate. As each batch cooked, we added burgers and hot dogs to our plates, until each person had some of everything they desired.

We marched through the open gate connecting the front yard to the back yard. The evening light sparkled on the surface of the pool. We loaded up with toppings, chips, potato salad, and baked beans from the tables in the back until our paper plates bent under the weight.

I took a huge bite of my burger—cheese, pickles, mustard, ketchup, mayo, if you please—and looked up to find Red standing next to my chair.

She examined my food with unabashed interest. “That looks mighty tasty, Miss Luella.”

“Please, call me Luella,” I said through the mouthful. “You want a burger? Or maybe some potato salad?” I gestured to the food.

Red beamed. “Okay!” She half-turned toward the food, then pivoted to face me again. “I almost forgot. Here—I brought you your mail." She tugged a stack of letters from her back pocket and handed them to me before wandering off in the direction of the grill.

I wiped my hands and patted my mouth with a napkin before inspecting the stack. "Junk. Junk. Junk. What's this?" I brought the last letter closer. "Millefleur Properties?"

Mama threw down her napkin and sat up straight.

I held the envelope at arm's length as if it might explode. "I already knew I had to get out of this house. She better not be trying to rush me." I grimaced.

"Open it!" said Pepper.

I ripped it open and fished the papers out. "Some kind of... legal documents? And a handwritten note." I laid the documents aside and read the note out loud. "'Dear Luella, I regret our meeting had to take place under such unusual circumstances.'" I let out a grim laugh at her choice of words. "'However, I feel that despite the difficult beginning, we can continue to have a long and fruitful working relationship.'" I caught Mama's gaze and made a face of disbelief.

"Nuttier than a fruitcake," Mama muttered.

"'To that end, I would like to make amends with you. Please find enclosed the deed to the house on Seabreeze Lane... '" I gasped. "The house?" I seized the legal documents and scanned the text. "What's a quit claim?"

"May I?" Raphael leaned over to take the papers. He murmured under his breath as he rapidly read through the papers, then he looked up and met my gaze. "She's transferring all claim on the property to you."

"Can she do that? I didn't sign anything!"

"You don't have to. It belongs to you now, automatically—unless you draw up something similar and quit your claim to the property."

Mama slapped the table. "That sneaking little—"

"Mama!"

Mama didn't finish her sentence, but she seethed. "She thinks she can hand you a house and everything's hunky-dory?"

"Oh, I don't know, darling. It is a free house, after all," said Queenie.

Rose waved a hand for silence. "Finish the letter."

"'Please find enclosed the deed to the house on Seabreeze Lane, and please accept my compliments on the auspicious launch of your no doubt illustrious new avocation. Sincerely, Hildegarde Millefleur.'"

Mama rolled her eyes. "Always the five-dollar words when a ten-cent would do."

Red strolled into the backyard, her plate buckling under what appeared to be a triple cheeseburger. "What'd I miss?" She plopped down on the back doorstep.

We couldn't speak freely in Red's presence, so I phrased it delicately. "A person who did me wrong has offered me a gift."

"What kind of gift?" asked Red.

"A big one," said Mama.

Red regarded me from over the top of the cheeseburger. "It got any strings on it?"

I glanced at Raphael, who shook his head. "Technically, no—"

"Take it," said Red, instantly. "Take the money and run."

"It's not money—"

"You know what I mean," she added through a large mouthful.

"Out of the mouths of babes," Queenie declared, as if that solved everything.

I regarded the papers dubiously. "I don't know . . . "

"I don't like it," Mama said. "It don't go halfway to repaying what she put you through that night."

My gaze took in the back of the house, from the gingerbread trim on the portico, to the tall trees that bowed over the fence, to the shivering surface of the pool. I stacked the papers one at a time, then slowly slid them into the torn envelope. "No, I suppose not."

Mama placed her hand on my arm. "Hang on a minute, girl. I didn't say you shouldn't take it. You got a real nice setup here."

"You think I should take it?"

"I don't forgive, and I don't forget . . . but I don't turn down a free house, either." Mama tugged the envelope out of my grasp. "Why don't I hold onto this so you can think it over and not do anything rash?"

"Your idea of rash might be a little different from mine, Mama."

Her eyes twinkled. "Maybe we're more alike than you know."

I let the subject slide so we could finish our meal on lighter topics. After Red finished her cheeseburger, she departed, allowing the rest of us to return to discussing all things magic-related—once I had securely bolted the fence gate to prevent any surprise visitors.

Rose swept our group with her gaze. "So what is it we're actually supposed to do with these powers?"

Queenie gestured with a ring-laden hand. "Sparkle Beach is our territory—and yours. Ours to protect, ours to defend—"

"Ours to surf!" Pepper pumped her fist into the air. "Yeah!"

"That, too," added Queenie.

"Define 'defend,'" said Rose.

All eyes turned to Mama. "It doesn't take too much imagination to picture what someone with powers could do if they took a mind to cause trouble." She leveled a pointed look at Raphael and me.

Pepper's eyes widened. "How often does that sort of thing happen?"

Queenie and Mama shared a look, as if calculating how much to tell and how much to save for later. "Not often," said Queenie.

Mama snorted. "Often enough."

Mrs. Millefleur's words echoed from our lighthouse confrontation: *You have no idea what's coming.* I shivered, and not from the night air.

Zephyr pressed against me, providing comfort with the warmth of her fur.

Queenie patted my shoulder. "Not to worry. There's never been anything your mother and I and"—she paused, clearly thinking of Mrs. Millefleur—"your mother and I couldn't handle. And now we have the rest of you!" She clasped her hands in satisfaction.

Mama winked. "Mostly we just use our powers for fun. Ain't that right, Queenie?"

Queenie waved a hand and conjured the shape of a dolphin from the pool water, then let it fall with a splash. "Exactly, darling. Most of the time." She drifted to the side of the pool and trailed a fingertip into the water. Under her touch, the water swirled into a perfect whirlpool. "Water of the blood, fire of the mind, earth of the body, air between all," she murmured.

Pepper left her chair and stood beside Queenie. She peered into the water. "Are you sure we have to talk about blood?"

A half-smile tilted Queenie's lips. "Don't be afraid, darling." She made a smoothing gesture and the water stilled. "Try it."

Rose flexed her fingers and looked on with interest. "What exactly are you doing?"

"Solidifying our connection to our territory. Letting it be known that we are its guardians." Queenie nodded to Pepper. "Go ahead."

Pepper inhaled deeply and set her lips in a firm line. "Water of the blood." She jabbed her finger into the water. The water bounced and churned, then tumbled into a lively spiral. Pepper breathed out and smiled.

Rose joined them. She held her hand over Pepper's whirlpool. "Fire of the mind." Silver fire ignited at her fingertips.

Raphael looked at Mama as if asking for permission.

She nodded with the sharp grace of a bird of prey.

He stood and joined my friends. "Earth of the body," he said. He splayed his hands and held them out, his artist's fingers fluttering over the water as if limbering up. "What do I do?"

Mama raised herself from the plastic lawn chair and took a place at the pool's edge. She scooped up a handful of dirt from the ground. "Think fast!" She tossed the dirt like a frisbee and it arced across the water.

Raphael reached with both hands. Instead of catching the falling earth, he froze it in midair over the water. He let out a relieved laugh as the dirt remained suspended. "Wouldn't want to muddy your pool."

"Luella?" Mama prompted.

I stepped to the pool and stood next to her, unsure of what to say or do. "Air between all?"

"Say it like you mean it, girl. Join everything together."

Rose's fire cast flickering light over the swirling water.

I hesitated. What if I did something wrong?

The thought—which should have stung me with doubt—instead prompted me to laugh. How could I doubt myself after everything that had happened? I seized Mama's hand with renewed resolve. "Air between all!"

"Air between all," Mama echoed. She squeezed my hand in return.

A croak and a bark announced the presence of Midnight and Zephyr. Midnight landed on Mama's shoulder. Zephyr dashed around the yard, completing a circle beyond our stations at the pool.

The floating dirt gathered itself into tiny clumps and began to rotate like an earthen galaxy in sync with the whirlpool. Silver flames dripped from Rose's fingertips and spun over the water, intersecting the levitated earth in elliptical patterns. Droplets of water broke free from the surface of the pool and danced in the air.

I concentrated on bringing the elements together. The wind rose, sending silver swirls through the space between the six of us. Strands of air bound the earth, fire, and water droplets, drawing them down to the open center of the whirlpool.

Silver light burst from the center of the pool and shot into the sky. It reached a zenith far above us and popped like a firework, sending a net of glitter shooting toward every horizon as far as the eye could see.

The glitter sparkled in the dark sky, then faded, leaving the night even blacker after the dazzling effect. The water stilled. Mama blew a burst of air in time to knock the falling dirt away before it landed in the pool.

"Nice save," said Raphael.

Midnight retreated to perch on the fence, and Zephyr came to my side.

Mama smiled. "That's a good night's work." She thumped my back with obvious pride, and walked off to gather empty plates and cups.

After we cleaned up, Rose, Pepper, Mama, and Queenie prepared to depart. I walked them out.

"Goodbye, darling. I'll see you Monday." Queenie's hugs came with an ever-present cloud of perfume. She squeezed my shoulders, then bustled away to her convertible.

I hugged Rose and Pepper in turn. "Say hello to Dog Mountain and the family for me."

Mama was last. "'Night, baby." Her hug nearly knocked the breath out of me.

"'Night, Mama." We released each other. Raphael and I waved as they got into Pepper's SUV.

The passenger side window rolled down and Mama leaned out. "Y'all don't stay up too late, hear?"

I rolled my eyes. "Goodnight, Mama."

She grinned and rolled up the window. The SUV trundled away down Seabreeze Lane.

Raphael and I returned to the backyard to enjoy the breeze and the darkness. Zephyr curled at my feet as Raphael and I sat side by side.

"What do you think?" I said.

"About what?"

"About the house."

His brow furrowed as he considered the question. "That's a tough question, isn't it?"

"She could have killed us."

"Is that an argument against a free house?"

"I don't want her to have the satisfaction of thinking she's bought me off. And yet . . . "

"And yet you love this house, and it nearly kills you to refuse." His hand slid over mine.

"Damn it, Raphael, why do you have to read my mind?"

His gaze flitted over my face, taking in my features. "I never got to thank you, by the way." His voice softened to a more intimate tone. "For saving me."

"My pleasure." I wondered if my eyes looked like his—soft and shining, pupils wide and dark like the new moon. My hand found the back of his neck and my fingers slipped over his hair.

He closed his eyes with a soft smile and tipped his head back ever so slightly, as if he were silently giving thanks to the stars above.

I closed the distance and pressed my lips to his. He returned the kiss with a fervor that stole my breath. A tremble started in my toes and shook its way upward through my bones, and the more we kissed, the more I trembled—

I broke away and stared at the pool. The water bounced, then jittered into stillness.

"Luella? Did I do something wrong?"

"No, not at all. Kiss me again."

He swept me into his arms and kissed his way down my cheek to my neck, leaving my view of our surroundings clear. "Raphael—"

"Mmm?" His nose nuzzled my ear.

The ground rumbled. The gravel on the pathway danced.

"Raphael, I think—"

"Mmm," he added, pressing his lips to my shoulder.

I shivered. If I didn't put a stop to this, he'd probably bring down the house.

My house.

I patted his back in a businesslike fashion. "Raphael, I think you're causing an earthquake."

He straightened, and the ground gave one last rumble under our feet. His gaze swept the trembling earth. "What can I say? You have that effect on me."

"We'll have to sort that out somehow." I kissed his cheek once, lightly. "Speaking of magic… it's a moonless night. I should take advantage of it."

"A little night flying?" He raised my hand to his lips.

"Practice makes perfect."

"Then you definitely don't need to go. You're already perfect."

I elbowed him. "Flatterer."

"I would go with you, but my powers seemed to be limited, at the moment, to throwing dirt around." He stretched, then stood. "May I borrow your kitchen while you're out? I'd like to give that gluten-free rugelach recipe a shot."

I stood as well, and hugged him. He smelled of sandalwood and the smoke from the grill. "You're too sweet."

He returned my embrace. "That's just the future rugelach talking. Now get up there and go catch a few stars. I'll have those rugelach ready for tasting when you get back."

I released him. The dark sky beckoned. Though my mother and my friends had left, and Lily was far away, I saw them all in my mind's eye as vivid as life. Wherever I went, I would carry them with me through a bond even greater than spells and glitter.

Zephyr barked, breaking my reverie. She dashed an eager circle around the pool.

I unfurled my wings like shining bolts of silver lace. "Ready, girl?"

She leaped into the balmy night air and I followed, the wind rising around us, causing the overhanging tree branches to toss and sway. Her white and silver coat shone like moonlight and stars as she capered up and away into the clouds.

My wings let me fly, but love—the true magic—made my heart soar.

The Midlife Elementals adventure continues in

Silver Charms!

Sometimes, a date from hell is just what you need…

Don't miss this laugh-out-loud paranormal romantic comedy series!

CPSIA information can be obtained
at www.ICGtesting.com
Printed in the USA
BVHW042319120722
641937BV00034B/232